THE DEVIL

&

SISTER FORD

BOOK THREE OF THE

INVISIBLE ENEMIES

SERIES

LYNDA D. BROWN

First Printing 2014

ISBN Number: 978-0-9850913-2-3

And the evil spirit answered and said, "Jesus I know, and Paul I know; but who are you?" Acts 19:15

Books by Lynda D. Brown:

Invisible Enemies Book one of the Invisible Enemies Series

Seed of Satan: Leah's Story Book Two of the Invisible Enemies Series

Powerful Prayer to Protect & Bless Your Family

Damien's New Bike Book one of the Kingdom Kids Series

The Author Chat Guide: How to Convert Your Published Book into an Audiobook

The Author Chat Guide: How to Promote Your Book on a Shoestring Budget.

Books are available in print,
eBooks and audiobooks.

Prologue

William felt a presence in his bedroom. When he turned over, he saw a man sitting at the edge of his bed. "Hello William." The man said softly. William sat up and rubbed his eyes. He reached over and grabbed his glasses from the nightstand and adjusted them on his face. "Is that you, Lord?" William asked with a yawn. Jesus grinned. "Yes. My son, I have heard the desires of your heart, even if you refuse to give voice to them. I know what you want and what you need, and I'm here tonight to bless you." Jesus said softly. William was curious as to which unspoken request Jesus was referring to.

"It's time for you to remarry son," Jesus said quietly. "Marry?" William stammered in disbelief. Jesus laughed. "Why ya gotta say it like that? I know how much you miss being married, old friend. You're still a young man, and I want to bless you with a son to carry on my legacy at

Grace Faith." Jesus calmly replied.

William leaped out of bed and stared at Jesus with horror. "A son, you mean like a baby? I'm way too old to be starting a new family with babies!" William retorted as he began to pace about his spacious bedroom. "I can't believe this, a baby, of all things!" He was walking back and forth across the room so fast; Jesus became dizzy watching him.

"Calm down William, you're only fifty-one years old. Abraham was nearly a hundred when I blessed him with Isaac, and Sarah was in her nineties, at least your Cecilia is only forty." The Lord said with amusement. William choked. "*My Cecilia?*" He asked irritability. "Since when did she become *my* Cecilia?"

Jesus chuckled. "Um, all knowing, remember?" He said pointing to himself. William rolled his eyes and climbed back into bed. "I see you're not in the mood to be serious tonight, so I'm going back to sleep," William replied grumpily, as he punched his pillow, turned over and pretended to sleep.

Jesus stared at his stubborn, lonely, faithful son and sighed. William was acting was just like the Israelites who wanted to stay in the wilderness and mourn Moses' death and not move forward to possess what He had for them. It was time for William to move forward and possess the things God had set aside for him and Cecilia. So with a heavy heart, Jesus waved his left hand over his son. "William."

William stiffened when he heard her voice. No, it couldn't be. He turned around and there she was sitting on lush green grass, surrounded by a group of small children. A cute little boy sat on her lap.

"Wanda," he whispered quietly, as tears stung the back of his eyes. William glanced around and was shocked to see that he was no longer in his bedroom, but in Heaven. He looked at Jesus. "Please don't do this to me; you're not being fair…" He pleaded. Jesus looked at his faithful son. "I love you William, and it hurts me to see you lonely. It's been almost twenty years son. It's time for you to let Wanda go." Jesus patted William's arm and walked away.

William turned towards Wanda. She put the little boy down and walked towards her husband. She reached out and caressed his face. William was surprised he could actually feel her touch. She gently wiped away the tears on his cheeks. "Honey, the Lord is right, it's time for you to let me go, and move on with your life. I'm so happy here William, I can't wait to share this with you, but every day I watch you struggle between your growing feelings for Cecilia and your lingering feelings for me. Baby, I want you and Cecilia to be happy. She takes real good care of you, and our daughters love her. Cecilia also needs you, she's been widowed for almost twenty years, and hasn't been with another man since Jackson died." Wanda said to her loving, but stubborn husband.

William just held his wife's hand. He didn't know what to say. He glanced over and saw a small bench that he could have sworn wasn't there a minute ago! They walked over to it and sat down. "How can you ask me to be with another woman, when I still love you? He asked quietly.

Wanda reached out and smoothed her husband's graying hair. "Because I'm up here sweetheart, and I can't come back. William, you're still a very attractive man, and you have needs that you have ignored for years. I love you and miss you too, but honey, I want you happy and *whole*. I know that Cecilia makes you happy and you make her happy. You two work so well together, and Grace Faith church is better and stronger because of you. We watch you all the time up here, cheering you on. We really enjoyed watching you defeat

Satan and his demons when they tried to destroy Abby. I was so proud of how you taught the congregation about spiritual warfare, and how the church used that knowledge, and stood up to the demon that materialized at the Church. God is very pleased with you, William and so am I."

William was astounded. "You really watch us up here?" He asked. Wanda nodded. "Oh yes, we can tune into what's going on down on earth anytime. You should see Michael and the angels as they prepare for battle, when the saints on earth begin praying and asking God for help. Millions of them take flight and fly off to do battle for the Lord!" Wanda said with great enthusiasm.

William was blown away. "Wow, and you get to see this?" Wanda grinned and nodded. William shook his head. "Amazing. I can't wait to get here and see it all myself." He said wistfully. Wanda took his hand and looked him in the eye. "It's not your time yet." She said firmly. "You still have a mighty work to do for God. Earth is in its last days, and God is going to use you, and the members of Grace Faith to help the lost and unbelievers. You are living in what the bible calls **perilous times**, and as the situation on earth gets worse, people are going to be crying out to God, really seeking Him, and He knows that you and Cecilia will teach them how to rightly discern His word, so that many souls will be saved." She told him breathlessly.

"Wanda, God wants me to marry Cecilia, and He wants to bless us with a son. Can you believe that?" William asked her. Wanda smiled brightly. "I know, and your son is going to be amazing." She whispered. William's mouth fell open. "You know?" Wanda nodded, and kissed him.

William closed his eyes, enjoying her sweet kiss. He wanted to ask her about meeting the saints in the Bible, but when he opened his eyes, he was shocked to find himself back in his own bed. Disappointed, but happy, he lay there thinking about what Wanda told him and then his thoughts drifting to his best friend, Cecilia Ford. A baby, Lord, what are you up to? He finally turned over and fell into a blissful sleep, dreaming of Cecilia and lots and lots of babies.

Jesus chuckled to himself as He left William's house. William had been the apple of the His eye, since he was a little boy. The Lord had called William at an early age, and he enthusiastically responded. William began preaching at eighteen, following in the footsteps of his father, grandfather and great grandfather. He met Wanda Anderson at vacation bible camp when they were both sixteen.

They fell in love that summer, and William knew, without any doubt, that she would eventually become his wife. Wanda's father and both of her grandfathers were preachers, so being a pastor's wife, was an easy transition. She had watched her mother and both grandmothers in that role.

In the late 80's, William followed God's calling and moved to Washington D.C. to take over Grace Faith church when the elderly pastor became ill. As a visiting pastor, William had preached there several times, and the congregation began to grow. After the Board of Directors voted him in as the new pastor of Grace Faith, he asked Wanda's father for her hand in marriage, and a year later, he and Wanda married.

Years later, Wanda began working with the children and the young adults in the church. After seeking God, Reverend Rawlins met with his church board and recommended that his wife take over the children and young adult ministry. Some of the elders in the church felt she was too young, and protested, but several months later, as the children and young adult ministries began to grow, they had to concede. Young adults began joining the church in droves, and the elders that once opposed her, began bragging about Wanda and her ministry to other churches. Children that had never been to church, began bugging their parents to take them to Grace Faith! God was doing great things using Sister Rawlins, and soon He blessed her and William with two sweet little girls of their own.

Unfortunately, tragedy struck, and Wanda Rawlins was killed in a car accident nearly twenty years ago. William still grieved for his beloved wife, but the Lord had decided it was time for William to move on. He had great plans in store for him and His beloved daughter, Cecilia Ford and it was time to put them in action.

Chapter One

Hannah Harris was busy checking the financial report her assistant had given her. Even in the midst of the recession that had gripped the country since 2008, business was great. Hannah thought about the scriptures in Genesis when God provided for Abraham, Isaac and Jacob during times of famine, and because of their obedience, they all received hundred fold harvest. If anyone needed proof that God's Word is true and still working today, all they had to do was see the financial report Hannah was looking at. God had blessed the church's employment and training center with a hundred fold return! She bowed her head for a moment to give thanks to God; she was so grateful that He was her source and not this fallen, corrupt **Babylonian** world system that Reverend Rawlins preached about during church services.

Five years ago, God gave Reverend Rawlins

a vision to purchase an abandon building near Grace Faith Church, and turn it into an employment and job training center. Reverend Rawlins chose Hannah to manage the center, now the center was one of the top agencies in the District of Columbia, assisting people looking for jobs.

Last year, Hannah's boyfriend and the center's attorney, Daniel James, shared with her the dream God had given him about starting a business school for church members and the people in the community that were interested in starting their own businesses. The school would be built on biblical principles. God instructed Daniel to handle the legal work free of charge for those interested.

The next morning, Daniel received confirmation that the dream was indeed God's will, when after waking up, Daniel turned on his television and saw a well known pastor talking about his Christian Business School. Intrigued, Daniel sat up and watched as the church held a commencement service for those that had completed the course. After the service ended, an excited Daniel logged onto the church's website to check out the program. Feeling confident that this was what God wanted, he printed out the curriculum to show his fiancée and the pastor. Daniel called Hannah after he logged off the site and went over to her house to discuss his vision and to show her the website.

After viewing the site, Hannah also got excited and she called Reverend Rawlins to request a meeting. They met with Reverend Rawlins a couple of days later, and he too became excited about the program and asked Daniel to contact the pastor to see if he could fly to Chicago, Illinois, where the school was located and check it out. When Daniel arrived, one of the school administrators showed him around and allowed him to sit in on several of the classes. Daniel was so impressed with the school, he set up a conference call between the pastor, Reverend Rawlins, and the school's administrator to discuss setting up an extension of the school for Grace Faith. Daniel worked diligently with the founders of the Chicago school, making sure Grace Faith had the same curriculum and dedicated business owners to teach the classes.

Nine months later, Reverend Rawlins announced to the church that the business school was now open and enrolling students. Several church members along with residents in the area signed up for the first session. The following semester, at least 100 students were enrolled in the school, and soon, Daniel and Hannah set up an online class.

Several of the neighborhood drug dealers, impressed by what the church was doing, stopped selling drugs and joined the church. During a Sunday service a couple of them confessed that they had received a *revelation* from the Lord, that what they had learned in the streets, working for Satan, God now wanted them to use that knowledge to set up *kingdom* businesses for the neighborhood.

Soon the neighborhood began to prosper, because of the positive impact from the center and the business school. The church also owned and operated a preschool thru 12th grade school that taught Christian principles and values, where 98 % of the students graduated and went on to complete college. Fifty former students moved back to the D.C. area, and opened businesses in conjunction with the church to give back to the community that they had grown up in.

Reverend Rawlins was following the Lord's command in Isaiah 61 to **rebuild the waste places.** Hannah knew that the Lord had blessed her church, and the church was blessing its members and the community. Whenever Hannah thought of Reverend Rawlins, she immediately thought of Sister Cecilia Ford, one of her dearest and closest friends. Sister Cecilia Ford was the *Prophetess* of Grace Faith Church, and hanging around Cecilia was beginning to rub off on Hannah. Whenever she thought of the woman or spoke her name, either Hannah's phone would ring and it would be Cecilia or she would pop up in person.

Sure enough, the phone rang and Hannah heard her assistant Carol greet Cecilia, and then she buzzed Hannah, to tell her Cecilia was holding for her on line one.

Hannah picked up the phone and was taken aback when she heard the excitement in her friend's voice. "Hannah, I had a dream about a wedding last night, and it was beautiful. I couldn't see the bride or groom, but I think it's you and Daniel." Cecilia said excitedly. Hannah picked up a piece of paper and began to fan herself. "Girl, I don't think Daniel is ready for marriage." Hannah laughed as she swirled around in her chair and looked out the window over the beautiful grounds of the center. "He tends to break out in a sweat anytime he hears the word. We've been dating for nearly two years now, and I think he's real comfortable with the relationship the way it is."

Hannah sighed. Cecilia laughed. "Well, I don't know what God is up to yet, but I can tell he's up to something. So stay on your toes. I sense something wonderful coming your way." Cecilia told her best friend. They chatted for a few more moments and made plans to have lunch tomorrow at Cecilia's bakery.

Before heading home, Hannah heard a knock on her door. When she lifted her head up, she saw a tall, dark handsome man hovering in her doorway. "Excuse me," the stranger said, "I came by here last night, but you were already closed. I'm a general contractor, and I need to hire some carpenters and painters for a couple of jobs I'm working on. Do you think you can help me?" He asked in a deep sexy voice. Hannah blinked, and then cleared her throat. *My goodness, this man is gorgeous*, she thought, before waving him into her office. "I have a couple of subcontractors that you may be interested in. We've used them before on several projects for the church and they always do a great job. I have some forms you'll need to fill out, and we also do a background and credit check on prospective contractors." She said, as she handed him a stack of papers.

The man stepped into Hannah's office and took the forms from her. In turn, he handed her one of his business cards, and his financial portfolio before introducing himself. "I'm Joseph Jenkins, from Raleigh Durham, North Carolina. I moved up here about six months ago and started a division of Jenkins Construction in the DC area. My friends call me Joe." They shook hands, and Hannah motioned for him to take the seat in front of her desk.

Hannah was impressed with Mr. Jenkins financial statement. She saw that he was a self-made millionaire. Hannah discreetly peeked over the paper in front of her to see if Mr. Fabulous wore a wedding ring, and her heart sank a little when she didn't see a ring, but she did see a faint line where a wedding band used to be. He must be a *playa* she thought. Then she immediately chided herself for unfairly judging him. Joe told Hannah what type of subcontractors he was looking for and he mentioned that he came to her agency, because several of his employees were members of Grace Faith Church.

Hannah was pleased to hear that, and the two engaged in a friendly conversation as Hannah went through her roster of carpenters and painters. She told Joe that she was thinking of expanding the job-training center to include carpentry and painting because of the number of new developments springing up in the area. Hannah was concerned that too many African American men and women were missing out on these opportunities because they didn't have the skills they needed to compete.

Joe looked at Hannah with excitement. "I was originally hired as an apprentice painter myself, but once the foreman on the job saw that I was willing to learn carpentry and other skills, he hired me full time and taught me everything I know. My family runs a training center back in Raleigh Durham where we teach men and women how to become subcontractors. I would like the opportunity to teach this trade to those that want to learn it." He stated emphatically. Hannah was very pleased to hear him say that. "So you wouldn't mind teaching someone how to do this business, even if that means you might have to compete with them?" She asked. Joe smiled, and Hannah nearly fainted from the brilliance of it. His teeth were white and perfectly straight. "I'm a firm believer that people should know how to build their own houses. I just completed mine on Collins Avenue, and the boys and I can't wait to move in. Living in a hotel with six year old twins has been challenging to say the least." Hannah stared at him. "So you're the owner of the huge two story brick colonial with the three car garage?" Joe nodded. Hannah laughed and extended her hand to him across her desk. "Well, welcome to the neighborhood, I live about three houses up from you on the left side of the street." She told him.

Hannah and Joe were engrossed in a lively conversation and didn't hear Daniel when he returned to the center. He had great news that he couldn't wait to share with Hannah. Without knocking, he turned the knob to Hannah's office and stopped short when he saw her talking to a very attractive man, who was busy filling out forms. Jealousy ripped through Daniel with a force that made him stagger backwards. Daniel's hand gripped the doorknob so tightly, that it began to throb. He took a deep breath and got a hold of himself, realizing that he was being silly. Daniel immediately took authority over the *spirit of jealousy* that was attacking him and bound it in the name of Jesus.

He cleared his throat to get Hannah's attention, and forced himself to smile. Hannah and the man stopped talking and turned around towards the door. Irritation quickly turned to disbelief as Daniel stared at the man chatting with his lady. "Joe?" Joe's mouth flew open as he stared at

Daniel. The two men rushed to each other and hugged, then followed it up with an elaborate handshake. Hannah watched the two men with a puzzled expression on her face, apparently they knew each other. Daniel turned to Hannah. "Baby, this is my college roommate Joe Jenkins. I haven't seen him in years. Man, how you been?" Daniel asked in delight.

Joe grinned at his old pal. He and Daniel had been roommates for four years at North Carolina Central University, back in Joe's hometown of Raleigh Durham, North Carolina. Back in the day, Joe and Daniel were *wild* young men, partying and chasing the pretty college women, as they finished their prospective degrees. After Daniel moved to New York after graduation, Joe finally settled down and married his college sweetheart, Deidra. Joe, busy with his new family and building his construction business, and Daniel, working hard to make a name for himself at the law firm where he worked, they had lost touch with each other over the years. Joe was surprised to see Daniel in D.C., and equally surprised when he called Hannah, ***baby***!

Daniel walked over to Hannah and dropped a sweet kiss on her lips. Joe grinned, because he knew Daniel was ***marking*** his territory. "When did you move back to D.C., Dan? I thought you were still in New York." Joe asked.

Intrigued that the two were old friends, Hannah leaned back down in her chair and watched the two men interact. "I moved back in the area a couple of years ago, joined this church and started my practice here." Daniel answered, as he sat down in the chair next to Joe. "What about you," he continued, "how's Deidra and the boys." The smile disappeared on Joe's face, as he lowered his head and quietly mumbled, "Deidra died of breast cancer almost three years ago." He said sadly. Daniel looked at Joe in disbelief. "**What!** Man, I didn't know. I can't believe it, Deidra's gone?" Daniel sadly shook his head. Thinking about the couple's twin boys, he looked at Joe. "How are the twins doing, how are they coping?" Daniel asked, remembering how badly he handled his parent's death. The radiant smiled that had captured Hannah's attention earlier, reappeared on Joe's handsome face. "The boys are doing great, thank God. My family has been wonderful, very supportive. They were with us when Dee died. My mom and sister's stayed with us when Dee took a turn for the worse. They took care of the twins while I was at the hospital with Dee during her final days. They took the twins to church with them, and I eventually started going back too, and rededicated my life to Christ. Dee did the same, and seven months later she died peacefully in her sleep." He told them. Daniel turned to Hannah. "Joe's parents are Bishop Joel and Ernestine Jenkins." He told her. "He's got seven brothers and five sisters, and they're all terrific." Hannah's mouth dropped open. Joel and Ernestine Jenkins were very popular and famous televangelist that Hannah enjoyed watching and partnering with. She peered closely at Joe and yes, she could certainly see the resemblance between him and his famous father.

Daniel turned to Joe, "How long have you been in D.C.? Daniel asked his frat brother. Joe stood up and handed the completed forms back to Hannah. He grabbed his cell phone and keys off her desk. "I moved here last year. I was staying on the other side of town, looking for the right neighborhood to build my house. After Dee died, I started my own construction company with two of my brothers. My sisters run the office. We've made quite a name for ourselves in North Carolina, building houses and commercial projects. Remember my brother Ralph? He owns the largest architecture firm in Raleigh and designs most of our projects. My twin brothers, work for him. My brother Marcus works with my parents in the ministry, and will take over once they retire. My sister Maggie owns her own bridal boutique.

The memories of Dee started to get to me, and I decided to get a start fresh and moved here to start a branch of Jenkins Construction in the D.C. area. I was telling Hannah that some of my employees are members of Grace Faith church and they suggested I come here and sign my company up to hire on more help." He told his friend. A mischievous smile appeared on Joe's face. He cleared his throat and said, "According to Hannah, we're neighbors. I built the house up the street from her." He told Daniel. Hannah tried to hide the grin that threatened to break loose. She knew what Joe was implying, and by the reddened of Daniel's face, so did he. Daniel threw back his head and laughed out loud. "Man, don't even try it. Hannah is *my* baby, and if it's one person I can count, it's my baby." Daniel said, as he made his way over to Hannah.

He sat down on the edge of her desk and took her left hand in his. Looking deeply into Hannah's eyes, he kissed it softly, winked at her, and lowered her hand, but continued to hold it. Daniel enjoyed showing people how much

Hannah meant to him. *Well, do something about it before its too late*; he heard a voice warn him in his spirit.

Startled, Daniel sat straight up! Panic struck Daniel's heart at the thought of losing Hannah to another man, and he silently repented for taking his relationship with Hannah for granted. He promised God he would take care of the situation as soon as possible, because he knew without a shadow of a doubt, that the Lord intended for him and Hannah to be together. Daniel thanked God for blessing him with such a beautiful and amazing woman. Hannah raised her left eyebrow at him, wondering about the peculiar look on his face.

Joe shook his head as he recognized the look on his best friends face. He had once displayed it on his own. Joe reached out and hugged Daniel, nodded goodbye to Hannah, and left, leaving the two love birds alone. Daniel came back around to Hannah's desk and once again perched on the side, positioning himself in front of her, and taking both hands into his, he looked at her and said, "Have I told you today how much I love you? Have I told you today how beautiful you are, not only on the outside but your heart, which is one of the sexiest things about you? Have I told you today, that if I didn't have you in my life I have no idea how I would keep breathing? Have I told you today, that when I wake up in the morning you're the first thing on my mind, and when I lay down at night, your face is the last image I see when I close my eyes? Have I told you Hannah that you are the love of my life and I thank God each and every day that He brought us together? Have I told you Hannah," he said softly as he slid off her desk, to the floor and down on one knee. "That I want to spend the rest of my life with you, to wake up with you next to me each morning and to go to sleep with you by my side each night? To get pregnant with you and watch our children grow inside you and raise them together and dedicated them to the Lord? Hannah Harris, will you marry me and share a life with me? He proposed to her softly.

Speechless, Hannah stared down at the man of her dreams. Tears stung the back of her lids and slowly trickled down her cheeks. She drew Daniel into her arms and kissed him deeply, sealing their agreement. "I would be honored to be your wife, get pregnant with you and raise our children together. I love you with all my heart," she whispered against his warm lips. She kissed him again with such passion that it took Daniel's breath away. Daniel once again heard the Lord. ***"Well done, my son. That was an excellent proposal. You've made my daughter very happy. Just look at her.***" Daniel watched Hannah as she tried to reapply her lipstick. She was having a difficult time because she kept grinning, her face radiating great joy. A warm feeling swept over him as he watched her. She's going to be my wife, he mused to himself in amazement. I can't wait to announce it to the world! Suddenly the Jared jewelry commercial appeared in his mind. He nodded, receiving the message loud and clear. "Baby, let's go to Jared's!"

After picking out a beautiful engagement ring for his beloved, Hannah and Daniel went out for dinner and discussed their wedding plans. Daniel's apartment lease was scheduled to expire in December, six months away. Hannah pulled up the church's website on her phone to check the calendar to see if the church was available for Christmas Eve, which happened to fall on a Friday. They decided to get married Friday, December 24th at sunset.

The church picnic was scheduled for the following day, and Daniel and Hannah decided to announce their engagement there, however, they wanted to do a more intimate announcement with friends and family, so Hannah called Daniel's aunt and uncle, Dr. Kenneth and Kathleen John, Reverend Rawlins and Cecilia Ford, and Hannah's sister and brother in law, Abby and Greg Taylor, and invited them over to her house for dessert. Two hours later, Hannah led her guest into her living room, where she had red velvet cheese cake and coffee set up for them.

Once everyone was seated, Daniel stood and reached for Hannah's hand. She rose and joined him in front of their guest, slipping her hand into his. Daniel turned to their guest. "This afternoon, I asked Hannah to become my wife and she said yes." He beamed. Cecilia, Abby and Katherine, squealed in unison and jumped up from their seats to hug Hannah. Hannah proudly showed them the 2.5 carat engagement ring she and Daniel picked out earlier that afternoon. It was a beautiful chocolate 3 stone ring layered in 14 k gold. It looked beautiful on Hannah's smooth slender, mocha brown manicured hand. Daniel's aunt hugged Hannah again. "Welcome to the family darling. Kenneth and I have been praying for you and Daniel." Abby smiled at her sister and nodded in agreement with Katherine. "We've all been praying for you two. We see how God has been using the two of you to fulfill his prophecy of Isaiah 61:4: ***And they shall build the old wastes, they shall raise up the former desolations, and they shall repair the waste cities, the desolations of many generations.*** You're an inspiration for the other singles in the church that look at you two as an example. Now they can see the manifestation of your faith. Sis, I'm so happy for you" She pulled her little sister in her arms and they held each other tight. Hannah felt so blessed.

Cecilia playfully shoved Abby out the way and grabbed her best friend and hugged her. Abby laughed and stepped back and watched them. She was glad that Cecilia was such a good friend to her sister. There was a time in Hannah's life when Abby and their parents had abandoned her. A lonely Hannah had returned home from college, moved into her own place and rejoined the church she grew up in. Hannah loved Reverend Rawlins. He had become not only a spiritual father to them her, but a surrogate dad, after her parents had killed each other, influenced by the evil spirits Abby's ex-husband's family had exposed them to. At the time, her sister Abby was a rising R& B star, having forsaken her gospel singing career to seek her fortune in secular music. Abby was also abusing drugs and alcohol, at the time, and didn't have time for her sister. When Hannah had no one else, the young widow, Cecilia Ford, had befriended her.

Cecilia whispered in her friend's ear, "I told you I saw a wedding in my dream. I'm so glad it's you, Hannah." Cecilia said as she hugged Hannah again. Reverend Rawlins waited until the two friends had stopped hugging, and he reached out to Hannah. "I'm so happy for you and Daniel; you two are perfect for each other. I'm glad you waited on God to bless you, Hannah." He said sincerely. Hannah hugged him back and held his hand. "Reverend Rawlins, I would love for you to walk me down the aisle." Hannah told him. Tears glistened in Reverend Rawlins eyes; he was so touched by Hannah's request. "I would be honored to walk you down the aisle, sweetheart. I just wish Ruthie and Leroy were still with us so they could share in your happiness."

Abby and Hannah looked at each other and their eyes glistened with tears, as they thought about their parents. "Always remember sweetheart," Dr. Kenneth John said, as he took his turn hugging Hannah, "Ruthie and Leroy will always be with you. Cherish the good memories, and the bad memories will fade."

After things settled down, the woman sat

together and talked about the wedding, while the men gathered around the fireplace. Daniel told them about his friend Joe. Reverend Rawlins was intrigued to hear that Daniel knew Joe's parents, Bishop Joel and Ernestine Jenkins. He was well acquainted with the popular ministers. Reverend Rawlins asked Daniel to invite Joe and his sons to the church picnic that was being held the next day, and Daniel assured him he would.

Their guest left an hour later and while Hannah was in the kitchen busy cleaning up, Daniel pulled out his cell phone and called Joe. He extended the invitation to Joe and the twins to come to the church picnic and meet the pastor and members, Daniel also told his friend that he had asked Hannah to become his wife, and she said yes. Joe congratulated him. After he hung up, Daniel reached over and pulled Hannah into his arms. "Okay, just six more months, and no more going home after dinner. Baby, I can hardly wait!" Hannah laughed and kissed her fiancé on the lips. *Her fiancé*! God had blessed her socks off once again! Two years ago, she was on her way to an appointment, and ended up owning her dream house. The owner had just built the house when her mother had suddenly fallen ill, and she decided to move back to North Carolina to take care of her.

While the movers were loading the woman's furniture into a huge moving truck, she noticed Hannah admiring the house and asked her if she wanted it. The woman, led by the **Spirit**, decided to bless Hannah with the two hundred and fifty thousand dollar house totally **free**! Hannah couldn't believe it. It was everything she wanted in a house!

Once she moved into her dream house, God had blessed her again by bringing Daniel into her life. They hit it off immediately and now, Daniel had finally proposed to her. She was glad that he wanted to live in her house, and she decided to add his name to the deed as a wedding gift to him. Hannah thanked God for allowing her to experience **heaven down here on earth.** She thought about her friend Frieda Wilson, who had died a brutal death, at the hands of the man she was married to. Frieda refused to wait on God for a mate, and had met this man on a matchmaking website called **Fantasylover.com.** Poor unsuspecting Frieda had unwittingly met and married a **fallen angel**, who had assumed the identity of multimillionaire Samuel Dawson, owner of the Cujo Family restaurants. Samuel Dawson had been held captive along with Daniel and thousands of other humans, who had unwittingly logged onto the matchmaking website and had their identities and lives stolen by demonic creatures, who were posing as humans on the site! After being freed, a frightened and humbled Samuel found Grace Faith Church, shared his testimony with the congregation and gave his life to Christ. Samuel enjoyed being a member of the church, and when he found out about the center, he had approached Hannah about teaching a cooking class for the center's adult education program.

Hannah told him that Cecilia held classes at her bakery, **Kingdom Creations,** so Samuel and Cecilia began working together, holding classes at Cecilia's bakery and Samuel's restaurant. Hannah thought about her best friend, and wanted her to be as happy as she was. Joe's handsome face came to mind and she looked at Daniel and grinned. "What?" He asked, as he reached up to put away the last glass. "Maybe you should introduce Joe to Cecilia tomorrow. I know he's a bit younger than she is, but I think they'd make a cute couple. What do you think?" She asked him. Daniel was quiet for a minute. "What kind of woman was Deidra?" Hannah asked curiously. Daniel thought about his girl Deidra, and with a shake of his head, he laughed. "Deidra was **off the chain!** We were **all** concerned when Joe hooked up with her. He's so quiet and conservative and she well, **wasn't!**" He said with a laugh. "My boy Joe likes **drama queens!** I will certainly introduce them, I'm sure the twins will fall in love with Cecilia, because she owns a bakery." He laughed.

After they finished the dishes, Hannah turned off the lights in the kitchen, and they walked hand in hand back to the family room. Daniel sat down on the comfortable sofa and pulled his woman down on his lap. "What happened to your plan to set Cecilia up with Samuel? They seem to work great together. The Progressive dinner fundraiser they did for the scholarship fund turned out great. We made over fifty thousand dollars, and the food was terrific." He said, as he nuzzled Hannah's neck.

Hannah closed her eyes and moaned softly as Daniel's soft kisses left a trail from her neck to her lips. Trying hard to stay focused on the conversations instead of his kisses, Hannah thought about the conversation she had with Cecilia about Samuel. She opened her eyes and looked at her fiancé. "Cecilia confessed to me that it's just too *creepy* for her to think about Samuel romantically, she keeps thinking about his evil alter ego, and how that thing killed poor Frieda."

Daniel shuddered. Romance now forgotten as he thought about Frieda Wilson's death and his own ordeal of being held captive, beaten and tortured by the shape shifting demon that Frieda had married. He shifted uncomfortably on the sofa and Hannah moved off his lap and sat next to him. "Have you spoken to her dad recently?" He asked. Hannah shook her head sadly. "Reverend Rawlins called him a few weeks ago; he's very worried about him. He said Dennis was finally getting used to Ohio, he had found a good church he likes up there, and the people are friendly. However, he's still concerned that Angelina and her *friends* will find him, he's also worried about his son. Apparently, after he was born, Angelina emailed him a picture of the baby. It really tore poor Dennis up." Daniel looked at Hannah in disbelief. "She emailed him? Did you guys tell Greg? He should be able to find Angelina through the IP address." He said excitedly. Hannah shook her head. "Yea, he knows, however, when he traced the IP address, it was for a Starbucks in the Los Angeles area. He had some of his guys staking it out for about two weeks, but didn't turn up anything." They sat there in silence for

24

a moment, each lost in their own thoughts about the events that had transpired that year.

Hannah and Frieda had been friends since fourth grade, and Hannah still felt responsible for encouraging Frieda to marry the fake Samuel Dawson, thinking he was the real deal. Now her friend was dead, killed by the man she thought was her husband, and even worse, poor Frieda died knowing the baby she had given birth to was actually a **Nephilim**, half human and half fallen angel. Hannah was still trying to come to grips with the enemy's scheme to breed humans with demons. Satan did this centuries ago, corrupting the human blood line during Noah's time. This is why God flooded the earth, to get rid of the abominations that the fallen angels had conceived with human women. Reverend Rawlins and Greg Taylor were diligently trying to contact the humans that had signed up for Leah Lewis' website, **Fantasylover.com.** Many of them had no clue that they may have inadvertently given birth to a monster! The babies that Frieda and bestselling author Leah Lewis had birthed, were extremely evil and dangerous. The church had set up an anonymous phone line for users who dated or married someone from the website. They had received thousands of calls and Reverend Rawlins, prompted by the Holy Spirit, met privately with select ministries all over the world, to share with them what the enemy was up to. The ministers met and strategized on the best way to help those dealing with the **hybrid babies**.

With the romantic mood broken, Daniel pulled Hannah up from the sofa so she could walk him to the front door. Their good night kiss lasted about five minutes, and when Daniel reluctantly pulled away from her, he winked and readjustment his pants before leaving. Hannah laughed as she watched him get into his Lexus. He blew her a kiss, and pulled off.

Chapter Two

Azazel paced back and forth in his lair down in hell. He was reeling from the report one of his field *imps* had given him. This particular imp was assigned to Reverend William Rawlins, and the creature overhead Jesus speaking with William about marrying Cecilia. Azazel was flabbergasted by the news and he was trying to come up with a way to thwart God's plan before sharing this dreadful information with *his* master. He understood the danger of William and Cecilia marrying, their church would be stronger and even more powerful than it already was. And if she conceived a child, like the Lord intended her to, the child would wreak *havoc* to Satan's Kingdom. Unable to come up with a scheme to stop the pastor and his lady, Azazel sighed heavily and vanished. He materialized seconds later in the huge, dank home of his master, *Satan*.

Bowing deep before his lord, who sat on his

own throne, a counterfeit of the Most High's in Heaven, Azazel remained bowed down until Satan acknowledged him. When Satan gestured for him to step forward, Azazel did so reluctantly. "What news do you bring me?" Satan snarled. Azazel stammered nervously. "Our enemy appeared to his servant, William Rawlins, and told him it was time for him to marry the **prophetess**, and He's prophesized a son will be born to them!" The fallen angel watched in fascination as his master's face turned inside out with rage. Satan leaped off his throne and roared with anger. Every creature in hell trembled with fear. Azazel discreetly moved away from Satan, fearing his master would attack him in his anger. "I will not allow this! This wedding can't take place and this child will never be conceived. I don't care if we have to destroy this whole city! Those two insufferable humans will not get married, under any circumstances!" Satan stated as he stalked around his throne. Azazel trembled nearby, waiting to be dismissed, but Satan glared at him. "Go and bring me the imp that's assigned to that woman. Bring him to me at once!" He demanded. Azazel bowed and instantly vanished. He shape shifted into a large raven and soared through the sunny blue skies of Washington D.C. Azazel circled the sky, headed for Cecilia's bakery. When he spotted it, he dove head first towards the empty grassy area of the large parking lot, and shape shifted into a human man.

He adjusted the Italian cut suit that appeared on his body, and taking a deep breath he walked into Cecilia's **Kingdom Creations** bakery. There was a short line of people standing in front of the glass counter, trying to decide which of the mouthwatering desserts they wanted. Even Azazel drooled as he looked at the delicious pastries displayed in the glass case. Since his released from the abyss, Azazel had developed a taste for human cuisine, especially sweets. He walked over and pulled a number from the machine on the side of the counter, and waited patiently for his turn, while discreetly searching for the invisible imp assigned to watch over the human woman. Azazel spotted the creature on the ceiling, sitting on a silver hanging light fixture. He made eye contact with the creature and telepathically communicated to him that Satan was demanding his presence. The imp nodded towards Azazel to let him know he received the message, and immediately vanished. Azazel knew he should accompany the imp, but he was determined to purchase some of the red velvet cupcakes that

29

Kingdom Creations was famous for.

When his turn finally came, he smirked at Cecilia, and ordered two cupcakes. Cecilia's heart skipped a beat as she waited on the nice looking man in the expensive suit. She could sense something evil in him and silently began to plead the blood of Jesus over her, her business and the customers in the shop. She called for warrior angels to protect her and her customers. With a fake smile, Cecilia quickly put two cupcakes into a small box and handed it to the gentleman. Azazel hid a grin as he reached into his wallet and pulled out a ten dollar bill. He knew the **Prophetess** could sense who he *really* was. Suddenly, a gust of wind burst through the shop, and Cecilia felt a calming peace flow through her. Unseen by the human eye, several large warrior angels materialized in the bakery, accompanied by Cecilia's guardian angel, Raphael. But only Azazel could see them. The demon glared at the room full of angels, and quickly grabbed his box of cupcakes from Cecilia and bolted from the store. Cecilia silently thanked God for protecting her, and the angels joined her in giving thanks and praises to the Lord.

Raphael, found a nice empty corner in the bakery and silently stood guard over his charge and her business. He knew she was being targeted, and he bitterly remembered how this same demon had sent his minions to attack her. When they didn't find her at home, the angry demons set her house on fire!

Back in Hell, the imp assigned to Cecilia, was joined by the imp assigned to Reverend Rawlins. They were given strict orders by their master. "Do whatever you have to do to stop William Rawlins from marrying Cecilia Ford. If those two end up married, I will rip both of you in half and feed you to my dog." He growled menacingly.

Cerberus, Satan's three-headed hell hound, turned his head when he heard his master mention him. The huge ugly beast looked at the two imps and licked his lips. The winged imps looked at the slobbering beast and trembled with fear. They bowed down to their master and instantly vanished.

Eligos, the demon assigned to Cecilia, returned to the bakery and was surprised to find Reverend Rawlins enjoying a cup of tea and a chocolate croissant in the kitchen. He heard a small pop and looked up to see Forneus, the pastor's imp, swinging next to him on a light fixture. They listened as Cecilia told Reverend Rawlins about the strange man that had come into the shop

31

earlier. "I sensed a presence of evil when I waited on him," she said as she wiped down one of the long metal tables. "He knew it too, because I saw a smirk on his face." She said worriedly. She turned and looked at her best friend. "William, I think those evil beings that kidnapped Daniel and Samuel have returned to wreak more havoc in our lives. I'm concerned about Hannah and Daniel, we can't let them ruin things for them." William nodded as he listened to Cecilia. He chewed thoughtfully on the delicious croissant Cecilia had made just for him. They were delicious as usual, and he knew that she always kept a batch available just for him.

William heard the Lord speak to him. "It's not Hannah and Daniel they're after, it's you and Cecilia." William stopped chewing and stared at Cecilia. The enemy was aware of God's plan for him and Cecilia to wed, and if they were already showing up, William knew Satan had a plan to try and stop what God had decreed.

He debated whether or not to share the revelation the Lord had given him, so he prayed for wisdom. He felt the Lord urging him to confide in Cecilia, so William put down the half eaten croissant and looked at Cecilia. "Cecilia, please come and sit here next to me. I know exactly why they're here." He said to her gently.

Cecilia wiped her hands on her apron and sat down next to William. She noticed the peculiar look on his face and when he reached over to hold her hand in his, Cecilia's heart began to flutter. William took his time, knowing with all certainty that this wonderful woman of God was meant to be his wife.

"You and I have been friends for a long time, CeeCee," he said, calling her by her nickname. "After Wanda died, you went from being my friend to my rock. I don't know if you realize how you kept me and the girls going after her death, and as always, I knew I could count on you to keep the church together while I went through the grieving process." William paused and looked deep into Cecilia's brown eyes. "Sweetheart, you mean more to me than I have ever told you or even allowed myself to think about. I tried to ignore my feelings for you, thinking I was being unfaithful to Wanda's memory, but last year, when the enemy attacked you and set fire to your house, all I could do for days afterwards was thank God that you were safe with me at my house. When you moved back into your own home, I was miserable. The time we spent together while your house was being rebuilt was very precious to me. My daughters saw how miserable I was, and they were angry with me because I allowed you to leave without telling you how much you mean to me. They love you dearly, and so do I." He stood up and gently pulled her into his arms and held her tight.

The two imps stared at the humans in horror! Oh no….he couldn't …. "Cecilia Ford, would you do me the honor of becoming my wife? I love you with all my heart and soul and I don't want to spend another year without you being a part of my life." Before she could answer, William bent down and kissed her deeply.

Eligos frantically looked for something to distract the couple. He spotted a tin canister of flour and he flew over and threw it down next to them on the floor. When the can hit the floor, William and Cecilia abruptly stopped kissing and looked around the kitchen. They spotted the canister next to them on the floor, and Cecilia looked over at the shelf where she kept the canister, and wondered out loud how it managed to fall near them from clear across the room.

Raphael instantly materialized in the kitchen, searching for the two imps. He saw them up on the ceiling and raised his sword, but the imps quickly vanished. A shaken Cecilia laid her head on Williams shoulder. "Baby, they have come back because they know the Lord has given me His blessing for us to marry." William said. Cecilia's head shot up and she looked at him. "He did? The Lord wants us to get married?" She asked softly. William looked at her and nodded. "There's more, honey, He wants us to have a child, and so do I." Cecilia's heart leaped. Tears formed in her huge brown eyes. A baby! She always wanted to have a baby.

After Wanda's death, Cecilia had found herself slowly falling in love with the sweet compassionate minister and his two daughters. Now William wanted to marry her and have a baby with her. God had just answered all of her prayers! William gently lifted Cecilia's face and kissed her again. He was really enjoying this. "Well?" He asked. 'Yes, yes, yes...I love you William with all my heart and soul, you and your daughters." She stopped and looked at him in concern. "Have you told them about this? She asked. William smiled and nodded. "Yes, I called and told them I was going to propose to you last night, and they can't wait to hear from you. Knowing those two, they're already planning the wedding and honeymoon for us." He laughed. Cecilia laid her head on her man's chest. Her man!! "I hope we're not going to steal the spotlight from Hannah and Daniel. They're planning a December wedding; did you have a particular date in mind?" She asked him. William nodded, "If I had my way, I'd say let's do it this week, but the girls would have a fit if I cheat them out of a wedding, but Cecilia, the enemy is aware of our plans, and I want you safe with me. Is three weeks too soon for you?" He asked innocently.

Chapter Three

William arrived back at the church feeling great. He had a spring in his step that he hadn't had in a long time. It had been years since he held a woman in his arms and kissed her, **really** kissed her, and he loved how Cecilia responded to his kisses.

Cecilia had not been with a man since her husband died of cancer when he was twenty-nine years old. After William's wife Wanda died nearly twenty years ago, he had not thought about remarrying until Cecilia stayed with him for nearly four months while her house was being rebuilt. It was wonderful to come home to a delicious home cooked meal, and have someone to talk to, and watch old movies with while eating popcorn. They went out to dinner and movies, socialized with his daughters and their husbands, and also their church friends. When Samuel began working with Cecilia for their joint cooking classes, he became a tad jealous, but she confided in him that it was still spooky to be around Samuel, and William's heart soared. Poor Cecilia had witnessed the fallen angel, disguised as Samuel, murder Frieda right in front of Dennis, the girl's father. William realized that the enemy was going to do everything to try and stop his wedding, but he was determined to make sure he and his beautiful fiancée would be married right away.

Before heading into his office, he stopped at his secretary's desk, and asked her to order a dozen red roses to be sent to Cecilia at the bakery. He grinned at the surprised look on her face as he dictated the note for the flowers: ***Looking forward to spending the rest of my life with you, Love William***.

He grabbed an apple, bit into it, and then looked at Agnes and grinned. "I just proposed to Cecilia, and she said yes." He told his stunned assistant. "Could you look at the church's calendar and tell me if there is a free Saturday afternoon available in three weeks?" He asked her. Agnes stared at him with her mouth wide open. She was thrilled that her dear friend finally **woke up** and realized that he and Cecilia were perfect for each other, but he was giving them only three weeks to plan a wedding? That made absolutely no sense!

Agnes glared at William. "Reverend, no woman in their right mind would even consider trying to put a wedding together in three weeks! I can't believe that Cecilia agreed to that." She said, appalled. William grinned. "I know its short notice, but I trust that between you, CeeCee, my daughters and the rest of the women in the church, you ladies will have us standing before the altar in three weeks." He noticed the disapproving look on her face and decided to come clean with her. "This morning the enemy showed up at her bakery. The Lord has warned us that they are going to try and do everything to stop this wedding, so that's why we're moving so fast. Beside, neither CeeCee nor I are spring chickens and it's been a long time for both of us, if you know what I mean." He said with a wicked grin on his face.

Agnes' mouth fell open once again. This was a side of her beloved pastor she hadn't seen in years. Laughing, she stood up and walked around her desk and gave him a big hug. "I'm so happy for both of you, and I'm going to personally make sure this is one of the best weddings every held at Grace Faith Church. William thanked her and hugged her back. They spent some time looking over the calendar, and after rescheduling some thing, they came up with a date in July. Agnes called Cecilia and confirmed the date with her, and once that was done, Agnes got busy. She called Samuel Dawson about catering the event, which he agreed to and then she called her friend Josie, who owned a florist shop.

William went into his office and briefly checked the messages on his desk, and not finding anything urgent, he sat down and called his friend Dennis Wilson, who was in town visiting. When Dennis answered, William got right to the point. "Dennis, they're back. Cecilia just spotted one in her shop. It appeared in human form, but she was able to discern what he was. I'm calling to give you a head's up, so you can watch your back." William told the man on the phone.

Dennis' voice cracked when he answered. "She contacted me again last week. She wants to introduce me to our son. I just can't get rid of this woman, William; she's tracked me down in two different cities." He said miserably.

William sighed. He tried to tell his friend that you can't run from the devil, but he wouldn't listen. "Well I'm glad you came back here, Dennis. Trying to stand against the enemy by yourself is suicide. Now you have the whole congregation backing you up, praying for you. We have some great prayer warriors in the congregation, and with God's help, He will protect you." William said evenly. "I know, pastor, but I just feel so foolish. How in the world did I fall for a demonic spirit? I was the head deacon of Grace Faith Church." Dennis said sadly.

Fed up with his dear friend feeling sorry for himself, William snapped. "That's just pride talking, man. None of us are strong enough to defeat the enemy in our own power. The Lord is the only one who can take on Satan and win. Besides, I'm going to need you three weeks." Reverend Rawlins said. "Three weeks? What's going on in three weeks?" Dennis asked his friend. "Cecilia and I are getting married!" William told him. "What! That's great and about time!" Dennis whopped, gratefully to hear some good news.

After chatting a few more minutes with his friend, William then called Greg Taylor to see how he was coming along with their special project; tracking down the Nephilim. Greg told his pastor that he did have some information and wondered if William could stop by his house on his way home. "Abby and Renee are over at Hannah's and RJ' and Greg Jr. are watching the NBA finals at a friend. It would be just us." William told him he would be there around five-thirty. Hours later, William told Agnes good night, and whistled on his way out the door. Agnes smiled and shook her head.

When William arrived at the Taylor's home, Greg opened the door to let him in. "I have the information in the family room, come on in." William followed Greg into the back room and got the shock of his life when he saw most of the men from the congregation waiting for him. "Congratulations! They shouted when William walked into the room! "What? How? Oh my!" William said, speechless.

Greg reached over and hugged his spiritual father. William had been his pastor and friend since Greg was a teenager. "Cecilia told Hannah and Abby about your engagement, and Abby told me. I got the guys together and we decided to throw you an impromptu bachelor party."

William couldn't believe the table was filled with all his favorite foods, buffalo chicken wings, pizza, beer, chips n dips, and Cecilia's famous red velvet cupcakes. The men crowded to congratulate him on his upcoming nuptials. When it was Daniel's turn to speak to the pastor, he gave him a hug and said. "When Hannah told me about your engagement, we were wondering if you and Cecilia wanted to do a double wedding in December." William looked at the young man.

"Cecilia and I are getting married on the 23rd of this month." He told him. "What!! That's in three weeks!" All the men exclaimed in unison. Dr. Kenneth John shook his head. "I can tell you're really out of practice when it comes to women. No woman in their right mind would agree to get married in three weeks, William." He admonished his dear friend.

William looked at his friend and grinned. "Cecilia did" He said smugly. Kenneth shook his head in disbelief. William looked at his dearest friends and decided to tell them the truth. "I'd like to share something with you, and I would appreciate if it didn't leave this room. There's a reason why we want to do this as soon as possible. This afternoon, Cecilia waited on a young man that came into her bakery and she immediately sensed evil in him. She believes that it was one of the evil spirits that attacked us a couple of years ago." He told them.

The room was so quiet you could have heard a pin drop on the carpeted floor. Greg looked at his pastor. "You think they're back, pastor?" He asked quietly. Reverend Rawlins nodded. "The Lord visited me a few nights ago, and blessed my marriage to Cecilia. He also told me that He's going to bless us with a son."

Once again the men stared at their friend. William chuckled. "I felt the same way, until recently. I thought I was too old to start another family, but the more I meditated on it, the more I began to look forward to having a baby in the house. When I proposed to Cecilia, I told her that the Lord wanted to bless us with a son, and she was ecstatic. However, when she told me about the enemy showing up in her shop, the Lord spoke to me and said that the enemy was aware of His plans for us to marry and have a child. After I heard that *revelation,* I shared it with Cecilia and told her I wanted her with me as soon as possible. I have to keep her safe. The enemy is gearing up to try and stop this wedding and I need all of you to be vigilant. Please keep us in your prayers to help us get through this." He asked them. He turned to Daniel. "Son, if the enemy can't get to me or Cecilia, they will attack those closest to us. Don't let down your guard. They are determined to try and wreak havoc on each of us."

William then turned his attention towards Dennis. "I hope you're planning on staying at my house until the wedding." Dennis looked at his old friend and nodded. "Yes, thank you. I was just telling the guys before you arrived that my so called ex wife contacted me again by email and sent me pictures of our son. She named him after me, and now she's threatening to sue me for child support if I don't contact her back. I've hired Daniel to help me and he's been doing research to see what my rights are. I don't mind paying child support to take care of my son; however, I don't want anything to do with *her*." He said emphatically.

"Reverend, the legal issues are very complicated. I just found out that my name is still on a marriage certificate in St. Louis MO, where Cynthia Reed married the demon that stole my identity. I've been trying to track her down so we can get an annulment, but so far, I'm not having any luck." He said dejectedly. Greg looked at his friend and soon to be brother in law and said. "Roger called earlier, he thinks he has a lead on her. She had a grandmother that she spent quite a bit of time with in New Orleans Louisiana, and he's flying down there first thing in the morning to search for her." He told him.

Daniel became excited and prayed, "Please Lord, help him find her! I would hate to disappoint Hannah by postponing our wedding until I get this divorce or annulment out of the way." His uncle, Dr. Kenneth John reached over and hugged his nephew. Daniel turned towards William. "Are we destined to fight these demons for the rest of our lives? He asked, discouraged. William looked at him with a sad smile.

"Remember what it says son, in Ephesians 6 verse 10: *Finally, be strong in the Lord and in the strength of his might. Put on the whole armor of God that you may be able to stand against the schemes of the devil.* Jesus told his disciples in Matthew 16 verse 19: *I will give you the keys of the kingdom of Heaven. Whatever you bind on earth is bound in heaven, and whatever you loose on earth will be loosed in Heaven.* When Jesus left this world to be with His father in heaven, he told the disciples. *Whatsoever things I do, you shall do and greater, because I go to be with my father.* Reverend Rawlins looked at everyone and said very seriously. "As long as you've made Jesus, Lord of your life, you'll always have to contend with demonic spirits. Remember, the enemy comes to kill, steal and destroy mankind, and as disciples of Christ, we are Satan's sworn enemies. Jesus made it very clear, that our job was to continue His work, healing the sick, taking care of the poor and casting out demonic spirits. Each of us that take that mandate seriously, and not only **hear** the word, but are **doers** of the word, have a target on our back. However, please don't let that discourage you, always remember we know how the book ends, and we win! You just have to be ready to fight the good fight of faith." He said somberly.

Greg looked at his spiritual father and nodded. "Yeah, just ask Abby. That's why she taught the church, and wrote her bestselling book, ***Powerful Prayer to Protect & Bless Your Family*,*** so others would know how to speak prayers of protection, and blessings over their families." He told his friends proudly. Greg turned towards William. "Reverend, I can have my men keep an eye on Cecilia until she moves into your house after the wedding." He offered. William thanked him, then cleared his throat before addressing his friends. "I'm moving into Cecilia's place after the wedding, and Dennis, I could either sell my house to you, or rent it to you, if you're interested." He told his friend. Dennis looked at him in disbelief. "Are you serious? I would love to buy your house. Your daughters aren't interested in keeping it?" He asked. William shook his head. "Both my girls have families and homes of their own. Also, as much as they love CeeCee, I didn't want them to feel uncomfortable with me living with another woman in the house where they were raised by me and their mother." He said softly. The other men murmured in agreement. One of the deacons proposed a toast to their pastor and afterwards, they spent the rest of the evening enjoying the food, and discussing church business, sports and how to deal with the Nephilim problem.

Meanwhile, on the other side of town, several women from the church were gathered at Hannah's house, celebrating Cecilia's engagement. After Cecilia called Hannah and told her about the reverend's proposal, Hannah reached out to Abby and they quickly pulled together a small party for Cecilia, complete with food and bridal magazines. Agnes, was there and she had everyone laughing as she told them about Reverend Rawlins.

"Girl, he was just grinning and telling me how he couldn't wait any longer than three weeks, because it's been such a long time, if you know what I mean, and he gave me this **wicked** grin! I was so shocked, I nearly fell out of my chair. He was thoroughly enjoying himself!" She laughed. They all laughed and looked at Cecilia who was blushing. She looked at Agnes. "Did he really?" She asked. Agnes nodded and gave her a hug. "Cecilia, I haven't seen him this happy in a long time. I'm so glad he came to his senses and realized you two are perfect together." She told her friend.

Cecilia looked at her friends, and thanked God for blessing her with them.

"According to William, God wants to bless us with a son." She told them. Her friends knew how much Cecilia wanted a baby, and they were ecstatic overjoyed for this mighty woman of God. Hannah hugged her and whispered in her ear, "Wouldn't it be great if we got pregnant at the same time so our can kids grow up together?" Cecilia laughed and hugged her back. "That would be awesome; however, since you and Daniel won't be married until December, my son may be about 6 months older than yours! I want to get pregnant on my honeymoon!" She declared mischievously. Hannah laughed and hugged her again. "I hear ya!" Everybody laughed.

Abby looked over at the two women and smiled, however, Daniel's aunt Kathryn noticed the strained look on her face. Concerned, she leaned over and whispered. "Are you okay? What's wrong?" Abby looked at the older woman and motioned for her to follow her into the kitchen. When they arrived, Abby shut the kitchen door and turned to Kathryn.

"I've been having bad dreams all week about Daniel and Hannah's wedding." She confessed sadly. "I'm not real sure what the Lord is trying to tell me, however, when Cecilia mentioned that the enemy was aware of her and Reverend Rawlins plan, my spirit began to jump all over the place." Kathryn looked at her with trepidation, she was well aware of Abby's gift of discerning spirits, a gift that was discovered when she was a young child, so Kathryn knew not to downplay Abby's concern.

"Have you spoken to Reverend Rawlins about your dreams?" She asked Abby. Abby shook her head. "Greg knows, and that's why he had the guys meet at our house to throw the reverend a little get together. Greg promised me that he would talk to both him and Daniel. I'm reluctant to even tell Hannah about the dreams, I just don't want to upset her, she's so incredibly happy." Abby told her sadly.

"What are the dreams about, Abby?" Kathryn asked, not sure if she really wanted to know. "I see Hannah and Daniel standing at the altar in front of Reverend Rawlins, it's a beautiful wedding, and the whole congregation is in attendance. Right before the ceremony begins, a huge wind blows the church doors open, and I see two medium sized funnel clouds, like mini tornadoes, rushing into the church, destroying everything. Pandemonium is everywhere, and once the tornadoes leave, the only one standing in front of the altar with Reverend Rawlins is Hannah, Daniel is gone, swept away by the storm."

Kathryn found a chair and sat down. "Oh Jesus, help us!" I knew I shouldn't have asked," she said wearily. "Honey, I'm no prophet, but it doesn't take one to see that your dream is telling you that something very bad is going to happen. I believe the enemy is going to try and stop their wedding too!"

Chapter Four

In New Orleans, Louisiana, Cynthia Reed James was busy cooking up a pot of seafood gumbo for her guest. After her marriage to the *fake* Daniel James fell apart, she packed up and left D.C., and moved to New Orleans in her grandmother's old house that she had inherited years ago. Cynthia was still bitter and scared about the events that had transpired in her marriage. After barely escaping with her life, she and her mom Anne, had fled to New Orleans to hide from her daughter, Danielle, and Danielle's half-brother CJ.

Cynthia had tried to forget about Daniel and their daughter and start her life over again; however, her mom couldn't handle the sexual abuse that she had suffered at the hands of her fake son in law, and after returning to New Orleans, Anne suffered a complete mental break down and Cynthia had to commit her to a mental hospital.

Cynthia was determined to move forward with her life and put the whole miserable incident behind her. She had looked up her old girlfriends when she arrived back in town, and it didn't take long for them to fall back into their old routine of getting together on Friday nights. The group of women had been friends since they were six years old and back then they called themselves the G.O.C. (Girl's Only Club, no boys allowed.)

Now, in their thirties, the women hosted a Girl's Night, once a month on a Friday and tonight was Cynthia's turn to host the event. Each host was responsible for creating a menu of food and drinks, and tonight she was serving her grandmother's famous seafood gumbo. She was also serving pitchers of her famous New Orleans style *Hurricanes*.

Cynthia left the gumbo simmering on the stove, while she lit candles and set up the bar in the family room. Cynthia felt right at home in her grandmother's house, and she was grateful that it had been left to her in the will. Before she married Daniel, Cynthia lived in St. Louis MO and had only used the house for vacations, but now, this was the only place where she felt safe. She glanced at her watch and realized her guest would be arriving in two hours. She checked the buffet table where she had the snacks laid out, and finally went upstairs to shower and dress.

When her guest arrived, Cynthia made sure everyone had a drink and was comfortable. The day before, her cousin Gayle called and asked if she could bring one of her co-workers, Sandy Lewis. Sandy was new in town, and she and Gayle had hit it off immediately. A few months ago, while having lunch together, Gayle was telling Sandy about the good time the ladies have on Friday nights, and Sandy hounded her with questions. So Gayle, feeling sorry for Sandy because she was new in town, called Cynthia to see if it was okay to bring her.

While the ladies sat around the card table playing spades, and listening to jazz from her iPod, Cynthia played bartender, mixing up her delicious Hurricanes and passing around appetizers. The ladies made Gayle's friend Sandy feel right at home, and soon, the conversations were flowing along with the Hurricanes.

Cynthia was in the kitchen, preparing to bring out her gumbo, when she heard the doorbell ring. She yelled out for someone to see who was at the front door, while she placed the gumbo, rice, jalapeno cornbread muffins and green salad on the large dining room buffet for her guest. When she finished, she removed her apron and stepped into the living room to see who was at the door.

An attractive African American man stood in her foyer talking to Gayle. Cynthia stared at the man; he seemed vaguely familiar. The man saw her and introduced himself. "Mrs. James, I'm Roger Bacon, and I work for Taylor and Taylor Investigations in Washington DC. May I have a word with you in private, please?" He asked politely. Cynthia immediately panicked. Oh no, they had found her!

Noticing the stricken look on her face, Roger, stepped towards her, to reassure her he meant her no harm. Cynthia quickly hid behind Gayle for protection. "Why are you here? What do you want?" She demanded, trembling with fear. Hearing the commotion in the foyer, the rest of the ladies stepped into the foyer and stood behind their friend.

Realizing he was surrounded by women determined to protect their friend, Roger, raised his hands in surrender. "Ladies, I promise I'm not here to cause trouble. I just have a legal document that I need to discuss with Mrs. James." Feeling braver with her girls having her back, Cynthia stepped out from behind Gayle and cautiously approached Roger. "What legal document?" She asked curiously. Roger reached into his right breast pocket and pulled out a piece of paper and handed it to her. She took it and turned away from him to read it. What she read made her gasp. It was a petition for an annulment! She turned on him. "Who sent you here with this?" She demanded fearfully. Roger was not comfortable discussing this with everyone staring at him, so he asked again, "Is there some place we can speak in private and I'll explain everything to you?" He asked.

Before Cynthia could reply, her friend and lawyer, Simone Montegut snatched the paper away from her and quickly read it. When she finished she turned and looked at Cynthia with a puzzled look on her face. "Your husband is dead. Why would you need to have your marriage annulled?" She asked her.

Cynthia glared at Roger, upset that his arrival had put her on the spot with her friends. With a deep sigh of resignation, Cynthia shocked her friends, "Daniel is not dead, he's alive. What happened between us was so crazy and bizarre, I couldn't think of a way to tell you guys what *really* happened. I found out that the man I was married to was not Daniel James, he was an imposter." She told them. They stared at her. "If he wasn't Daniel James, then who was he?" Simone asked, puzzled. Not sure how to answer, Cynthia turned helplessly towards Roger. "The person Cynthia married was a con artist," He told them, embellishing the truth for her. "He was responsible for stealing people's identity and duping women into marrying him. I represent the real Daniel James, who's engaged to be married in less than six months." He told the group.

Roger reached into his breast pocket and pulled out an ink pen that he handed to Cynthia. "Mr. James would really appreciate you signing this document, so both of you can legally move on with your lives." Before Cynthia could take the pen he offered her, Simone, shook her head at Roger. "I'm Cynthia's attorney, and I need to look into this further before I can advise my client to sign this. Do you have a business card or phone number where we can reach you?" She asked firmly.

Roger reached into his breast pocket and pulled out his business card. He circled his cell phone number and handed the card to Simone. Simone thanked him and escorted him to the door. "Give me two days to check this out, and I'll give you a call. My client has suffered much heartache and distress because of this situation. Her husband, this Mr. James, should probably hire an attorney too, so that we can get this resolved. I have to protect my client's best interest." Simone told him, before closing the door in his face. Roger stood on the outside porch, stunned.

The other women laughed, not believing the gall of Simone, who had a reputation of being a very aggressive defense attorney. The ladies returned to the dining room, and made a beeline to the buffet, where Cynthia had laid out the food. While the other woman were busy fixing their plates, and refreshing their drinks, Simone pulled Cynthia into the kitchen and confronted her. With arms folded in front of her, she glared at Cynthia. "Alright," She demanded. "What in the world is really going on? I can't help you if I don't know EVERYTHING!" She told her friend sternly. Cynthia nodded. "I need to be honest with everyone. Let's grab a plate and a drink and I'll tell you the whole ugly story about my marriage." She said reluctantly. Cynthia reached into the fridge and grabbed a pitcher of Hurricanes. "By the time I finish with my story, you guys are going to need something a lot stronger than this."

They went back into the dining room, where the other ladies were busy eating and whispering amongst themselves about Cynthia's mysterious marriage. "Tonight, I'm going to tell you the **true** story about my marriage, and all I can say is this: Be prepared to be totally blown away. What I'm about to share with you is the truth, and I have proof to back up what I'm about to tell you." Cynthia said miserably.

Intrigued, the ladies waited while Cynthia and Simone filled their plates and found a seat. "Everything I told you guys about how I met Daniel is true." Cynthia began. "I met him on a dating website, **Fantasylover.com** and after we met in person, we really connected. We got married a few months later and moved to D.C., that's when things began to fall apart. First my mother dropped in unexpectedly and went behind my back and convinced Daniel to allow her to move in with us. She and I were barely speaking at the time. However, things really got crazy after Leah Lewis came to my house and accused me of sleeping with her husband." "**The** Leah Lewis, the author, you knew her?" Everyone asked in unison. Cynthia nodded. "Leah had hired a private detective to follow her husband Claude. She suspected that he was having an affair. When the trail led back to me, Leah came over and accused me of sleeping with him, however, once she realized I had just had a baby, she..." "A baby!" Her cousin Gayle yelled. "You didn't tell us you have a baby. Where is it? Is it a boy or girl?" She asked her cousin excitedly.

Cynthia held up her hands to quiet the group down. "I'm getting to that, just bear with me; this is very painful to talk about." She said tearfully. The women forced themselves to settle down while Cynthia collected herself. Clearing her throat, she continued. "Like I was saying, when Leah realized I had just had Danielle, and I showed her the family portrait we had taken, she broke down and explained to me that her husband had been disappearing for weeks at a time, and the detective she hired had followed him to my house. After she realized, I wasn't the one her husband was cheating with, she called me the next day and asked if I would accompany her to the detective agency that gave her the wrong information; however, it was all just a setup.

Leah had the limo driver take us to an office that was owned and operated by this church in D.C. called Grace Faith. When we arrived, a woman named Hannah came out to greet us, and with her was my **husband** Daniel, who I thought was in St. Louis on a business trip! Now, ya'll know I went off, right?" She asked her friends.

They all nodded, they would have gone off too!

"I turned and slapped the mess out of Leah for setting me up; I couldn't believe she played me like that. Anyway, after security pulled me off of her, they separated us and put me in a room until I cooled off. The guards then escorted me into the main conference room with the others. The Hannah lady called her brother in law, Greg Taylor, he owned the private investigation company that Leah had hired to follow her husband, and he explained to me and Leah that we were married to the same man!" Cynthia stopped and took a sip of her drink.

"What, how could you two be married to the same man?" Simone asked. "Did they look alike?" Cynthia shook her head no, then continued her story. "At first, neither Leah nor I wanted to believe that, but Greg had me call my husband on his cell phone, while the **real** Daniel was sitting across from me. When I called, **my** Daniel answered and confirmed that he was still in St. Louis. They had me keep him on the phone, while Leah called her husband, Claude. My husband placed me on hold, and we all heard him answer his phone as Claude, Leah's husband! We were so outdone, that we both hung up and just stared at each other." She paused to catch her breath, while the ladies murmured amongst themselves.

Cynthia sadly shook her head and looked at her friends. "Trust me, you haven't heard anything yet, this gets much worse. After we hung up, there was a pastor in the conference room with us, I believe his name was Reverend Rawlins, and he began to explain to Leah that this was all her fault. Her and those damn books! He told her that she had opened up a *demonic spiritual realm*, and evil spirits had come through a portal and taken on the form of men."

Sandy laughed out loud. Everyone turned and looked at her. She coughed politely and looked at them. "That's just crazy! You guys don't really believe that do you?" She scoffed. Cynthia stood up. "I told you I had proof, didn't I? Wait right here." She quickly left the room and ran up the steps to her bedroom. She returned a couple of minutes later carrying a huge box filled with pictures and newspaper clippings. She also had her IPad with her. Cynthia sat back in her chair, and passed around the family pictures of her, the man she was married to, and their lovely daughter Danielle.

Cynthia continued her story. "The man Leah and I married was a *fallen angel*. Reverend Rawlins told us that this fallen angel was one of the original *watchers*, angels that the Lord had sent to earth after he created humans, to watch over them. Instead, this demon and one hundred and ninety nine of his buddies began to lust after human women, and they decided to breed with the women, and start a new race of men that carried their *angelic* bloodline. Their offspring were called The *Nephilim*, and they were huge, giants actually."

She opened up her bible and found Genesis 6 and read that chapter out loud. Simone picked up her drink, took a long sip and laid the glass back on the table. "C'mon Cynthia, you're way too intelligent to take that literally. Men wrote the bible, not God. I'd rather have you believing in that voodoo crap your grandmother use to do, instead of this junk." She scoffed disdainfully. Pain swept across Cynthia's face, and Simone immediately felt bad. She knew how much Cynthia loved her deceased grandmother and she quickly apologized. "I'm sorry honey, I know you believe in all that stuff, but it's just not real, none of it!" Cynthia shook her head. "Simone girl, you don't have a clue. One of the reasons this demon choose me, was *because* of my voodoo heritage from Granny! They knew my daughter would inherit that same evil, and trust me she

64

did." Gayle looked at the picture of the sweet little infant girl and shook her head. Thinking her cousin was losing her mind like her mother had, she felt bad for Cynthia.

"Then what happened?" Her friend Deborah asked. Cynthia looked at her. "After the pastor explained all of this to us, Greg, the private investigator, showed us a DVD that he recorded, that showed Leah's husband and their child flying around the kid's nursery. They could also become invisible." She told them. There was an uneasy silence in the room as the ladies looked at each other. Realizing they didn't believe her, Cynthia grabbed her IPad and logged onto the Internet. After she signed into her YouTube account, she searched for a minute, and after finding what she was looking for, she clicked on the video and turned the IPad around for all to see.

Her friends gathered around the device and watched as a beautiful pregnant woman yelled at a doctor in a hospital emergency room and when security attempted to apprehend her, the woman immediately transformed into a huge hideous, black winged creature. The creature glared at the hospital staff, and then *flew* towards the ceiling, shattered the skylights, and disappeared. Before her guest could respond to what they had seen,

Cynthia clicked on another video that featured best-selling author Leah Lewis, who was severely battered and bruised. Leah was speaking to the press from the hospital, and they listened in horror as the woman described the brutal beating she endured by her husband and his attempt to kill her. Cynthia's friends were mesmerized as they watched Leah, who could barely keep her head up, share with the press the information Reverend Rawlins had explained to her about how she had inadvertently opened a demonic realm and released these deadly creatures. The video ended with Leah pleading to her fans to stay away from her new movie and to stop buying and reading her books.

Cynthia turned off the IPad and continued her story. "Reverend Rawlins told us that Satan was once again trying to re-create a Nephilim race of men and angels by using Leah's website. Apparently, when humans registered for the site, they were kidnapped and held against their will, and one of the demons would assume their identity. They would then mate with a human in the hopes of giving birth to the *Nephilim*. My daughter, Danielle and Leah's son, CJ, are both Nephilim, and if I didn't believe it when the pastor told me at the meeting, I became a believer when I returned home to get my daughter. I raced home to pack so I could leave before my husband realized that I knew everything. When I went to my daughter's room, Leah's son and Danielle's half-brother, CJ was there, waiting for me. This four year old kid had a huge *machete* and he tried to kill me. This is how I got this scar." She pulled up the sleeve on her blouse and showed her friends an ugly raised scar. They gasped in disbelief.

Tears fell from Cynthia's eyes, as she continued. "My beautiful baby girl was cheering her brother on while I fought to get the machete away from him. Luckily, my mom came in, saw what was going on, and was able to drag me out of the room. Then CJ and Danielle flew out her bedroom window and disappeared. I haven't seen my daughter since, and I hope I never do." She finished emphatically.

The women looked at each. What Cynthia told them made absolutely no sense, yet they saw her scar and they could see how reliving whatever happened, still upset and terrified her. Cynthia passed around newspaper clippings, and her friends read newspaper articles about millions of people disappearing, and reports about babies that were able to do some amazing things. Cynthia looked at her friends. "What's really scary is that Leah's website is still up and running, and people are signing up every day!" She said with a shudder. Simone wasn't sure what to make of all this, but there was one thing she did know. The *real* Daniel James had some explaining to do if he wanted to get out of this marriage!

Later, while Gayle and Cynthia were in the kitchen cleaning up, Simone and Sandy sat out on the front porch with the other ladies, sipping their drinks. Sandy turned to her. "Do you really believe all of that, I mean with you being an attorney and everything? She asked her discreetly. Simone turned and looked at the woman next to her. "Honestly, I'm not sure what to think. I've known Cynthia since we were six, her granny was strange, always concocting potions and putting spells and hexes on people, but we just thought she was eccentric, but this..." She waved her hands around. "I don't know what to think." She admitted. Simone turned to her sister Valerie. "What do you think?" She asked. Valerie took a sip of her drink before answering. "Before Cynthia had her mom hospitalized, I stopped by here one day to see Cynthia, but she wasn't home. I did, however, have a very strange conversation with Anne. She confided in me that she had been raped by two *demons*, and she swore that one of them was Cynthia's husband. Cynthia had told me her mom was delusional, so I really didn't pay much attention to what she said, but now, after hearing this." She shrugged her shoulders and took another sip of her drink.

Cynthia stepped out on the porch carrying a fresh pitcher of Hurricanes. She overheard Valerie. "Val, what my mom told you was true. After mom and I escaped and moved here, she finally broke down and told me that she had been sleeping with my husband for months, before I gave birth." Cynthia said wearily as she sat down to join the women on the porch.

"What! No way. Anne was sleeping with Daniel?" Simone asked in disbelief. Cynthia nodded. "She thought she was in love with him, but one night, the same night I gave birth to Danielle, he took her home and raped and beat her until she became unconscious. When she came to, another man was in our apartment with Daniel, and the two of them took turns assaulting her. When she threatened to tell me everything, and go to the police, she said Daniel transformed into a monster, fangs and all, and threatened to kill her. She knew that he was more than capable, so she kept quiet, and endured his attacks until

69

we fled. That's the real reason I had to have her committed, she just couldn't deal with **that** anymore. I wanted to be mad at her for sleeping with my husband, but ya'll know my mama, she'll sleep with anybody if she thinks they'll take care of her, but even *she* didn't deserve that." Cynthia said, holding back a sob.

Chapter Five

The ladies finally left Cynthia's house about one in the morning, and after Sandy arrived home, she immediately shape shifted into her true form and vanished, reappearing seconds later in Hell. She bowed down in front of her master, and reported to Satan what transpired at Cynthia's house.

Satan was furious! Thanks to that meddling pastor, William Rawlins, the humans were aware of his plans. He angrily stomped around his throne, trying to devise a plan to stop the annoying pastor once and for all. He turned and looked back at Sandy. "Stay close to the human woman and keep me informed. I will not allow their marriage to take place. Daniel belongs to me! Seduce him, kidnap him. Do whatever you have to do to stop that wedding!" He ordered, as he glared at the creature. The demon nodded and vanished.

Satan then summoned Azazel. "We got rid of that annoying pastor's last wife when she interfered with my plans for that human, Abby Harris. I want you to do the same with that prophetess! Father didn't say I couldn't **kill** her and I want her dead!" Satan said with an evil smirk." Azazel bowed down to his master and immediately vanished.

Azazel transformed himself into a huge black crow and soared through the skies towards Cecilia's bakery. When he arrived, he flew into a tall tree, across from her shop and perched himself on a thick branch. Azazel had an excellent view inside the bakery, and he carefully watched Cecilia's every move.

He searched the store for the imp assigned to Cecilia, and when he spotted him, he telepathically communicated with the imp, and together they waited for an opportunity to attack!

Cecilia was in the bakery's kitchen busy kneading dough for her pies, when the Holy Spirit whispered to her. She listened carefully as the *Spirit* advised her to cover herself with the blood of the *Lamb*, because the enemy was near. She quickly obeyed that still small voice and when she asked for angelic protection, *Raphael*, her guardian angel instantly materialized in the kitchen. She couldn't see him with her natural eyes, because he was invisible, but she immediately became calm as she felt his presence near her.

As the line of customers grew, one of the sales clerks called out for assistance, so Cecilia wiped her hands on her apron and stepped behind the counter. She was amazed to see so many people in the bakery on a Wednesday afternoon. Cecilia stood behind the cash register while her two sales clerks waited on customers. Soon, only two customers were left and when the last customer stood in front of Cecilia to pay for his donuts, he casually reached into his pocket and pulled out a gun!

"Lady, all I want is your money, don't do nothing stupid and make me shoot you." The gunman said quietly. Cecilia noticed that the young man's eyes were red, and he was shaking and scratching his arms. Realizing that he was probably strung out on the cheap heroin that was circulating in the neighborhood, she reached into the cash register and pulled out a handful of money. Cecilia was determined not to let him see her fear. "Here, that's all I have. Please leave, and young man, I'm going to pray for you because this is **not** God's will for your life." She told him as she handed him the money.

Azazel hopped up and down on the tree branch, as he watched the drama in the bakery with glee. He had spotted the young man sleeping in his car across the street from the bakery's parking lot, and he sent a mental *command* for him to rob the bakery. Azazel showed the junkie *visions* of hundreds of dollars in Cecilia's cash register and safe, enticing the strung out junkie. When Azazel heard Cecilia tell the man she was going to pray for him, he immediately sent the robber visions of his childhood.

Anger quickly rose up inside the man, and he glared at Cecilia. The man's father had been a preacher, a very bad one. When he was a child, his father would beat him mercilessly over the simplest infractions, while telling him over and over, "I'm going to pray for you." The man raised the pistol to Cecilia's head. "I don't need your stinking prayers lady, I don't believe in your God, but let me show you what I do believe in." He sneered. The two frightened clerks ran screaming into the back of the shop and hid in the kitchen. One of the clerks whipped out her cellphone and dialed 911. Cecilia quietly bowed her head and prayed. With a wicked grin, the gunman pulled the trigger, but before the bullet left the chamber,

Raphael, her guardian angel, waved his hand, and the gun misfired. Dumbfounded when the gun just clicked, the man stared at the pistol in shock.

The invisible imp in the shop, quickly flew over to the man and sat on his shoulder. He reminded him about the knife in his back pocket. The robber sneered at Cecilia, and reached into his back pocket, grabbed his knife and swung it towards her throat!

But Raphael quickly bought his sword down on the man's arm and the knife fell harmlessly to the floor. The junkie stared down at the knife on the floor and fear gripped him. *What in the world?* He knew he had bullets in his gun, and the woman should be dead, but she wasn't, and when he tried to stab her with his knife, it just fell right out of his hands. Terrified man grabbed his donuts and ran out of the bakery. Cecilia quickly followed, and slammed the door shut, locking it. She leaned her head against the door, and loudly thanked and praised Jesus for sparing her life.

Katie, one of Cecilia's sales clerks, peered out from the kitchen and saw her boss standing by the door. She looked on the floor, searching for blood, but didn't see anything; she looked at Cecilia, a look of horror on her face. "What happened?"

Cecilia flipped the shops door sign to *Closed* and walked back towards the counter. "The Holy Spirit gave me a heads up when I was back in the kitchen. He told me to be vigilant, so I began to *plead* the blood of Jesus over us and asked God to loose angels to protect us. God is faithful, which is why I'm still here." She said quietly. She motioned for Katie to follow her to the kitchen where the other clerk was still cowering under a table. Cecilia reached for her coat. "You two can go home; you'll get paid for the whole day, but I'm closing the shop early. I'm going to head over to the church and talk to Reverend Rawlins about what happened here."

Glad to be getting off work early with a full day's pay, the two girls grabbed their coats off the coat rack. Still frightened, Katie said, "Uh, we'll wait until you're ready to leave so we can walk out together. I called the police, should we wait for them? What if that guys is still out there, waiting for us on the parking lot?" She asked fearfully.

Cecilia gave a short laugh as she walked over to the window and looked out at the empty lot. "He's gone. Give me a minute and we'll leave together. We'll be here all day waiting for the police to arrive. I'll call them from the church; let's just get out of here. "

Cecilia turned off the lights, and took the money bag out of the safe that was hidden in the kitchen. She put the bag in her purse so she could deposit it in the bank, before heading over to the church. Cecilia set the alarm and the ladies walked out the back door of the bakery. She watched as the girls got in their cars, and they all left the parking lot together.

Cecilia stopped at the bank, deposited her money, and then drove straight over to the church. When she arrived, Reverend Rawlins was having a meeting with his ministerial staff. Cecilia saw that Hannah and Abby were there, so she quietly took a seat in the back of the pastor's office, and lowered her head and prayed for guidance from the Holy Spirit, while William finished up his meeting.

Seeing the strained look on his fiancée's face, William quickly adjourned the meeting. While the ministers were leaving the room, William dashed over to Cecilia. "Baby, what's wrong?" He asked her tenderly. Biting back tears, Cecilia tried to smile at him, but failed miserably. Hannah and Abby also saw the tension on their friend's face, so they went over to see what was going on. Cecilia looked around to make sure no one else was in the room, and after taking a deep breath, she told them what happened at the bakery.

Stunned looks appeared on their faces after Cecilia finished her story. William was furious and Hannah and Abby were alarmed. They couldn't believe the enemy attacked Cecilia again in her shop! William pulled his fiancée into his arms and hugged her tightly. He didn't want to let her go, ever. He sent up a prayer of thanksgiving to his Lord for sparing Cecilia's life. Then he asked the Him to help them.

*"My son, gather your prayer warriors and intercessors together and instruct them to pray for protection for you and Cecilia. It is the enemy's desire to kill Cecilia before you two can marry. I have given **all** saints the authority and dominion to contain the enemy, so use this power that you have been blessed with."*

William bowed his head and thanked the Lord for wisdom and instructions. He then relayed the message to Cecilia, Abby and Hannah. The two sisters gasped in shock. The enemy wanted their friend dead! Abby was in charge of the prayer warriors and intercessors, so she turned to Reverend Rawlins, "I'll contact all the warriors and intercessors and we'll get started immediately." She offered. Reverend Rawlins nodded his approval and turned to Cecilia. "I don't care how it looks, or what anybody says, Cecilia, darling, I'm moving in with you tonight. I'll pack a few things and then move the rest of my stuff over this weekend. I refuse to allow the enemy to take you away from me." He said firmly.

Cecilia's heart soared. "Thank you, sweetheart," she whispered in his ear, as he continued to hold her close. Abby swallowed the huge lump in her throat, and tried to fight back the tears that threatened to fall. She still blamed herself for Wanda Rawlins death. The Lord quietly spoke to her spirit. *"Beloved, there is no need to continue blaming yourself for her death. Wanda knew that she was in a spiritual battle, and sometimes soldiers are lost. She fought the good fight of faith and is now enjoying her reward, abiding here with me."* Abby bowed her head and thanked her Father.

Hannah choked up as she watched her pastor holding her best friend. She wished Daniel was with her, but he was in Chicago working on a case for one of his clients. She quickly sent him a text message to call her when he was available. They all turned when they heard a knock on the door, and Abby's husband Greg and Roger Bacon, one of Greg's employees and a member of Grace Faith church, entered the office.

Greg immediately felt the tension in the room and quietly asked what was going on. Reverend Rawlins told him and Roger about the attempted robbery at the bakery. Greg hugged Cecilia and offered to station some of his men around her house and the bakery around the clock, but she declined, and told them that she's putting her trust in the Lord.

"Right before this guy came in; I was in the kitchen kneading dough, when the Holy Spirit warned me that danger was near." She told them. Cecilia turned to Reverend Rawlins. "Sweetheart, I know you want to move in and protect me, but I have to make sure your reputation is protected too. I don't want anyone to think we're doing anything wrong, so I have an idea, why don't we get married this Sunday after the afternoon services." Cecilia suggested brightly. William looked at her. "Are you sure? I have absolutely no problem with that at all. We've already got the marriage license, and the rings, but are you really sure this is what you want?" He asked, concerned. Cecilia smiled and hugged him. "This marriage is more important to me than the wedding. Furthermore the flowers, the cake and my dress are ready. What do you say sweetheart?" She asked her fiancé.

William looked at her and a huge grin covered

his face. "I say, lets do it!" William kissed his blushing fiancée again. He couldn't get enough of her sweet lips. He turned to Dr. John, who was the church's associate pastor. "Kenneth, are you up to performing our wedding Sunday?" Kenneth looked at the two of them and nodded. "Absolutely, and I'm honored that you both asked me to perform the ceremony," He said sincerely.

William turned to his best and oldest friend, Dennis Wilson. The two of them had grown up together. "Dennis, would you be my best man?" He asked his friend. Dennis, who loved William like a brother, reached over and gave him a huge bear hug as an answer. William then turned to Greg. "Greg, CeeCee and I have discussed this and we want to know if you would walk her down the aisle and give her away?" William asked. A huge grin broke out on Greg's face. He stepped over to Cecilia and gently kissed her on the cheek. "I would be honored to walk you down the aisle." He said gently, as Cecilia reached up and hugged him.

Chapter Six

Cynthia was at the law office of Beausinger, LaChance & Montegut, where Simone Montegut was one of the senior partners. They were looking over Cynthia's marriage license and her daughter's birth certificate to make sure Daniel's signature was on them. Satisfied that everything appeared to be in order, Simone reached over and picked up the report her private investigator had compiled on the *real* Daniel James.

She immediately zoomed in on his financial information, and was pleased to see how well he was doing. She knew that Cynthia wasn't hurting for money, because her grandmother had left her well off, but she knew her friend stilled suffered from her sham of a marriage, so Simone was determined to make Daniel pay his way out of the marriage. She told Cynthia what she was thinking, and Cynthia hesitated.

" I don't know, Simone, this man was a victim just like I was, and he's still haunted by what he went through, I could see it in his eyes when he told us what happened to him." She said quietly. Simone took a deep breathe, and tried to control her temper. She still refused to believe the ridiculous story that Cynthia had told her and the girls, and she was convinced that Daniel was lying about being held captive by *monsters*. "Honey, I understand your concerns," she said soothingly to Cynthia, "but someone needs to be held accountable for what you went through. I'm not at all convinced that the man you married is not *the* Daniel James you met in D.C. If he wasn't, then who were you married to?" Simone asked her friend quietly.

Cynthia sighed. "See this is why I didn't want to tell you the truth. I know it sounds crazy and unbelievable, but I swear to you Simone, everything I told you is true." When Simone saw the tears forming in her friend's eyes, she felt bad, but she was determined to make Cynthia see the truth.

"Cynthia, why don't we drive to DC so that I can talk to Daniel James and this pastor; I'm certain I can get the truth out of them. I'm not buying this whole demons and monsters charade, I deal in cold hard facts." She said stubbornly. Cynthia shook her head and trembled with fear. "Simone, please don't ask me to go back there. What if CJ or Danielle is there? They'll kill me the minute they lay eyes on me." She shuddered. "I'd rather just sign the stupid annulment and move on with my life, isn't that what you told me to do after I told you my marriage had ended?"

Simone got up from behind her huge oak desk and walked over to Cynthia who was gazing out the large picture window that overlooked Jackson Square. "I spoke with the girls last night, and they want to go and support you. We can find out what's really going on, and then I'll know for sure if signing the annulment would be the right thing for you. Personally, I don't care if Daniel was a victim; I'm only concerned about you. He has that Hannah woman to lean on, and you have nobody." Simone said bitterly.

Cynthia continued to gaze out the window. Suddenly an image popped in her mind of Daniel and Hannah holding hands and jealousy roared its evil head. She remembered how *fine* the real Daniel was and maybe, just maybe, he *would* be interested in her! Simone was right. Why should *she* be the only one suffering?

She turned to her friend. "Okay, let's do the

road trip to D.C. When do we leave?" A sinister grinned appeared on Simone's face. "This Friday." She said evenly. Cynthia nodded and turned back to continue gazing out the window.

Meanwhile, back in D.C., Daniel was meeting with Greg Taylor and Roger Bacon to hear about Roger's trip to New Orleans. Roger shared with them what happened when he met Cynthia, and when he finished, Daniel was crushed. "Do you really believe she'll try and fight the annulment?" He asked anxiously. Roger looked at him and nodded. "Cynthia's friend, Simone Montegut is her attorney and she's a real bulldog." Roger said as he reached into his briefcase and pulled out some papers. He laid them on the desk for all to see.

"Look how many cases this woman has won, and according to my sources, she'll win her cases by any means necessary." He turned and looked at Daniel. "I believe that Simone is going to talk Cynthia into fighting the annulment." He stated quietly. Both Greg and Daniel looked at him in shock. "What? Cynthia knows the truth, that it wasn't me she was married to." Daniel said in disbelief. "Why would she do this?" He asked Roger.

Roger sighed. "All I can tell you is she's still very

afraid because of what happened to her, and she may even be dealing with some post traumatic stress. I honestly don't know what to tell you, man." Roger told his friend.

Greg shook his head. "Maybe she just needs some closure. Think about it, she lost a husband and a child, and it looks as if you've lost nothing. If her attorney convinces her to fight this, you might have to postpone your wedding for a year or more." He told Daniel. Daniel sat down with a thud and held his head in his hand.

How could he tell Hannah, the love of his life, that they couldn't get married in December? Daniel's cell phone rang, and when he pulled it out of his pocket, he looked at the number on the screen. It was Hannah.

He excused himself from the guys and spoke briefly to her. When he finished, he rejoined the men back at Greg's desk. He turned to Greg. "So where do we go from here?" He asked quietly. Greg shook his head. "Nothing we can do until we hear from Cynthia, but in the meantime, trust God and go on with your wedding plans. Maybe she'll come to her senses, sign the annulment and move on with her life. Unfortunately, with the enemy lurking about, you and Hannah will have to stay on your toes." He told Daniel. Roger gathered up the papers on the desk and put them back in his briefcase. "I was able to leave Simone and Cynthia my business card, so if I hear from them you'll be the first to know." Daniel nodded his head and Roger turned and left the office.

Greg looked at Daniel; he could see his mind working overtime. "What are you thinking?" He asked him. Daniel laughed, but it was a heavy laugh. "Hannah told me about the attempted robbery and burglary at the shop the other day and that Reverend Rawlins and Cecilia are getting married Sunday, you don't know how I wish that was me and Hannah." He said as he slumped down dejectedly in a chair.

Greg tried to hide the grin that threatened to spread across his face, but he wasn't successful. Daniel looked at him. 'What's so funny?" Daniel asked him crossly. Greg laughed out loud. "I'm sorry man, but I know that look of frustration. You and Hannah are anxious to uh, *consummate* your relationship right?"

Daniel had to laugh; he knew that *was* a huge part of his frustration. He loved Hannah, and he couldn't wait to show his virgin bride just how much he loved her. "Daniel, if the Lord told you to marry Hannah, then nothing in the world can stop that except for you and Hannah. Always remember, *His will be done*, and if God is for you, who can be against you?" He reminded his soon to be brother-in-law. Daniel nodded. "You're right, thanks for reminding me." Greg stood up and hugged his friend. "We are all in this good fight of faith together, and we have to keep each other strong."

Chapter Seven

On Friday morning, Cynthia and the girls piled into the large GMC Yukon that Simone rented for their road trip, and within an hour they were on the highway. They prepared for the long seventeen hour drive by stocking the Yukon with DVD's for the DVD player. They filled a huge cooler up with water, and soda, and Gayle's new friend Sandy was so grateful that they allowed her to accompany them; she brought along a huge basket of goodies for the girls to eat. The girls had all travelled with Simone before, and they knew she was a stickler for keeping to her schedule. She had already mapped out the places where they would stop for bathroom breaks, and places to eat lunch and dinner. According to her, they would arrive in Washington D.C. first thing Saturday morning.

Cynthia tried to have a good time with her friends, but truth be told, she was scared to death.

She prayed that the *demon toddlers*, Danielle and CJ, were nowhere near DC and even though Simone and the rest of the girls really didn't have a clue what they were walking into, she knew. What she dealt with two year ago still gave her nightmares. Simone drove for nearly five hours straight before stopping in Knoxville Tennessee for lunch. When she headed towards downtown, they looked at each other and rolled their eyes. They knew Simone, who had a passion for BBQ, was taking them to her favorite restaurant, Calhoun's.

When they arrived, they were not at all surprised that Simone had made a reservation and they were seated immediately. Everyone ordered their favorite items off the menu, and two hours later, full and satisfied; they walked back to the SUV and piled back in.

Simone turned the huge SUV towards the highway, and Gayle, noticing how fidgety Cynthia was, leaned over to her and whispered, "What's wrong?" When Cynthia raised her head to reply, Gayle was stunned to see tears in her friend's eyes. "I still don't think this is a good idea," Cynthia whispered to her in a low voice. She didn't want Simone to hear because she knew her friend would disregard her fears. "I'm just praying that my daughter and her brother are nowhere near DC. We're walking into a hornet's nest and honestly, Gayle, I'm afraid for our lives." She said sadly. Gayle looked at her in shock. "What? Why would you think our lives are in danger?" She whispered back as she glanced at the back of Simone's head, hoping that she couldn't hear them.

Cynthia reached down and grabbed her IPad and turned it on. She logged onto YouTube and found a video from a local DC news station. "Check this out." She said grimly, as she reached inside the bag again and pulled out a set of earplugs and handed them to Gayle, who put them on and clicked on the video. A newscaster appeared on screen and spoke about the deaths of two young nurses who had worked at the hospital where the incident with the woman *transforming* into a winged creature happened. Next a picture of a young man appeared on the screen and the anchorwoman reported that he had committed suicide the day before the two nurses died. The camera then panned over to show his distraught family. His parents spoke to the reporter.

"Earlier that day, he was at Mercy Hospital to visit a sick friend, and when he arrived home; he was excited about something he had videotaped at

93

the hospital. However, after he died, we couldn't find his cell phone, and after his funeral, one of his friends confided to us that he had not only witnessed the incident at the hospital, but he recorded it and uploaded it to YouTube. It was his footage that made the news." His mom said sadly.

Cynthia clicked on several more videos about the incident at Mercy Hospital and Gayle couldn't believe what she was seeing. As she stared at Cynthia, a cold chill ran through her body. 'You need to show this to Simone." Gayle whispered quietly to her. Cynthia shook her head. "She still won't believe it, you know how she is. If she can't touch it, smell it, or taste it, it just doesn't exist. All I can do is pray and hope that those awful things have moved on." She said desperately.

Simone pretended like she couldn't hear the conversation between Cynthia and Gayle, but she did and was hurt my Cynthia's words. Simone gritted her teeth; she was more determined than ever to prove to Cynthia that she had been a victim of some kind of elaborate hoax. Simone was going to stop this nonsense about monsters and demons once and for all.

Several hours later, as the first rays of sunlight began to rise; Simone pulled into her sister Lisa's driveway and parked the SUV. Lisa was out of town with her husband and their three kids for the week, and after Simone had called and confided to her about Cynthia's situation, she offered the girls her five bedroom house.

The girls grabbed their stuff and climbed out of the huge truck and went inside the beautiful house. Simone claimed the master bedroom suite, while the other women paired up to sleep in the remaining bedrooms. Eleven o'clock that morning, everyone gathered in the spacious kitchen and Simone pulled out a frying pan, while Gayle reached into the cabinets to grab plates and glasses, while Val and Deborah unloaded the groceries they had purchased on their way to Lisa's house.

Cynthia asked Sandy to help her set the table on the large redwood deck, and within minutes the girls were munching on pancakes and bacon and eggs. After breakfast, Simone took charge of the day's itinerary, eager to get this situation with Cynthia resolved. "Okay, let's plan our strategy." She said, putting on her attorney hat. "I'll call Greg Taylor, the owner of the private investigation company, and see if we can get a meeting with him and the real Daniel James later today, Gayle since you've been up here a couple of times to see Lisa, I'm putting you and Sandy in charge of finding that pastor at uh..." she looked over at Cynthia. "Help me out, what's the name of the church again?" Cynthia shivered, and wrapped her thin brown arms around her body. "Grace Faith." She said quietly. Simone gritted her teeth, trying to keep from snapping at a still frightened Cynthia. "Can you pull out your tablet and get the address for them please?" She asked through clenched teeth. Cynthia nodded and pulled out her tablet. Simone turned to her sister Valerie. "Val, I need you and Deborah to stay here and man the phones. I'm hoping this whole mess will soon be straightened out so we can get back on the road and be home by Monday." She said with an air of confidence. Gayle glanced over at Cynthia, who just shook her head.

Simone picked up her cell phone and the business card that Roger Bacon had given her in New Orleans and dialed the number on the card. A woman answered and Simone asked for Greg Taylor and gave the woman her name. Seconds later, Greg came on the line, and after he and Simone greeted each other, she got right down to business.

"My client, Cynthia Reed James and I would like to meet with you, Daniel James and his attorney, if, of course, he's not representing himself." Simone said dryly. Greg laughed. "No, he has an attorney, and he's anxious to meet with you and Cynthia so they can settle this matter and move forward with their lives." Greg said evenly.

"Wonderful, are you available at one o'clock this afternoon?" Simone asked, determined to control the conversation. "One o'clock is fine. Would you care to meet here at my office, or at Daniel's office?" Greg asked her. Simone thought for a moment before answering. She remembered that Cynthia had found out about this monster/ demon nonsense at Daniel's office, so she decided that was the best place for Cynthia to confront her demons, so to speak. Simone requested the meeting be held at Daniel's office and Greg agreed.

Greg immediately called Daniel after he hung up with Simone and told him about the meeting. Daniel was thrilled that Cynthia and Simone were in DC, and he prayed that it would be just a matter of time before Cynthia signed the annulment papers and he and Hannah could be married in December, right on schedule. After talking to his assistant about reserving the conference room for eleven o'clock, he then went searching for Hannah. This was news he wanted to tell her in person. He found her down in the cafeteria area, going over the menu with the head cook. Hannah and Reverend Rawlins had opened up the cafeteria as a place for their employees to have lunch, and for those with experience in the food service business to have a good paying job. It also served as a working class room for the new culinary classes that Cecilia and Samuel taught.

Daniel waited patiently until his fiancée finished her meeting, and when she did, he greeted Ms. Pat, the elderly cook, and then took Hannah by the arm and escorted her out to the hallway for some privacy. "Cynthia is in town with her attorney, and they want to meet here with me at eleven this morning. Will that work for you?" He asked anxiously. Hannah nodded and pulled her man into a brief hug. She knew how concerned he was about Cynthia not signing their annulment papers, but Hannah had faith in God. Reverend Rawlins had taught his congregation and his ministry teams these words of wisdom: When God gives you a promise, you're going to have to deal with the problems associated with that promise, and once you deal with that, God moves you into a place of provision. **Promise. Problems. Provisions.**

Hannah had seen it happen time and time again. She knew the enemy was trying to keep her and Daniel apart, but Hannah was ready for battle. Nothing was going to keep her from marrying the man the Lord had chosen for her! She had waited way too long for this. But Hannah remembered the pain and hurt on Cynthia's face last year when she came face to face with the real Daniel, and saw that he was in love with someone else. Hannah wouldn't inflict that kind of pain on Cynthia again, so she told Daniel that she would be at the church while Cynthia was there. Daniel really wanted Hannah by his side, but he too, remembered the pain and outrage on Cynthia's face when she saw him and Hannah together, so he nodded in agreement. After promising to see each other later that afternoon, Hannah left to meet her sister at Grace Faith church.

Daniel walked down to the large conference room where his attorney and Greg Taylor had arrived. Daniel's attorney was a member of the church and he knew exactly what was going on, however, he was concerned about convincing Simone Montegut, who had a reputation as a tough litigator that his client was as much a victim as hers.

When Simone and Cynthia arrived, Greg went out to greet them and they followed him into the large conference room. When they stepped into the conference room, both Simone and Cynthia's heart skipped a beat when they saw Daniel sitting at the table. Cynthia had almost forgotten how fine Daniel was, and by the way Simone hesitated before strutting into the room, Cynthia knew that she found him attractive as well. Once the introductions were made, and everyone was seated, Simone immediately went on the offensive.

"Thank you for meeting with us on such short notice, but Cynthia would like to get this matter resolved quickly so that both she and Daniel can get on with their lives. Now, that being said, why don't we dispense with this *fairytale* of monsters and demons taking over Mr. James' body and marrying my client and having a child with her?" Simone asked sharply. She glanced down at her stack of papers and pulled out a sheet and placed it on the table for all to see. "I've taken the liberty of comparing Daniel's financial information with Cynthia's financial information and to get this divorce done, here's what we're asking for in maintenance and child support." She said firmly, sliding the paperwork across the polished oak table.

Daniel started to protest, but his lawyer kicked him under the table to quiet him, and calmly reached over to take the paper offered by Simone.

He studied it carefully, jotted down a few notes on his notepad and put the paper back down on the table and smiled gently at Cynthia. "This figure looks very reasonable, however, before we can talk about maintenance; let's talk about the child support, shall we?" He asked, glancing slyly at Simone, who shifted uncomfortably in her seat.

"My client denies paternity of the toddler," he stated as he glanced down at the paper Simone had drawn up, "Danielle Marie James, and to establish custody we need to ask your client where the toddler is. Is she in good health and how soon can we see her and get her tested?" He asked calmly. Simone and Cynthia looked at each other.

Simone hadn't seen this coming. "Unfortunately, Ms. Reed-James doesn't have custody of her daughter. She has no idea where she is." Simone admitted. Daniel's attorney nodded and looked at Cynthia. "How can you ask for support for a child you don't have custody of?" He asked her gently. Cynthia trembled fearfully, not at all liking where this line of questioning was headed. She turned to Simone. "I don't know where Danielle is, and I don't **want** to know. That child tried to kill me!" She wailed fearfully. Daniel's lawyer turned back to Simone and played his trump card. "Ms.

Montegut, I know the story that Mrs. Reed-James told you and I know that you don't believe it. So this is how we're going to play this out: Your client can either find her daughter so that we can do a paternity test, or we will notify Child and Family Services that a child is missing, and your client can explain to *them* where her daughter is." He said softly, as the two women looked at each other in surprise. "Or you can listen to what my client and Mr. Taylor have to say about your client's daughter and what they are doing to try and find these special children." He told her sternly.

Simone's back arched. She couldn't believe the gall of this man, but when she looked at Cynthia's stricken face, Simone decided to back down and see what they had to say. She turned and looked at Daniel. "Alright, I'm willing to listen to this fairytale you guys have conjured up," she sniffed disdainfully. Daniel turned to Greg. "Why don't you show her the tape?" He asked him.

Greg walked over to a file cabinet and unlocked it with a key he kept on his key ring. He removed the DVD and walked over to the flat screen television on his wall and pushed the DVD into the player. Seconds later, the room was filled with CJ's laughter and Simone watched in horror as the little boy vanished right in front of her on the screen, and seconds later, the boy's father also disappeared. When Claude reappeared from out of nowhere, as he searched for his son, Simone jerked back and screamed. She couldn't believe it! Cynthia turned and looked at her triumphantly. "See Simone, I told you!" Simone stared at the television screen, and watched as father and son flew around the boy's bedroom. When the DVD stopped, everyone turned and looked at Simone, who continued to stare at the screen. She was in shock.

"Simone, Simone," Cynthia said as she gently shook her. Greg, Daniel and his attorney looked at Simone with concern. They knew how shocking the DVD was for everyone who had seen it, but Simone's eyes were glazed over, and her beautiful café au lait skin was pale. Daniel got up to get her a glass of water, and his attorney knelt down beside her chair and spoke softly to her, reassuring her that everything was going to be alright.

Greg pulled out his cell phone and called Reverend Rawlins to see if he was available to come to Daniel's office. A few minutes later, Simone finally came around, and she gratefully sipped the ice water Daniel handed her. She returned the glass to Daniel and looked at him.

"What are they?" She whispered in a haunted voice. Daniel pulled up a chair and sat down next to her. "They're demons, Simone. I was held captive nearly six months by these things before I was able to escape. What you've witnessed was them in human form, and trust me, you don't want to see what they look like in their *natural* form. The child, CJ appears to be human, but he's a hybrid, half human and half demon." He told her quietly.

Greg walked over to the large screen and pointed to the man who was standing next to Claude. "This one is also a demon in human form. Leah Lewis thought that he was just her houseman and her husband's friend. She also didn't realize, until it was too late, that her son's nanny was a female demon, a *succubus*. Poor Leah was attacked by all three of them when she returned home from her meeting with us that day. She died later that evening from her injuries, but before she passed, she held a press conference to try and warn her fans not to go see her new movie and to stop reading her books. We know that Cynthia doesn't know where her daughter is, because we don't have a clue where any of these children are. Our best guest is that *Satan* has hidden them until he's ready for them to resurface. Our pastor is on his way over to explain this to you, if you like." Simone shuddered and turned towards Cynthia. "I'm sorry I didn't believe you. Tell me what you want to do next." She said softly.

Cynthia looked at Daniel and Greg. She knew these two men were sincere, and she didn't want to hold Daniel back from starting his life with his fiancée. Cynthia turned to Daniel's attorney. "Where are the annulment papers? I'll sign them right now." She said firmly. Daniel squeezed her hand in thanks, while his attorney pulled the paperwork out of his briefcase and handed it to Cynthia. She and Simone looked over them, and then Cynthia signed them, freeing Daniel to marry the woman of his dreams.

Chapter Eight

While Simone and Cynthia were at Daniel's office, Gayle and Sandy had located the address of Grace Faith Church on Google, and borrowed Lisa's car and drove over there. When they arrived, they were surprised to see a large group of women gathered there. Once inside, they realize they had crashed a party. Gayle attempted to sneak back out, but one of the ladies waved them in and handed them each a plate of food. The woman looked at each other, shrugged, and began to eat the delicious food. As they walked around and mingled with the crowd, they soon found out they were at a bridal shower for one of the church members. "Who's the lucky bride?" Gayle asked the young woman who had invited her and Sandy to join her at a table. The member beamed at the two ladies. "Sister Cecilia Ford, that's her there in the light blue dress, she's marrying our pastor, Reverend William Rawlins tomorrow. They've been friends for years, and we're just thrilled for them." She gushed happily, as she pointed at Cecilia.

Sandy nearly choked on her food. Oh no! She knew that Satan would have her head if she allowed that wedding to take place tomorrow. She sat there and tried to come up with a plan, while pretending to enjoy her food. Gayle continued to chat with the church member and suddenly, Sandy remembered that she had something in her purse. She glanced around for a restroom and spotted one close to the bride to be. Sandy excused herself and went into the ladies room.

When she came out, she made her way over to the group where the bride was, and slipped behind them for a few minutes. After returning back to her seat, Sandy leaned over and told Gayle she was ready to leave. They thanked the church lady for inviting them and left. Standing outside, they looked at each other. "What now?" Gayle asked. Sandy shrugged. "I have a friend that lives here; we use to hang out at a bar called Pico's. Wanna see if it's open?" She innocently asked her friend.

Back at the church, Hannah and Abby were in the kitchen, preparing to bring out the ice cream and cake while Cecilia sat talking to Kathryn. Suddenly Cecilia stopped in mid-sentence, clutched her head, groaned and keeled over. Kathryn stared down at her dear friend in shock. "Cecilia, Cecilia," She cried out in fright. Everyone stopped talking and turned around to see Cecilia passed out on the floor and Kathryn kneeling beside her, lightly slapping her face to try and bring her around. "Call an ambulance!" Abby shouted as she and Hannah made there way over to their stricken friend. "Cecilia, can you hear me? Cecilia!" They all shouted, but Cecilia didn't respond. Hannah whipped out her cell phone and called Reverend Rawlins. "It's Cecilia." She said quickly when he answered. "She's unconscious, and we can't get her to wake up. The ambulance is on its way, meet us at the hospital." Hannah told him. When the paramedics arrived they immediately began to work on the unresponsive woman. After checking her vitals, they loaded her onto the stretcher and into the ambulance. "Looks like she may have had a stroke, you guys can meet me us at Memorial." The attendant said, before closing the ambulance door. The ladies all ran to the parking lot, jumped in their cars and followed the ambulance to the hospital.

On the other side of town, William Rawlins was beside himself. Greg refused to allow his distraught pastor to drive, so he drove William and Daniel to the hospital while Daniel's attorney stayed behind and completed the paperwork with Simone and Cynthia.

When the men arrived at the hospital, the emergency room clerk told William that Cecilia was being admitted to the ICU. They took the elevator to the unit on the third floor where they found the ladies from the bridal shower. Abby rushed into Greg's arms and Hannah into Daniel's. Everyone started talking at once, and finally William raised his hand and they quieted down.

He turned to Kathryn who had been sitting with Cecilia before she collapsed. "Kathryn, what happened?" He asked her gently. "I honestly don't know what happened. One minute we were sitting there laughing and chatting, and a minute later this strange look came over her face and she just passed out. She hasn't opened her eyes or said anything since." Kathryn said tearfully. Once again all the ladies began chattering at once and William held up his hand trying to quiet them down. Before he could say anything, Kathryn's husband Dr. Kenneth John, came out of Cecilia's room and approached his friend and pastor. "I'm afraid Cecilia is in a coma." He said grimly. The ladies all began to moan and wail. William was so shocked, he had to sit down. A coma!

Chapter Nine

Simone and Cynthia left Daniel's office and were driving back to Lisa's house. Simone was still shaken by what she witnessed on the DVD. "I could really use a drink, why don't you call and find out where everyone is." Simone suggested to Cynthia. Cynthia called Gayle who informed her that she and Sandy were at a bar called Pico's. Gayle told her it was a great place, so Simone drove to Lisa's house and picked up the other girls and headed over to Pico's.

When they arrived, Gayle waved them over to the table where she sat with Sandy, and within minutes everyone was seated and placing their orders with a waitress. Gayle offered her friends some chicken wings and stuffed bacon and cheddar potato skins while they waited for the waitress to come back with their food and drinks. The bar was filled with people, and the ladies noticed there were several good looking men

111

watching a baseball game. A guy looked over at the group of ladies, and he noticed Simone and made his way over to her table.

"Simone Montegut?" He asked quietly. They all turned and looked at the tall, dark and very sexy African American man towering over their table. He stood well over six feet five inches and he wore an Armani suit that showed off his fabulous body. Simone cocked her head to the side, trying to figure out how this guy knew her name, and how she could have ever forgotten his. He smiled at her, and they all swooned at his beautiful smile and even white teeth.

"I guess you don't remember me. You represented one of my brothers a couple of years ago in a dispute with his business partner. I'm Joe Jenkins; you represented my brother, Ralph." He said politely.

Recognition showed in Simone's eyes. She smiled at the man. "Oh yes, I remember the Jenkins clan. You're from Raleigh Durham North Carolina, right?" Joe laughed. "Yeah, clan is right, it's a lot of us. How have you been? Are you living in DC now? Simone shook her head and offered him a seat. He sat down and she introduced him to her friends.

"I'm down here working on a case for a friend.

Are you here with your beautiful wife?" She asked him, remembering the woman who clung to him and constantly glared at her, whenever she had to meet with the family, while working on his brother's case. Joe sadly shook his head. "My wife died from breast cancer two years ago. I moved here a couple of months ago with my twin boys." He said softly. Everyone genuinely expressed their sorrow, but they couldn't believe their luck. This fine, sexy man was single! But it was obvious that he only had eyes for Simone, he barely glanced at the other ladies.

Sighing, the others went back to nursing their drinks and eating their appetizers. "I own a construction company here and I just closed a huge deal. My brothers came down to celebrate with me. Would you ladies mind if we join you?" He asked hopefully. When they said yes, he stood up and waved his brothers over. The ladies looked in astonishment as six tall handsome men walked over to join them at the table. Joe introduced his brothers to the ladies, and once they were all seated, the guys ordered another round of drinks and more food.

While his brothers were busy chatting up the other ladies, Joe pulled his chair closer to Simone. "I hope we're not too overwhelming." He said as he sipped on his drink. Simone looked at her girlfriends; each of them glowing from the attention of his brothers. "Oh, I think they'll be just fine." She said dryly. Joe laughed.

They chatted quietly, and soon Simone found herself smitten with the fine, sensitive man sitting next to her. She tried really hard to concentrate on what he was saying, but all she could do was stare at his kissable lips, imagining them pressed hard against her lips and other places. The thought made her so hot that she blushed. Val turned to ask her sister a question and was rendered speechless when she looked at Simone. It had been years since Val had seen her workaholic sister flirting with a man. Val looked over at Joe and he seemed just as smitten as Simone. Val grinned. "Hey Simone, what time are we scheduled to leave tomorrow?"

Simone tore her gaze away from Joe and looked at her sister. "We should be on the road by six am so I can be at work on time Tuesday, why?" She asked. "Because we've been invited to a BBQ at Joe's place!" Val said excitedly. Chris looked at his brother, and with a sheepish grin said. "I hope it was okay to extend the invitation, bro." He said as he gazed wistfully at Val. Joe laughed as he watched his brother slobber over Simone's sister. He could truly relate. It had been a long time since he was even attracted to someone since his wife's passing. "We would love to have you ladies join us for our family BBQ. You can meet my twin boys." Joe laughed. Phyllis, who was sitting between Cynthia and one of Joe's handsome brothers turned to him. "How many brothers and sisters do you have?" She asked curiously. He laughed. "I have seven brothers and five sisters. It's thirteen of us, but we have two sets of twins in the family."

The ladies gasped. Joe looked at Simone with a naughty grin on his face. "We breed quickly!" He said and she laughed at his huge understatement.

Around ten p.m. Simone yawned and looked at her wristwatch. It was way past her bedtime, and even though she hated to break up the party, Simone was tired. She picked up her purse and stood up and the other ladies followed suit. "Guys, thank you for such a wonderful evening. I haven't laughed this much in a long time." She said to Joe and his brothers. The guys stood up and Joe tossed some money on the table for a tip for their busy and very attentive waitress. "We'll walk you ladies out." He said as they headed towards the door. Joe paid the huge tab without blinking an eye, and then casually linked his arm through

Simone's as they walked out to the parking lot and over to her SUV. Joe reached into his pocket and pulled out his business card and wrote down his home address and phone number. "I'm going to fire up the grill at noon, so you ladies just come by when you're ready. If something comes up and you can't make it, please give me a call, okay?" Simone nodded and they chatted a few more minutes to allow his brothers to say their goodbyes to her friends. "I'm really looking forward to meeting your sons." Simone said shyly. Joe grinned. "I hope you feel that way after you meet them, they're huge pranksters. My brother Charlie has taught them all of his old pranks from back in the day, and once they get started, it's like being in an episode of Punk'd! Those two give my parents plenty of grief when they're babysitting for me." He said dryly. Simone laughed and Joe knew he was a goner; at that moment, he knew that somehow this woman was destined to be his wife!

Back at the hospital, visiting hours were over and William finally relented and let Greg and Abby drive him home. Cecilia was in a private room in ICU, and even though she was in a coma, she could hear and sense those around her. She sighed heavily after William and the gang left, she had tried for hours to make them understand that she could see them and hear them but for some reason they couldn't hear her.

A few hours later, Cecilia opened her eyes and noticed a brilliant light shining over her. Then she saw a very handsome man literally perched on the foot rail of her hospital bed, like a canary in a birdcage. He was peering down at her with an inquisitive look on his face, and when he noticed her staring at him, he looked at her and smiled.

"Well, well, welcome back Cecilia, I'm your guardian angel." The man said cheerfully. Cecilia felt the hair rise on her arms and the back of her neck. "No, you're not," she said evenly, "I know who you are. Don't try and fool me with that shining light crap, I'm aware of all the forms you come in Satan." Cecilia stated emphatically. Exposed, Satan sneered and transformed into his true hideous self. Cecilia stared at his long, unkempt hair, the deep scars and pockmarks on his face and the tattered black wings that hung loosely at his side. She knew from the description in Ezekiel 28:12 that Lucifer had been a beautiful angel, before he was kicked out of Heaven and cast down to earth as Satan, the accuser of the Christians.

He flew down from the bed post and angrily

117

stalked around the room, while she watched him, curious to know what he was up to. She didn't have to wait long.

"I know who you are too, Cecilia Ford, and I'm sick of you and your precious gift. I'm a prophetess, I can see into the future!" He mimicked nastily. "You think you're so special, don't you? Do you really believe *Father's* lies about how much he loves and cares about you?" He asked, as he stalked over to the head of her hospital bed and leaned his hideous face close to hers. "If he loves you so much, tell Him to heal you so you can walk out of here!" He challenged her.

Cecilia smiled to herself and quoted Matthew 4:7 ***"It is written: Do not put the Lord your God to the test."***

Furious Satan glared down at her. He wanted to kill her, but knew he couldn't himself. All he could do now was torment and harass her. This was his first battle with this mighty woman of God face to face, and he was alarmed that she had absolutely no fear of him! "William doesn't really want to marry you; God is *making* him marry you!" Satan taunted, hoping to throw her off guard. "It is written, ***"It is not good for man to be alone. I will make a help meet for him. Gen. 2:18"*** Cecilia calmly quoted. Satan flew into a rage, and disappeared.

The next morning Cecilia felt someone nudging her and when she opened her eyes, she saw that **he** was back again. This time he didn't mince words with her. "Poor Cecilia, isn't today your wedding day? Too bad you can't climb right out of that hospital bed and head to the church. William will get tired of waiting for you and find himself another wife." Satan snorted with laughter. Realizing that today was indeed her wedding day, Cecilia turned to her accuser. "Go away, Satan, I command you in the mighty name of Jesus." She demanded wearily. Incensed, Satan *had* to vanish.

When William walked into her room later that morning, accompanied by Dr. John, she tried in vain to get his attention. Cecilia tried to move her arms and legs but couldn't. She tried speaking but no sound came out. William stood at the foot of her bed observing, while the doctor examined her and made some notations in her chart. When he finished, he turned to William. "All of her test came back normal, there's no swelling or leakage from the brain, and frankly there's no medical reason why she hasn't awaken." He looked at Cecilia, then back at his friend William. "I believe this is a spiritual attack, William, some kind of demonic oppression. Maybe it's time for the saints to start interceding and praying for Cecilia" Dr. John said solemnly.

William blinked back tears as he stared down at his beloved fiancée. "Today was supposed to be our wedding day and my baby is lying here helpless and I can't even help her." He said sorrowfully. Kenneth John took his good friend by the arm and gave it a light squeeze. "You knew the enemy was going to try and stop the wedding and apparently he's succeeded, for now. But don't count Cecilia out too soon, she's a fighter. We're going to bring her back and you two will get married as soon as she's strong enough." His friend said.

William nodded as he sat down in the chair next to Cecilia's bed and placed her limp hand in his. It was warm to the touch. Cecilia tried squeezing William's hand, but couldn't. Tears of frustration formed in her eyes and slowly ran down her cheeks. William was astounded when he saw them and he stood up and leaned over her. "Baby can you here me?" He asked urgently. Cecilia tried to nod, but couldn't, so more tears fell from her eyes.

William raised his head up to the ceiling. "Father, please help me. Tell me what's wrong with Cecilia; what do you want us to do?" He prayed out loud. William bowed his head and continued praying while he was waiting for an answer from God.

Satan appeared and once again perched on the end of Cecilia's hospital bed. He stared at William and Cecilia with contempt. Cecilia tried desperately to get William's attention so he could see the Prince of Darkness. Feeling her distress, William suddenly lifted his head and looked around. He could sense an evil presence in the room, and he noticed Cecilia's trembling hand. Now he was convinced that his fiancée was under some sort of demonic torment. William began loudly and boldly declaring that he and Cecilia were the righteousness of God, and he commanded Satan, in the name of Jesus to let Cecilia go and to leave immediately. Stunned, Satan glared at the mighty man of God, and vanished. William felt peace fill the tiny room, and once again he looked down at Cecilia and was stunned to see her gazing back at him with a smile on her face. He bent down and gently kissed her lips and whispered, "Baby, if you can hear me, blink once for no and twice for yes."

Cecilia blinked twice. William was elated. "Was the enemy in here harassing you?" He asked and again Cecilia blinked twice. William quickly hit the button to notify the nurse, and soon a nurse and Dr. John came into the room. William explained that Cecilia was able to communicate by blinking her eyes. He stepped back while Dr. John asked Cecilia some questions that she was able to answer by blinking her eyes, while the nurse was busy checking the patient's vital signs. When they finished, Dr. John made some notes on her charts, patted William on the back and left. William sat back down and took Cecilia's hand. "I'm not leaving your side. Next time he comes in here; he's going to have to go through me to get to you." He said defiantly. Cecilia finally understood that the enemy was attacking her through her mind. Feeling safe with William there by her side, Cecilia finally closed her eyes and slept.

Chapter Ten

Joe's BBQ was in full swing by the time the women pulled up in front of his house. Simone was impressed with the beautiful two story brick home that Joe had built for his family. It had everything she always wanted in a home; a huge bay window in the living room that overlooked the beautiful landscaped yard, a large porch that wrapped around the entire house, and a brick 3 car garage. When they walked around to the back, the girls were amazed by the number of people that were there. Joe was manning the large brick barbeque pit, and laughing with his buddies, when he looked up and saw Simone and the girls heading his way. His heart skipped a beat as he looked at her. She had her hair in a ponytail that hung past her shoulders and a red sleeveless sundress that stopped right above her knees and a pair of red and white sandals. He wiped his hands on his *Kiss the Cook* apron and quickly made his way towards them. Simone, saw the look on his face and blushed, as she smiled warmly back at him. It had been a long time since a man had made her feel this good.

Joe introduced the women to his family and friends. While his mom and sisters were checking Simone out, Joe looked around for his twin boys. He'd seen them a few minutes ago playing with their cousins. He spotted them over by the swing set and waved them over. Curious, the twins ran to their dad and he proudly introduced them to Simone and her friends. Simone smiled at the two boys. They were spitting images of their dad and each other. Joe had mentioned to her that they were identical, just like his twin sisters and brothers.

Six year old Travis and Trevor Jenkins politely shook hands with the pretty lady standing next to their dad. They noticed the huge grin on their dad's face and they looked at each other in surprise. It had been years since their dad had looked at a woman the way he was looking at Simone. Trevor, who was the eldest by seven minutes, turned and looked at his grandmother and aunt to see what they thought. He could see they were also checking out the woman that Joe had taken by the hand, and was leading over to introduce to his dad and brothers. Trevor's grandmother Ernestine Jenkins was about to say something to her daughter, but she noticed her grandson watching her, so she smiled tightly and turned and went into the house. Travis, however, was intrigued with the pretty lady, so he followed his dad and Simone over to the group of men, and watched his dad's face light up again, as he introduced the woman to his grandfather and uncle.

Ralph remembered Simone and gave her a quick hug. Simone called her friends over and introduced them to Joe's dad and his brother Ralph. She looked down and noticed one of the twins staring up at her and she knelt down and said, "Now which one are you?" Travis shyly looked down at his sneakers and softly said, "I'm Travis." Simone introduced him to her friends and little Travis basked in the attention of the ladies, as they commented on how cute he was, and how much he resembled his dad.

Travis still missed his mom, and this was the first time his dad had introduced a woman to him and his brother since her death. Travis wondered if the pretty lady was going to be his new mom. He laughed as Simone tried to keep up with the names of Joe's cousins, nephews and niece and he decided right then and there that he liked her.

A couple of hours later, Simone sat at one of the picnic tables with Joe and his sons. She was busy wiping sauce off Travis' chin, when she heard Joe welcome someone that had walked up to the table. She turned and nearly fell off the bench, as she found herself face to face with Daniel James and a woman that she assumed was his fiancée. Daniel was just as shocked to see her and he nervously looked around and spotted Cynthia sitting with Marcus, Joe's brother. She nodded at Daniel stiffly and he returned the gesture and abruptly took his fiancée by the hand and moved on. Puzzled, Joe looked at Simone and with a sigh; she quietly told him that she had come to D.C. to see Daniel about annulling his marriage to her friend Cynthia.

Intrigued, Joe looked over at Cynthia, who had also spotted Daniel and appeared to be as uncomfortable as Simone had been. Joe leaned over and whispered quietly to Simone that he and Daniel were old friends and frat brothers. He also told her how much he liked and admired Hannah Harris, Daniel's fiancée. "I didn't know that Daniel had been married, he never mentioned it to me." Joe said evenly. Simone turned and watched Cynthia as she acknowledge Daniel and Hannah.

"Trust me, Joe, it's a long story." Simone said softy.

When Hannah saw Cynthia, she let out a sigh of resignation. She had hoped the woman had returned to New Orleans after signing the annulment papers. However, Hannah gasped when she saw the two women who were at Cecilia's bridal shower, Gayle and Sandy.

Sensing the powerful woman of God's stare at her, Sandy ignored her, and continued her conversation with one of Joe's brothers. But Hannah wasn't standing for that. She let go of Daniel's hand and marched over to Sandy and confronted her. "Hey, I know you, you were at Cecilia's bridal shower yesterday. I saw you hovering around her right before she collapsed. What did you do to her?" Hannah demanded angrily.

Everybody stopped eating and turned to look at the two women. Sandy glared at Hannah with narrow eyes, but before she could speak, Gayle jumped to her friend's defense. "Hey, back off lady. Sandy didn't do anything to your friend, we were barely there an hour." She said heatedly. But Hannah refused to back down and she stepped right up in Sandy's face. "Who are you?" Hannah asked suspiciously. Sandy stood up to her. "I suggest you get out of my face, because you don't have a clue who you're messing with!" Sandy said coldly.

Daniel stared at Hannah in surprise as she confronted the strange woman, but just as he was about to intervene, something held him back. Suddenly he felt a sick sensation in the pit of his stomach. Visions of the demonic creatures that once held him captive appeared before him, and he knew without a doubt that what Hannah was confronting wasn't human! Daniel stood next to his fiancée and held her hand. "Show yourself in the name of Jesus!" He commanded Sandy. The woman glared at him and immediately morphed into an enormous, hideous winged creature!

Joe's family and friends, were expecting a hair pulling fist fight between the two women, but when Sandy transformed into her true form, they screamed and fled. Ernestine Jenkins quickly gathered her grandkids and ushered them into the house. Simone and the others stared at the hideous creature in shock. Gayle, who had been standing next to Sandy, quickly moved away from the creature and hurried over to Cynthia, who was trembling in fear! "Oh no," Cynthia moaned out loud, "not again!"

Bishop Joel Jenkins, surprised to see an evil

demon actually manifest itself, stood beside Hannah and Daniel as they bravely confronted the demonic entity. He took over and stepped in front of the creature, and with a commanding voice he said. "Demon, I command you to leave now, in Jesus' name!" He boomed loudly. The hideous creature threw back its head and screeched loudly. It stretched out its huge claw and suddenly grabbed a stunned Simone, as it slowly backed away from the group. Joe lunged toward the creature, but it was too quick for him and clutching a terrified Simone to its chest, it flew off into the sky.

Sensing that her life was in grave danger, Simone began kicking and thrashing so violently, the creature lost its grip on the terrified woman, and Simone plunged towards the ground. Thinking quickly, Ralph grabbed a tablecloth from one of the tables, and he and his brothers quickly grabbed the ends of it, and spread out, positioning themselves underneath Simone, who landed right in the middle of the makeshift safety net. Joe helped her out and held her tightly, as a trembling Simone broke down and cried in his arms.

The demon flew to the top of the nearest tree and perched there, glaring down at the humans below. It turned towards Hannah and Daniel. "This time, we're going to destroy you and that damn church of yours! Tell your pastor that his beloved Cecilia will never wake up. She belongs to us now!" It cackled wildly. The thing turned its attention to Cynthia. "Your precious daughter Danielle misses her mommy. I'll bring her to you in New Orleans; she can't wait to see you again!" The creature said with an evil laugh, then it spread its massive black wings and flew off into the night.

After a moment of stunned silence, everyone began to talk at once. Joe was so outdone; all he could do was hold onto a trembling Simone and stare at his dad, Hannah and Daniel. "What in the world was that?" He asked. Cynthia, still trembling with fear, looked up into the sky, searching for more of the hideous creatures, and when she didn't see any, she turned and ran into the house. This was exactly *why* she didn't want to come back to D. C.!

Once everyone was inside the house, Joe's brother Marcus, who was also a minister, calmly led the crowd into the family room. They were all shaken to the core. Bishop Jenkins tried his best to calm everyone down, assuring them that the demon was gone, while Daniel and Hannah decided to call Reverend Rawlins. Reverend Rawlins was still at the hospital with Cecilia, and when he answered, Daniel told him what happened. William asked for Joe's address, and told Daniel he was on his way.

William hung up with Daniel, then immediately called Agnes, his secretary to come and stay with a sleeping Cecilia. Thirty minutes later, he arrived at Joe's house with Greg and Abby Taylor. Abby rushed over to her sister and hugged her tightly. She couldn't believe it when Reverend Rawlins told them that Hannah had just confronted a demon! Daniel introduced his pastor and friends to Joe's family.

The adults sat down in the family room to discuss what they had seen. Hannah shared with them how her spirit jumped when she saw Sandy, and Abby stared at her baby sister in awe. Hannah appeared shaken, but she was determined to tell Reverend Rawlins what the demon said about Cecilia. After she finished, a grim look appeared on the Reverend's face. Once again a demonic spirit had infiltrated his church and attacked the woman he loved.

"This is war!" He declared furiously. Bishop Jenkins nodded his head at Reverend Rawlins. "I've heard about you and your church. You've done a terrific job teaching your congregation about spiritual warfare and how to stand against the enemy. You should be real proud of Ms. Hannah and Daniel; they stood right up to that thing and refused to back down!" He said sincerely. Reverend Rawlins pulled Hannah into a brief bear hug. He would have been devastated if something had happened to her. "This isn't the first demon our Hannah has had to face down, but we'll leave that story for another time." He told Joel proudly.

Cynthia crossed over to Reverend Rawlins and hugged him tight. "Thank God you're here. I tried to tell my friends about these creatures but they wouldn't believe me. Would you please tell them what you told me and Leah about these things before they killed her?" She asked him tearfully. Reverend Rawlins patted the distraught woman on her back and led her to a chair where she sat down. Joe's brother handed her a glass of water. After taking a few sips, she took a deep breath and turned on her cousin Gayle. "This is your fault! You brought that woman into my house, now they know where I live. I can't go back home, because I'm afraid they will kill me!" She said heatedly. Gayle hung her head down, and tears rolled down her cheek. "I'm sorry. I had no idea who or what she was. She was just someone that I worked with, and she kind of attached herself to me." She explained sorrowfully.

Reverend Rawlins looked at her closely. "Did she know that you were related to Cynthia?" He asked her. Gayle shook her head. "Not at first, but now that I think about it," She said thoughtfully, "she did hear me discussing our girl's night get together at Cynthia's house, and she asked me if she could tag along. I agreed because she had just moved to New Orleans, and didn't have any friends. She was very nice at work." Gayle said sadly. Simone, who was still wrapped in Joe's arms, looked at Reverend Rawlins. "Are we in danger from this thing? Will it come back and attack us?" She asked him, with a haunted look on her face. Reverend Rawlins nodded grimly "I'm not going to lie to you; you're in a lot of danger. Are any of you saved? Do you have a relationship with Jesus?" He asked them quietly. Simone and her friends shook their heads, no.

Joe looked down at the woman in his arms and softly said. "Jesus is your only protection from this type of evil sweetheart." Valerie, Simone's sister, looked at the group and said scornfully, "I don't believe in *your* God, I'm a Buddhist, and Simone doesn't believe in *anything* but her own intellect. Gayle is dating a Muslim and is thinking about converting, so no we're not believers of your Jesus!" She spat out contemptuously.

Reverend Rawlins, refusing to be drawn into a debate with the young woman, gave Greg a knowing look. Greg turned toward Joe. "Do you have a DVD player in here? I have something I think everyone should see." He said grimly. Joe led him over to the player and Greg removed a DVD from his shirt pocket and inserted it into the machine. Joe turned on the television and handed Greg the remote. Greg turned back to the group. "You may want to sit down before I play this. A year ago, author Leah Lewis hired me to investigate her husband, Claude, a journalist with Reuters News Service. When my team began following him, we discovered some things about this man that wasn't natural. My guys would see him go into a store and when they followed, he wasn't there. We would check all the exits and nothing. It was like he just vanished! It wasn't until I was monitoring their son's nursery with a camera that I had hidden there, that we finally realized what we were dealing with." He turned towards the television and pushed Play on the remote control. A child's nursery room appeared on the screen.

Simone, having seen the DVD while negotiating Cynthia's annulment, turned her face into Joe's chest. After being in the clutches of that creature, Simone couldn't bare looking at the DVD again. Cynthia also didn't want to watch, so she buried her face in her hands. Her skin crawled when she heard little CJ shout "Hide Daddy!" She shuddered when she heard the others gasp in horror. Memories of the kid attacking her with a huge machete, while her own beloved daughter cheered him on, made her cry. She nearly jumped out of her skin, when she felt someone arm tap her arm, and she looked up into the caring eyes of Marcus Jenkins.

They had really connected earlier, before the incident with the demon. Marcus opened his arms out to her, and a grateful Cynthia fell into them and buried her head in his chest. He comforted her with soothing whispers, as he watched, along with the others in disbelief at the scene that was unfolding on the huge flat screen. Those had hadn't seen the video before, screamed when Claude and CJ began flying around the room! When the DVD ended, Greg turned off the television and removed the DVD from the player and put it back into his pocket. Everyone turned to Reverend Rawlins, who turned towards

Daniel. "Would you mind telling them what happened to you?" He asked his friend quietly. With a nod, Daniel told the group about logging onto Leah Lewis' dating website, *Fantasylover. com* and being attacked in his home. When he woke up he found himself being held prisoner in an underground dungeon. He told them how he had been beaten and tortured for months, until he finally had the courage to call out to Jesus for help. He told them that Jesus appeared as a blinding light, and when Daniel woke up he was inside Grace Faith Church.

When Daniel finished, Reverend Rawlins told them about Frieda Wilson, the daughter of one of his deacons and a close friend. Frieda had unwittingly logged onto the website and met a man that she thought was Samuel Dawson, the multimillionaire businessman who owned the Cujo restaurant chain, but the real Samuel Dawson, was held captive next to Daniel in the dungeon. Once they realized what Frieda was really married to, they tried to get the woman away from him, but Frieda was unwilling to give up the lavish lifestyle the demon had provided for her, and she refused to stay away from him. Unfortunately, the demonic creature ended up killing her, right in front of her horrified father and Cecilia. He told the group that Frieda, like Cynthia, had given birth to a child that was half human and half demon, a **Nephilim**, from Genesis 6 in the Bible, and that Frieda's own father, was also duped by the demons. Frieda's new husband had introduced him to his *aunt*, who was actually a female demon, called a *Succubus*. She eventually gave birth to another Nephilim. When Reverend Rawlins finished, the Jenkins family looked at each other in shock and disbelief.

Joe looked down at Simone and said, "There's no way I'm letting you go back to your sister's house with that thing on the loose. You can stay here." He said firmly. He didn't have to worry about getting an argument out of any of them, because after seeing the video and hearing Daniel and Reverend Rawlins testimonies, they were scared out of their wits! Simone finally lifted her head and looked over at Reverend Rawlins. Realizing how close she was to being killed, Simone asked him, "Would you please say the salvation prayer with me, Reverend Rawlins, I want to be saved." She said tearfully.

"Me too" her friends said in unison. Some of Joes' family members and friends that hadn't given their lives to Jesus, chimed in as well.

Everyone that is, except Valerie. She looked at them and laughed. "You guys can't seriously believe this. C'mon, the director of Leah's movie held a news conference after her death, and told the world that the video of the woman turning into a monster, was part of the movie. Get a grip!" She said heatedly. Reverend Rawlins ignored the stubborn woman and he bowed his head and led the group to Jesus! Once again, what the devil meant for evil, God, ever faithful, turned the situation around for His glory!

A few hours later, Reverend Rawlins, Daniel, Hannah and Greg and Abby left, and Simone and the girls helped Mrs. Jenkins and Joe's sisters clean up. Joe and his brothers gathered up sleeping bags and extra blankets to make room for their guest. Not only did the girls stay, but so did Joe's cousins and friends. Ernestine was glad that Simone and her friends, made the decision to give their lives to Christ, however she was concerned with Joe's growing feelings for her and her grandson Travis' sudden attachment to the young lady.

While her daughters took the other ladies upstairs to their rooms, Ernestine asked Simone to stay and chat with her for a moment. "My son and grandson seem to be quite taken with you,

Simone." She said evenly. Simone smiled at the older woman, she also noticed that Joe had his mother's beautiful brown eyes. "You're son is a wonderful man and I just adore your grandsons, Mrs. Jenkins. But I can see that you're concerned about Joe. I've enjoyed spending time with him, but I'll be leaving to go home to New Orleans in the morning, but if you want me to be honest with you, I really don't want to leave, and it has nothing to do with being afraid of that thing." She said wistfully, as she looked at the handsome man standing on the back porch chatting with his dad. Ernestine was startled to hear the sadness in Simone's voice as the young woman stared longingly at Ernestine's second eldest child. When Joe introduced her to Simone earlier, Ernestine realized that her son was falling for the beautiful attorney, but now, Ernestine could see that the feeling was mutual. She also liked the way Simone interacted with her grandsons. Little Trevor was like his grandfather Joel, independent and slow to warm to others, but Travis was just like his daddy, sensitive and quick to fall in love. Travis had barely left Simone's side, and Simone loved every minute of the little boy's attention. Before the showdown with the demon, Joe had called the boys in to take their baths and get ready for bed. Trevor, who had pretty much kept his distance from Simone, had shyly hugged her. Ernestine watched as Joe, as he watched the woman he was falling in love with, tenderly hug and kiss his sons goodnight. Ernestine knew how much Travis missed his mom, and she worried about how Simone's departure would affect the little tyke.

"Simone, you're the first woman my son has introduced to the twins and the family, since his wife's death. Oh, he's dated a couple of women that my daughters fixed him up with, but none of them captured his attention like you have. Tell me about yourself, you're so good with the boys, do you have any kids?" Ernestine asked innocently. Simone laughed and sat down at the kitchen table across from Joe's mother. "No, I'm kind of married to my job. I'm a partner in a law firm, and I've been working hard these last couple of years building my clientele. I haven't been out on a date in three years, my last relationship ended when I realized the man I was involved with, was more interested in the money I made, instead of me, so I kicked him to the curb and immersed myself in my career. However, after spending time with your family, I've realized how much I *do* want a family, and those twins, well, let's just say, they certainly have my **biological clock** on overdrive!" She said with a laugh.

Ernestine laughed along with her; she was very impressed with the smart, attractive young woman and finally understood her son's attraction. She reached over and covered Simone's hand with hers. "Well, I hope we see you again. You have truly been a breath of fresh of air, even with all the drama we had this evening. I'm glad Joe insisted you stay with us, I would be extremely upset if something happened to you and your friends." She said sincerely. Simone stood up and hugged the woman. "I hope your family knows how lucky they are to have you. My mother passed away when I was a senior in college, and then my father died the following year. My sister Valerie and I have been on our own for years, and as you saw tonight, she can be quite a handful!" Simone said with a laugh. Ernestine hugged her back. "Now, off to bed with you. Your room is next to the twins on the second floor." Simone bid the older woman goodnight, and went upstairs. As soon as Simone was out of earshot, Ernestine looked up to heaven and winked. "Okay, Lord whatever you're up to, count me in!"

The next morning after a hearty southern breakfast, the girls gathered their belongings and said goodbye to the Jenkins family. Simone spent some quiet time with the twins and she promised them she would come back and visit. She tearfully hugged and kissed both of them and she was surprised at how hard it was for her to leave.

Joe finally took her hand and walked her to her SUV. "Thanks so much for coming, Simone. My family really enjoyed meeting you, and my boys have fallen head over heels in love with you." He said quietly. Simone squeezed his hand. "They're wonderful boys Joe, and you're an amazing father." She said as she leaned her head against his big strong shoulders. She really didn't want to leave, but she knew she had to get back to New Orleans and her practice. "Promise me you'll call the minute you get home, so I know you made it safely?" He asked her. She nodded and wrapped her arm around his neck and gave him a deep soulful kiss. "I'm so glad I met you, Joe Jenkins." She whispered softly. Joe held her tight, not wanting to let her go. 'Trust me, the pleasure was all mine." He replied. Joe had to resist the urge to snatch her bags from the SUV and carry her back into his house. Before they could kiss again, Cynthia and the girls arrived with Joe's brothers, and after another round of goodbyes, Simone climbed into the truck and with one last wistful look at Joe, she drove off.

Ralph stood next to his brother and put his arm around his shoulder. "She's amazing man." He told his brother. Joe nodded, "Yep, there goes the future Mrs. Joe Jenkins!" Ralph grinned. He knew his brother well and knew Joe was serious. "So how are you going to court Simone, since she lives in New Orleans and you live here in D.C.?" He teased him. Joe looked at his big brother and grinned. "With God all things are possible!" Joe reminded him.

Chapter Eleven

Satan returned to his dark, dreary lair in Hell, still sulking about William commanding him to leave the hospital. He angrily decided to confront his Father, so he flew to the third Heavenly realm. When he arrived the **sons of God** were there presenting themselves to Him. God noticed him immediately, and said "Where have you come from, Satan?" His *fallen* son glared at him. "I have been patrolling the earth, watching everything that's going on." He answered angrily. God looked at him and chuckled. "Have you noticed my servants at Grace Faith church? There's none quite like them, they're totally devoted to me and they hate evil." God replied. Satan sneered at his Father. "So you think they love you because of who you are? Please, you pamper them like pets, making sure nothing bad ever happens to them. I want to destroy that pastor and his prophetess!" He demanded angrily. God threw back his massive head and laughed at Satan. "William and Cecilia are more than capable of withstanding anything you throw at them. Why don't you just admit that they defeated you with my Word?" The Lord chuckled.

Incensed, Satan stared at his father. He *really* hated him. Michael and Gabriel saw the hatred in Satan's eyes, and they quickly moved in front of him. Michael looked at the brother whom he had once loved, and said. "It's time for you to go, *Satan.*" He said emphasizing his brother's fallen name. Satan looked at him and swore. Gabriel, who was still upset by his brother's betrayal, shook his head He stepped in front of Satan and said quietly, "Now."

Enraged, Satan vanished and returned back to his lair in Hell. He flung himself down on his makeshift throne, and contemplated how he could destroy Cecilia and William before they married. One of his *soldiers* timidly step forward and asked for permission to speak. The demon bowed down to Satan. "Sir, I have a plan that I think will upset the human woman so much, she may refuse to marry the pastor. She may even stop trusting in Father." He said confidently. Intrigued, Satan listened intently as the soldier shared his plan. When the demon finished, Satan was elated. "Yes, I think this will certainly do the trick." He said, as he threw back his head and laughed. The demons, glad to see their master in a better mood, laughed with him.

The next morning when Satan appeared in Cecilia's hospital room, William was nowhere to be found, and the woman was still asleep. Satan perched himself on the foot rail of her bed and patiently waited for her to wake up. When she began to stir, he began his attack. "You're *not* who you think you are. You're nothing special and I'll prove it!" He sneered, as he waved his hand and created a large black funnel cloud. Cecilia's hospital room began spinning around and around, and she held on tightly to the bed. When the wind finally slowed down, she realized they were no longer in her hospital room, but in the cozy little three bedroom ranch house in St. Louis Missouri that she grew up in.

Cecilia and Satan hovered unseen in her parent's living room, and Cecilia's heart ached when she saw them, they had been deceased for years. Cecilia knew how much her parents loved her and each other, so she was surprised to hear them in the middle of a heated argument. She couldn't remember a time that they ever raised their voices to each other. "You should send her to your sister in Little Rock," Cecilia heard her dad tell her mom. "With my job laying me off today, we can't afford to keep her with us."

Cecilia rolled her eyes and laughed at Satan. "Oh, please. You've gotta do better than that. My daddy was never laid off, he was an excellent provider. The scriptures are right about you: *Whenever he tells a lie, he speaks in his native language for he is a liar and the father of lies.*" Cecilia said, quoting John 8:44. A furious Satan lifted his arm and the scene immediately changed. This time, Cecilia looked down and saw herself sitting in the living room of the small house her and her husband Jackson had owned. She was twenty-five years old and sobbing inconsolably while holding a blue baby blanket. Tears glistened in her eyes, as she looked down at a young broken hearted Cecilia, who had just suffered a miscarriage. Satan glanced over at her and noticed the tears in her eyes. With a wicked grin, he waved his hands again, and this time Cecilia saw a man reclining in a chair, watching television. Her heart ached, as she realized it was her late husband Jackson. Cecilia saw herself washing dishes in the kitchen, while her husband relaxed in front of the television. Her husband had nearly dozed off, until a commercial came on with a beautiful buxom blonde.

Cecilia watched in horror as her husband glanced around to make sure she was still in the kitchen, then he unzipped his pants and fondled himself as he leered at the blonde woman on the screen. Pain ripped across Cecilia's face. Satan waved his hand again, and this time, her husband Jackson and a blonde woman were in a hotel room making love. When Jackson loving moved the blonde woman's hair away from her face, as he showered her with kisses, Cecilia was shocked to see it was her best friend Carol!

Cecilia and Carol had worked together years ago and Carol and her husband Frank, often double dated with Cecilia and Jackson. The foursome did everything together and Cecilia loved her like a sister and now Satan was showing her *this*? To increase her pain, Satan made sure Cecilia could hear the conversation between Jackson and Carol. "You're so beautiful," Jackson muttered, as he left a trail of kisses from Carol's mouth to the indent of her navel. "Frank is so lucky, I wish Cecilia was as beautiful as you are. She's pretty, but she's just too dark. My mother warned me about marrying a dark skinned woman, she told me that our kids would look like *tar babies*." They both laughed as Jackson positioned himself on top of her and made love to her.

Cecilia became physically ill as she believed what she was seeing and hearing. Suddenly two of God's ministering angels, *Mercy* and *Goodness* appeared and glared at Satan. Cecilia saw them, and they spoke to her. *Don't believe this, the devil is a liar and you know this.* Peace fell over Cecilia and she shook her head to clear it, then she turned on Satan. "You're a liar and I don't believe any of this. In the name of Jesus, I **command** you to leave right now!" Cecilia screamed at him in anguish. Satan chuckled. He knew her power was weakening, because her faith was strong, but she was operating in unbelief. Poor Cecilia didn't really know what to believe!

"Sure, I'll leave, but before I do, I gotta show you just one more thing, **Ms. Prophetess**." Satan replied mockingly, as he waved his hand a final time. Cecilia saw a handsome young man working at a hospital. He wore a lab coat and had a stethoscope around his neck. Cecilia assumed he was a doctor. "Meet Jackson and Carol's son Jack. Yes, she named him after **your** husband, even though she was married to Frank. The poor fool died thinking Jack was his son. Now quote me some *scriptures* for that." Satan laughed. Cecilia gasped as she looked at the young man. He did indeed favor her late husband and Carol. Cecilia was stunned. "I guess your precious *Nazarene* forgot tell you that **Prophetess**!" Satan gloated, as he winked at her and disappeared.

Chapter Twelve

A despondent Cecilia found herself back in her hospital bed, still reeling from what Satan had shown her. *Mercy* and *Goodness* tried to reason with her, but she refused to listen to them and they left. When the door to her room opened, she didn't even bother to see who entered. A hand reach for her chart and then an unfamiliar voice asked her how she was doing. Carol finally turned to the person speaking to her, and was rendered speechless when she realize she was looking at the doctor from the vision that Satan had shown her!

"Good morning, Mrs. Ford. I'm Dr. Stanton. I'm a part of the team assigned to you." He said kindly. Cecilia stared at him so hard, he became uncomfortable. "Is there something wrong, ma'am?" He asked in concern. Cecilia shook her head and tried to speak. This time she was successful. "Forgive me, you just look so familiar. My husband and I were friends with a couple years ago. Their last name was Stanton, Frank and Carol. Do you know them?" She asked hesitantly. Her heart sank when she saw the grin appear on the young doctor's face. "Yes ma'am, my parents are Frank and Carol Stanton, but we live in St. Louis MO, we've never lived in DC. I'm on staff at BJC Hospital there."

Cecilia smiled sadly at the young man. "My husband and I grew up in St. Louis. I moved up here almost twenty years ago after he died. Your mom and I use to work for Washington University and your father and my husband Jackson, worked for General Motors." She told him quietly. Young Dr. Stanton pulled up a chair and sat down next to the woman. "Oh my goodness, are you CeeCee? My mom is always talking about a CeeCee that she used to be friends with." Cecilia nodded. "Yes, that's me. How are your parents?" She asked him hesitantly. "My father died about five years ago of cancer, but mom is still alive. She owns a small boutique in the Central West End. I'll call her when I finish my rounds, and let her know you asked about her." He assured her gently. Cecilia smiled at the young man. She was truly impressed with him, even though her heart was breaking as she searched his face, looking for signs of her deceased husband in him.

After Dr. Stanton left, Cecilia reached over and picked up the nurse call button. When the nurse arrived in her room, Cecilia smiled at her and said hello. Surprised that her comatose patient was now talking, the nurse immediately called for Dr. John. When Kenneth arrived in her room, he squeezed her hand to welcome her back, and asked how she was feeling. She assured him that she was fine and after the nurse left, she shared with him everything that Satan had done to her and showed her.

"I need to see William, Kenneth. How soon can I be released?" She asked desperately. Kenneth patted her hand. "Let me examine you first, and then I'll call William. Now what was the young doctor's name that came in to see you?" He asked curiously. When Cecilia told him, Kenneth frowned, not recognizing the name, but he wrote it down on his note pad. Forty-five minutes later, Dr. Kenneth John declared Cecilia fit to go home, and he had his nurse call William. After he left, the nurse helped Cecilia shower and dress. She was busy packing up her clothes when William came in. He was thrilled to see her up and about, and he gently took her into his arms for a long, sensual kiss. Cecilia's head reeled from the passion of the

155

kiss of the man she loved so deeply. When they finally came up for air, William held her tight, not wanting to let her go.

Comforted by her fiancé strong arms, Cecilia told him everything the devil had said and shown her. "William, I can't believe that Jackson had an affair and a child with my best friend." She said sadly, "Why would he do something like this to me?" William stroked her back, as he reminded her. "The devil is the father of lies and you know this. If you want to know the truth, we'll just ask the *Father*. Let's get you out of here and head over to the church, so we can both seek Him." He told her, as he grabbed her bag with one hand, and helped her into the wheel chair that the nurse had brought for her.

When Dr. John returned to his office, he called his secretary. "Could you page Dr. Jack Stanton, please? Jack Stanton was in the staff lounge, when he heard his name over the intercom. He walked over to a phone and called the operator, who connected him to Dr. John's office. When Dr. John came on the line, he introduced himself and asked the young man to come to his office immediately. Dr. Stanton agreed and hung up the phone. Realizing that meeting the chief of staff would blow his cover, the young doctor shape-shifted back into his demonic form, and instantly *vanished* from the hospital!

Reverend Rawlins and Cecilia arrived at the church and went inside to his office. When Agnes saw her, she leaped up from behind her desk and pulled Cecilia into a huge bear hug. "Thank God you're okay, CeeCee, we've all been so worried about you, the saints have been praying up a storm. When William told us you were under demonic oppression, the warfare prayers William has been teaching us went *up*, and now you're back and looking great." Cecilia smiled at her old friend and hugged her back. "Thank God, I'm a member of a church that believes in good strategic warfare praying." She said sincerely. William took Cecilia's purse and coat and laid them in his office. "We're headed over to the sanctuary, Agnes, can you see that we're not disturbed?" He asked his secretary. Agnes, wondering what was going on, nodded. "Yes, of course Reverend."

William and Cecilia arrived at the altar and knelt down to pray in the spirit. They remained like that for nearly twenty minutes. Finally they received a word from the Lord. He spoke audibly to them both. *"Remember to test the spirits: Beloved, believe not every spirit, but try the spirits whether they are of God: because many false prophets are gone out into the world."*

Cecilia and William looked at each other. "I didn't do that and I ignored the *angels* who were trying to tell me exactly the same thing. I allowed my *emotions* to get in the way." She said miserably. William pulled her into his arms again to comfort her, murmuring words of love and encouragement. "Cecilia, while you were in the hospital, God revealed to me that Satan asked for permission to *sift you,* he's determined to prove that he can break you down and convince you that you are not who God says you are." He lifted Cecilia face to his and stared in her eyes intently. "But remember sweetheart, one can put a thousand to flight, but two can put ten thousand to flight. Let's get married after the service tomorrow. Together as one, we can defeat this enemy and cast him back to the pits of hell!" William said evenly.

Cecilia looked at William, and hugged him. "I would love that, but I need to try and find Carol in St. Louis and ask her about her son Jack." She replied quietly. Just then William's cell phone rang. He started to ignore it, but when his *spirit* leaped, he reached into his coat pocket and pulled it out. He looked at Cecilia while answering it. "Hey Kenneth, what did you find out?" He asked his friend.

"Tell Cecilia that I finally tracked down this Dr. Stanton. I paged him over the intercom, and when he answered, the sound of his voice made my skin crawl. He never reported to my office and I think he was an imposter, sent in by the *enemy* to confuse Cecilia." He told him. William thanked him and hung up the phone and shared the information with Cecilia. A vision immediately appeared to Cecilia and the face of the man that was in her hospital room suddenly morphed into a hideous creature!

Cecilia gasped and looked at William. "The Holy Spirit just revealed to me that it was a creature from Hell that visited me! It was all a lie, everything that *thing* showed me was a lie!" She said as she sagged against William with relief. Jackson hadn't cheated on her after all and that thing was not his son! Cecilia was relieved, and then she became angry. With a determined look on her face she turned to William "Yes, sweetheart, let's get married tomorrow, I can't wait to become your wife. If it's a war Satan wants, *it's on!* I know the battle belongs to the Lord, but we're going to be right here, praying Him on!" She said as she leaned her weary head on her fiancé's very capable shoulders.

William kissed the top of her head and said, "You're going to stay with me tonight. The guest room is already set up for you, and this time tomorrow you and I will be man and wife. " He rose and pulled her up beside him. "C'mon, let's get you home and in bed." Cecilia raised her eyebrow at him and had a wicked grin on her face. William burst out in laughter. "Okay, that didn't quite come out the way I meant it to." He laughed as they left the sanctuary arm in arm.

Chapter Thirteen

After the short drive from Joe's house, Simone and the ladies arrived back at her sister's house, gathered their belongings and headed back to New Orleans. It was quiet in the SUV as everyone was lost in their own thoughts about the events they had witnessed the night before.

Cynthia was terrified about returning to her home, and on the drive back, she told her friends that she was going to put her beloved Grandmother's house up for sale. She just couldn't stay there, knowing that the creature she knew as Sandy, had spent time in her house. Her skin crawled as she thought about the evil shape shifting demon. Simone offered to let her stay with her, until she could find a new place to live, and Cynthia gratefully accepted. She was also seriously thinking about moving to D.C. and joining Grace Faith Church, so she could be under the teaching of Reverend Rawlins. She had discussed it with Marcus, and he thought it was a good idea. Reverend Rawlins and his congregation were well versed in spiritual warfare and she would learn a lot. Cynthia was quite smitten with the handsome young man, and when she told him the whole ugly story about her marriage, he didn't judge her, bur reassured her that everyone had a past.

Gayle was still upset about befriending Sandy and wrecking her cousin's life. Cynthia had apologized for blaming her, but Gayle still felt guilty. Val, on the other hand couldn't believe that her sister and her friends had fallen for the crazy pastor's story about demons and devils. She shook her head, suspecting that it was her sister's way of getting close to the handsome, wealthy Joe Jenkins. At first, Val had been jealous that Joe had fallen for her sister and not her. She would love to have a multimillionaire falling head over heels in love with her, however, when she meet his twin boys, Val quickly decided Simone was a better choice for him. Joe's kids were cute, but she wasn't interested in being anyone's mother, not now, not ever! She did, however, enjoy spending time with Joe's brother Christopher, and the night of the *demon attack*, she had tiptoed down the hall to his room and tried to seduce him. He had kindly rebuffed her, and she angrily cussed him out, and stormed back to her own room. Val was still embarrassed so she didn't tell her sister or friends, but she was *still* seething over his rejection.

Val knew that once Simone really embraced this Christianity thing, she would start nagging her to get saved and get her life together, but at twenty-four, Val didn't want that. She wanted to have fun partying, and getting high. Val had a secret that her sisters and friends didn't know; she was bi-sexual and enjoyed sleeping with men and women! She had met a beautiful Nigerian woman at a club one night who turned her out! They hooked up a couple of time, and the Nigerian beauty finally told Val that she was a high price call girl, servicing some of the richest men and women in the United States and Europe. She took Val along on some of her dates, and soon, Val was hired by her friend's madam to service her ultra-rich clients. She *dated* world class athletes, movie stars and music moguls. *Threesomes* were her specialty, and this is how she was able to live a very lavish lifestyle.

Unbeknownst to the others, Val and Sandy went out bar hopping after they met at Cynthia's house last week, and they wound up making love at Val's condo. While her sister and friends were repulsed by what Sandy shape shifted into, Val was delighted. She was a big fan of Leah Lewis' novel, **My Demon Lover**. She had read the book several times and rushed to see it at the movies when it was released.

Val had gotten so horny when Sandy transformed into the flying creature, she tried to seduce Chris Jenkins. After he rebuffed her, Val returned to her room and played with herself, as she thought about her night with Sandy. Val hoped that she would see her friend again. She sighed as she grabbed a pillow, and leaned back into her seat to take a nap. She was taking acting classes at Tulane University in New Orleans, because she wanted to be an actress and she felt that now would be a good time to move to Los Angeles to get her career started. She finally drifting off to sleep, dreaming about Sandy.

Sixteen hours later, an exhausted Simone pulled the rented SUV into her driveway. She gently woke her sister and friends and they all climbed out of the truck and followed Simone into her house. Since it was after two in the morning, everyone decided to stay at Simone's, before heading to their own homes, later that morning. When they went inside, they checked the house to make sure Sandy wasn't lurking about. Convinced that the house was safe, Simone went upstairs to her bedroom, took a shower and climbed into bed and immediately fell into a deep sleep.

Val was in her old bedroom, and after showering, she lit some incense and fired up a blunt, that she had hidden away in the bedroom closet. After she finished smoking, Val crossed her legs to meditate. She was deep in her trance when Sandy appeared before her in human form. Val jumped up and embraced her and the two began passionately kissing, and fondling each other. They tumbled into Val's bed. "Shh... we have to be quiet." Val whispered to her lover. "I can't let my sister and the others know you're here. They're still tripping because of what that pastor said about you. By the way, what *are* you?" Val asked, as she lay naked beside Sandy. "I'm whatever you want me to be, baby." Sandy answered seductively, as she kissed and licked Val's body from head to toe. Val closed her eyes, and lost herself in Sandy's lovemaking. She didn't see the shadows that were moving around in the room, quietly watching her and Sandy, as they waited patiently for *their* turn to have sex with the human woman.

Later that morning, in D. C., Reverend Rawlins

and Cecilia woke up in each other's arms. It was a beautiful Sunday morning, a magnificent day to have a wedding. William refused to leave Cecilia alone in his guest room the night before, and finally he convinced her to stay with him, in his bed. He assured her they would wait until their wedding night to make love, but until they were man and wife, he refused to leave her side. Cecilia enjoyed waking up in the arms of the man she loved, and William smothered her with long sensuous kisses as they lay in each others arms. They finally got out of bed before things got out of control. William stationed himself outside the bathroom door while she showered, and she did the same while he showered. When they were dressed, Cecilia went downstairs to make breakfast, and William was right behind her.

After a hearty meal, they drove over to the church and Cecilia carried her wedding gown in a long plastic bag. Hannah and Abby were already there to escort her to the room where the brides prepare for their wedding. They assured Reverend Rawlins they would not let his bride out of their sight.

Hannah was busy arranging Cecilia's hair and veil, when they heard a knock at the door. Katherine was surprised to see Daniel standing there in a tuxedo, carrying another long plastic bag. He grinned and asked for Abby, who came to the door. He handed her the bag and asked, "Would you please give this to Hannah, and tell her I'll see her at the altar?" Before Abby could respond, Daniel left. Hannah looked at her sister and then at the bag in Abby's hand. It was from Hannah's favorite bridal shop. The ladies crowded around as Hannah unzipped the bag and pulled out a beautiful white lace wedding dress, with a lovely veil. She gasped at the dress in disbelief, it was the one she had fell in love with in *Brides* magazine a few months ago! Hannah noticed a small white envelope attached to the veil, and with trembling hands, she opened it and read the note out loud. ***Hannah, I don't want to wait until December to make you my wife. If you feel the same way, please meet me at the altar for a double wedding. I love you, Daniel.*** Hannah squealed with delight. She couldn't believe it; her dream was finally coming true, she was going to marry the man of her dreams *today*!

Abby laughed. "Well I guess that means yes! C'mon let me help you get dressed and do your hair." But Hannah turned to Cecilia. "Are you okay with this? Today is your big day, and I don't want to intrude." She told her best friend sincerely. Cecilia hugged her tightly. "I would be honored to share this special day with my best friend. Now, hurry up and get dress. Our *husbands* are waiting for us!" Cecilia giggled happily.

An hour later both brides were ready and they looked gorgeous. They heard the organist playing the wedding march and soon there was a knock at the door. Greg, who was giving away *both* brides, offered each woman an elbow, and he escorted them into the sanctuary. Both Cecilia and Hannah gasped when they saw the beautifully decorated church. They looked over at their women's group and both mouthed 'thank you' to the thrilled women, who had decorated the church and the downstairs area for the reception.

The church was filled to capacity with the entire congregation filling the pews, as the brides made their way down the aisle to their husbands. Deacon Wilson and Joe Jenkins stood next to the grooms as their best men, and Abby, Katherine and Agnes followed the brides as maids of honor.

Dr. Kenneth John, the church's associate pastor stood at the altar to officiate. When the brides arrived, Reverend Rawlins and Daniel took their brides by the hand and stood in front of Dr. John. He performed the ceremony flawlessly and soon, both grooms were kissing their new wives. There wasn't a dry eye in the house.

Chapter Fourteen

Simone woke up and glanced over at the alarm clock on her nightstand. It was nearly one o'clock in the afternoon. Shaking the drowsiness away, she grabbed her robe and headed for the kitchen to put on some coffee. As she passed her sister's room, she noticed the smell of incense burning. Simone narrowed her eyes at her sister's door; she had asked her sister over and over again not to burn incense at night, in case she fell asleep with the stuff still burning.

Irritated with her irresponsible little sister, Simone banged on Val's door and demanded she open it. When she didn't get a response, Simone turned the doorknob, and stepped inside. The tongue lashing she was about to give her sister, gave way to shock as she looked at Val's bloody, naked body lying across the bed! The whole room was covered in blood. Simone stared in disbelief at the deep lacerations on her sister's body. She screamed in anguish as she rushed over to her sister's lifeless body. The other girls jumped out of bed and rushed to Val's room. They stared in horror, as Simone held her sister's torn naked body.

Feeling a sense of déjà vu, Cynthia began to tremble uncontrollably, but a quick thinking Gayle raced back to her room, grabbed her cell phone and called 911. Within minutes, the New Orleans police arrived, and after securing the crime scene, they began to bag and tag evidence found in the room. When they finally finished, the police allowed the coroner to remove Valerie's body.

After her initial shock wore off, Simone realized that the detectives were *very* interested in their whereabouts, since there was no sign of forced entry and Val's door wasn't locked. They *all* had access to the murdered woman's room and being an attorney, she knew that the first thing police looked at was accessibility. Simone reached for her cell phone and called one of her law partners. He immediately came over and stayed in the kitchen with each of the women as they were being questioned. Unable to find a motive or any physical evidence linking the girls to the murder, the police finally left.

After the police left, Simone went into the kitchen, and joined her friends at her huge round kitchen table. One of her neighbors had kindly put on a pot of coffee with chicory. Simone grabbed a mug and poured herself a cup with a dash of warm milk. She was numb. When the attorney finally left, Cynthia looked at Simone and said, "You *know* who did this, don't you?" She asked her friend quietly. Tears spilt down Simone's face as she nodded. "She was the only one of us that wouldn't accept Jesus. They must have attacked her while we were sleeping, I just can't believe this." She said in a hollow tone. Then a horrible thought struck her and she grabbed her cell phone and called Joe's number. She was concerned about him and the twins. When he answered, she let out a sigh of relief, and then burst into tears.

Gayle gently took the phone away from her and spoke to Joe. "We're here at Simone's house. Her sister Val was attacked and killed sometime this morning. Simone found her a couple of hours ago. The police just left. We think it was Sandy or whatever she is." She said quietly.

Joe was stunned. "No. Oh my God. Are the rest of you okay?" He asked, concerned. "The police questioned us because there was no forced entry.

Joe, I think Simone would really appreciate it if you could be here." Gayle said quietly. Joe ran his hand over his face. "Tell her I'm calling my pilot now and I'll be there in a few hours." He assured her. Joe and his family were still at Reverend Rawlins and Daniel's wedding reception. Joe found his family and told them what happened in New Orleans. Everyone stared at him in disbelief. Joe turned towards his parents. "Could you stay with the boys? I'm waiting on the pilot to call me back, and then I'm flying to New Orleans to check on Simone." He said anxiously. "Yes, of course son," his mother assured him. "See if you can convince her to come back with you, she shouldn't be in that house alone." She added.

Joe shook his head grimly. "I don't know if she'll be allowed to leave the city, the police didn't find any signs of forced entry and they *all* had access to Valerie's room." Concerned by his brother's statement, Ralph looked at him. "I'll fly up there with you, I know Simone's law partners." Marcus, was worried about Cynthia. "I'm going too. That thing is *really* after Cynthia and I want to make sure she's okay." He said determinedly. Joe nodded and they quickly left the reception.

Joel and Ernestine wondered if they should tell Reverend Rawlins and Daniel what was going on, but seeing the two newlyweds celebrating with their brides, Joel searched for Greg Taylor and when he spotted him, he waved him over and told him what happened.

Chapter Fifteen

When Joe and his brothers arrived at Simone's, she opened her door and fell into his arms and wept. Joe held her, while Marcus and Ralph went into the house searching for the others. They found them in the kitchen, still sitting around the table. When Cynthia saw Marcus, her heart fluttered in her chest and she ran to him. He wrapped his arms around her and held her tightly, grateful to God that she was alright. Ralph watched his younger brother. He had seen how smitten Marcus was with Cynthia when they were at Joe's house, and though he was glad that his brother was there to protect and comfort the young woman, Ralph was worried about Marcus, who was quiet, reserved and still a *virgin*.

Marcus was a minister at their parent's church and a great man of God. When Marcus answered the call on his life, and followed his dad and grandfathers into the ministry, everyone knew that once Joel and Ernestine retired, Marcus would take over their huge multimillion dollar ministry. Joe had confided in Ralph about Cynthia's marriage to the demonic spirit that had impersonated Daniel, and Ralph felt bad for the woman, but he didn't want her derailing the plans God had for his brother. Cynthia led Marcus outside, and they sat on Simone's back porch to speak in private, so Ralph sat down at the table with the remaining ladies, and gently asked them to tell him what happened.

After they told him, Ralph could see why Joe was concerned. Whoever killed Val had had set the girls up to take the fall for her death. Ralph sat quietly for a moment and asked the Holy Spirit for guidance. Suddenly one of his friends *popped* into his mind and Ralph pulled out his cellphone and dialed a number.

When the person answered, Ralph stood up and walked out of the kitchen and into the beautifully decorated dining room. He sat in one of the chairs and explained to his friend what started at Joe's house, and ended with the tragic death of Simone's sister in New Orleans.

Fifteen minutes later, Ralph hung up the phone and went into the living room in search of Joe and Simone. He found them huddled together on the couch, with Simone lying in his brother's arms. A vision *popped* into Ralph's mind, and he saw his brother standing at the altar with Simone, she was wearing a beautiful white wedding dress! Ralph thanked the Lord for confirming what he had suspected; Joe had declared his hearts desire and *spoke it* into existence! Simone Montegut was destined to become his brother's wife!

Ralph sat down on the couch beside Joe and Simone. "I just spoke to a friend of mine. She's a judge here in New Orleans, she's also a born again Christian. I explained to her what happened at Joe's and the situation here, and she's on the phone to the police as we speak. I'm waiting for her to call me back to see if she can get permission for you and your friends to travel back to D.C. with us. It's not safe for you to be here, we can protect you better at Joe's house. Our family has already decided to stay a bit longer until this situation is resolved." He said, as he looked over at Simone. Joe shifted Simone around in his arms so that she was facing him. "Baby, if you get the okay, will you come back to D.C. with me?" He asked her quietly. Simone sniffed and nodded. "Yes, but I don't want to put you and the twins in danger." She said anxiously.

Ralph smiled when he heard that. It really

touched him that Simone was more concerned about Joe and his sons then she was her own safety. At that moment, Ralph was both envious and delighted for his brother. He knew that his brother had finally chosen the right woman. As for Joe, his heart soared as he heard the woman he had come to love voice concern about him and his sons. He silently thanked God for bringing Simone into his life; he promised God that with His help, he would protect her with his life.

Ralph's cell phone rang, it was his friend. He excused himself and went into the dining room to take the call. When he finished, he stepped into the kitchen and asked the ladies if they would join him in the living room with Joe and Simone. Once everyone was seated, Ralph told them that his friend had called the chief of police and asked about the status of the investigation. She informed him that the police didn't have any evidence to support holding or arresting them, so they were free to fly back to D.C. Everyone agreed they would be safer with the Jenkins instead of on their own in New Orleans. They each called their jobs and requested a leave of absence, citing a family emergency.

Gayle called the guy she was dating and told him about Val's death, and explained to him that her life may be in danger, so she needed to leave town for a while. When he protested, they ended up arguing and in the middle of his rant; she told him how selfish he was and that she was done with him and angrily clicked off her phone!

Ralph discreetly chuckled. He had spent time with Gayle while she was at his brothers, and he found himself drawn to the feisty, beautiful woman. They had enjoyed some great conversations and a laugh or two while she was in D.C. But Ralph kept his feelings in check because he was waiting on God to bless him with the *right* wife.

The women decided to go home and pack some clothes and personal items, so Ralph and Marcus accompanied them. They went as a group to each house, and waited patiently as the women packed, and made arrangements for someone to pick up their mail. When they arrived at Gayle's condo, Ralph was blown away by the beautiful art work that covered her walls. When he asked her who the artist was, he was shocked when she shyly admitted that *she* had painted the pictures on her wall. They were absolutely stunning, she had pictures of landscapes and portraits of people. The painting of a family reunion really caught his attention, the images were so lifelike.

Suddenly another vision appeared, blocking

out the artwork. He saw himself and Gayle sitting in a nursery, and she was holding an infant wrapped in a blue blanket! Ralph was so shaken; he reached out and grabbed the chair in front of him. *Gayle?* Then Ralph heard the words he had been waiting for the Lord to utter for years: *"It is not good for man to be alone. I will make a helper suitable for him."* Ralph shook his head, to clear it, he was convinced he was hearing things. "Is that you, Lord? " He mumbled quietly under his breathe. Ralph heard God chuckle deep in his spirit. *"So now you want to question me? You've never, ever questioned anything I've spoken to you before, son."* The Lord answered. Ralph excused himself, and stepped outside on Gayle's nicely decorated patio. He looked up in the sky. "I know you're voice, so I know this is you, but Gayle? Are you sure, Lord?" He asked anxiously. Again he heard laughter. *"Yes, she's the one I've chosen for you."* Ralph nodded weakly.

Ralph was in shock. Finding a wife was the last thing on his mind; he had been so consumed with this new threat against his family. But as he continued to ponder it, he had to smile. This is just how the Lord operated, *suddenly*! His dad once preached about how God will suddenly bless you when you least expect it. This revelation from heaven had thrown him for a loop. He went back inside the house, and tried desperately to pull himself together. He tried not to stare at Gayle, as she went upstairs to her bedroom to pack, as he wondered why God had chosen *her* to be his wife. Ralph pretended to look at the pictures, but his mind raced with thoughts and images of the beautiful artist that had created the paintings on the wall. Marcus, noticing that his brother seemed off balance, walked over to him and whispered, "What's wrong? You look like you've just seen a ghost."

Ralph laughed and turned to his brother and nodded towards Gayle who was coming downstairs with her suitcases. "I've just seen my future!" He said with a smile. Surprised, Marcus watched as Ralph walked over and took Gayle's suitcases. As the pair stood next to each other, they made a stunning couple. Ralph was six feet and six inches tall, and Gayle, who had kicked off her heels, as she raced around her condo to pack, was at least five foot ten. Marcus turned his eyes toward heaven and whispered, "Thank you Lord, I was beginning to think he was going to live his life as a monk!!" He chuckled.

Two hours later, they arrived at the New Orleans airport and boarded the private jet.

The woman looked around the cabin with its polished woodwork and plush leather seats in awe. Simone turned to Joe and whispered to him, "Just how rich are you?" She asked, half joking. He laughed as he put on his seatbelt. "Actually the jet belongs to all of us. We bought it for our corporation. Ralph and I use it for business, and dad and Marcus uses it when they travel to preach or attend meetings." He told her.

Simone looked at him in surprise. Then she glanced back and looked at Marcus, who was sitting next to Cynthia. "Marcus is a minister?" She asked in a hushed tone. Joe grinned. "Yep, he'll be taking over when my mother and father retire." Simone leaned back into the soft leather seat and contemplated the information Joe had just shared with her. She thought about everything poor Cynthia had been through, and decided that Marcus was the perfect person for her to be with. He was strong and loving, just what her dear friend needed. A thought crossed her mind and she laughed out loud. Joe looked at her, puzzled. This made her laugh even louder. She leaned over to him and whispered. "I wonder if Marcus has told Cynthia that he's a minister. Her grandmother was our town's **voodoo priestess**. She was famous for her love spells, hexes and such!" Simone giggled. Joe glanced back at his brother and Cynthia. "Oh *that's* interesting, I wonder if she has shared that information with him." They both laughed. Simone reached over and took his big strong hand into hers. Joe raised her beautifully manicured hand to his mouth and kissed the back of it. Simone silently thanked God for saving her and bringing this wonderful, strong man into her life.

She leaned against Joe and stared out the window, seriously thinking about her future. She couldn't stomach the thought of living in her house anymore, knowing that her beloved little sister had been murdered there. Simone had left her cell phone number with the coroner, requesting they call her when the police released her sister's body. She knew she would have to return to New Orleans to bury her sister, but Simone decided that after the funeral, she would talk to her partners about buying her out of the law firm, then contact a realtor to list her house for sale. It was time for her to start over somewhere else, and she couldn't think of a better place to be than with Joe and his sons in D.C.

Chapter Sixteen

Hannah woke up in her husband's arms. Today was her first day as a married woman. She still couldn't believe that Daniel arranged it so they could join Cecilia and Reverend Rawlins in a double wedding; she knew the congregation was still buzzing about it. She turned and looked up at her husband and saw that he was still asleep. She giggled quietly to herself, realizing that one of the things she was curious about regarding her husband had finally been answered. She had married a man that *didn't* snore!!

Hannah was so comfortable in Daniel's arms that she wanted to stay in bed with him all day. She thought about their wedding night, Daniel knew she was a virgin, and he had been very gentle and patient with her. Hannah had worried that because Daniel was an experienced lover, she wouldn't satisfy him, but once things got heated between them, she didn't have *anything* to worry about. Her husband bought out a passion in her she never knew she had, and she was *so* glad that she saved herself for the right man and for her wedding night. Her thoughts then turned to her best friend Cecilia, and Hannah prayed that her wedding night had been just as spectacular as hers. Hannah wanted to call both Cecilia and Abby, but she knew that her marriage bed was *sacred,* so she shared her feeling with the Lord, telling Him everything. *I'm glad you waited too.* She heard deep in her spirit. Hannah grinned, as she snuggled up close to her husband and fell back asleep.

On the other side of town, Reverend William Rawlins woke up and smiled down at his wife. He loved her with all his heart and soul. He silently praised and thanked God for Cecilia. Jesus appeared in his room and stood next to the bed and smiled down at him and Cecilia. *"I love you too, William and I'm glad that you and Cecilia are finally together and happy."* Tears glistened in Williams eyes as he glanced up at his Lord and Savior. "Thank you for helping me get pass my lingering feelings for Wanda and moving on. Please tell her that I love her too." William said, without opening his mouth. The Lord reached down and patted his son's shoulder. *"She was the loudest one in Heaven cheering you two on as we watched from above. Wanda is thrilled for you and Cecilia.*" The Lord said quietly, then he vanished. William gently brushed the hair back from his wife's face and marveled at the fact that he was a married man. He knew he was blessed and suddenly, William was looking forward to starting a new family with this amazing woman. He continued to watch her sleep, thinking about the passionate night they had shared. *I want to spend more nights like last night with my bride before she becomes pregnant.* He looked up towards heaven. "I hope you heard that, Lord!" William heard, "*I hear you, son.*"

Abby Taylor woke up around eight o'clock, Greg was still snoring beside her. She looked at her handsome husband and gently touched his face. She was anxious to know how Hannah's wedding night had been, but she respected her sister's privacy. Abby wondered if the twins were up, her daughter was an early riser, but her twin brother RJ could sleep until noon. Abby was about to turn over and snuggle up to Greg, when her stomach lurched. She jumped up and ran into the bathroom, and made it just in time before throwing up. She was so sick, she couldn't close the door and within seconds, Greg appeared in the doorway. Abby was sitting on the side of the tub, weak and exhausted.

"Baby, what's wrong?" Greg asked, as he grabbed a face cloth, wet it and gently wiped her face. Abby was grateful for the cool rag against her flushed skin, and when he finished, she tried to stand up, but became nauseous again and had to sit back down. "It must have been something I ate at the reception." She said weakly. Greg helped her up and led her back to their bedroom. He made her get back in bed, even though she protested.

Renee heard the commotion in her parent's room and knocked on their door. When Greg told her to come in, she entered, and immediately became alarmed when she saw her mom in bed. She rushed over to the bed and sat down next to her mom. "What's wrong mama?" She asked concerned. Realizing her daughter still had nightmares because her biological father, and Abby's first husband, Randy Nelson, had kidnapped and hid her for nearly a year, Abby patted her daughter's arm and reassured her she was okay. "It was probably something I ate last night." Abby said gently. A skeptical Renee looked at her mother. She knew Abby was a picky eater like she was, so she quickly dismissed what her mom said. Renee looked over at Greg and saw that he was also concerned. Suddenly a thought popped in Renee's mind, and she looked down at her mom. "Um, are you sure you're not pregnant?" Renee asked. Abby stared at her daughter like she had lost her mind. "Pregnant? Now where would you get that idea?" Abby said grumpily. Renee laughed out loud. "Momma, I'll be sixteen in two weeks, we can talk about stuff like this, besides..." She bent over and whispered something in her mother's ear.

Abby looked at her in surprise. "Are you sure?" She asked her anxiously. Renee looked at her and nodded. Greg had a confused look on his face. "Well what is it?" He asked. Abby looked at her husband. "Maybe you should run to the drugstore and pick me up a pregnancy kit, sweetheart. Renee reminded me that I missed my period last month." Greg's mouth fell open. "Are you serious?" Abby nodded. Renee bent over and kissed her mom on the forehead. "I really hope you are, I would love to have a baby brother or sister. Greg, can I go with you? I can show you which one to buy."

Greg raised his eyebrow at his stepdaughter. "What do you know about pregnancy test, young lady?" He asked sternly. Renee laughed and gave him a big hug. "I'm going to be sixteen in two weeks, and we study this kind of stuff in health class." She said as she headed for her room to get dressed. Abby and Greg stared at each other; their baby girl was growing up!

Greg went into the bathroom, and washed his face, brushed his teeth and returned back to the room to get dressed. Abby had fallen back to sleep, so Greg dropped on his knees to say his morning prayers and declarations, then he asked the Lord if Abby was sick. He couldn't bear the thought of something serious being wrong with his wife. Instead of answering him directly, Ephesians 3:20 floated in his mind: ***"Now to Him who is able to do immeasurably more than all we ask or imagine, according to his power that is at work within us."*** Greg was floored! He quickly got dressed, planted a kiss on his sleeping wife's forehead, and yelled to Renee that he was ready to go.

Twenty minutes later, Greg and Renee returned from the store. RJ was in the kitchen pouring milk into a cereal bowl. He shoved a spoonful of cereal in his mouth and looked at his stepdad and sister. "Where have you two been?" He asked, as he chewed. "We went to the drugstore for mom, she's not feeling well." Renee said as she walked over to the sink and washed her hands. She reached into the refrigerator and pulled out eggs, bacon and sausage. She then reached into the cabinet and pulled out some pancake mix. RJ immediately perked up. "Are you going to cook breakfast?" He asked hopefully. Renee nodded. "Yep, I have a feeling we're going to be celebrating this morning. Can you reach into the freezer and get a couple of cans of orange juice, please" She asked him.

Glad that his sister was about to prepare some real food, RJ turned towards the freezer, but stopped short when he noticed the pregnancy kit in Greg's hand. He slowly turned and stared at his sister in horror. When Renee saw the look on his face she laughed. "Geez RJ, that's not for me, it's for mom!" Renee said as she shook her head. RJ turned back around and stared at his stepdad. "Is mom pregnant?" He asked incredulously. Greg was on his way upstairs, but when he heard the shock in RJ's voice, he turned and looked at his stepson. "Wouldn't you like to have a baby brother or sister, RJ?" He asked, concerned by the tone in his stepson voice.

"Aren't you guys, you know, kinda old to be having a baby?" RJ asked with a serious look on his face. Greg stared at him. "You think we're old?" He asked him, trying hard not to laugh. "Well yeah, mom's like almost *forty*!" RJ retorted. Renee rolled her eyes at her brother. "That's not old; some women have babies in their fifties. I read about a woman in her sixties that got pregnant!" She told him smugly. RJ scrunched up his nose, "Oh that's just gross!" He said, gagging. Greg just shook his head and went upstairs to wake Abby, while Renee continued to school her twin on the facts of life.

Thirty minutes later, Greg and Abby joined the kids down in the kitchen. Abby had a huge grin on her face and Greg was actually strutting. Seeing the look on her parent's faces, Renee hugged and congratulated them, but poor RJ just stared at them, horrified. His parents had made a baby, which meant they *do* actually have sex! *Oh Gross!*

Chapter Seventeen

When the Jenkins brothers, returned to Joe's house with the ladies in tow, Ernestine was waiting for them at the front door. She embraced Simone, who was so moved by the woman's compassion, she broke down in her arms. Ernestine quietly led her into the kitchen, while one of Joe's sisters showed the girls where they would be sleeping. The brothers had turned Joe's large basement into a comfortable four bedroom sleeping area. They had borrowed beds and furniture from a couple of Joe's display units. Each sleeping area had two beds and the brothers decided who was going to bunk with whom. Joe moved his mom and dad into his large spacious master bedroom suite, so they could be close to his sons, while he bunked with his brothers in the basement.

While his sons were in New Orleans picking up the girls, Joel had driven to Wal-Mart and purchased baby monitors for every room in the house. He had also contacted Joe's alarm system specialist, and had him check the system to make sure it was in working order. He wasn't taking any chances, because the Holy Spirit had advised Joel to be *vigilant.* Ernestine had taken her bottle of anointing oil and poured it around Joe's property, claiming the blood of Jesus over it, and commanding God's mighty warrior angels to surround the property, their vehicles and every occupant of the house and keep them from the **evil** one.

Joel and Ernestine were mighty warrior angels for the Lord and this was not their first time battling the prince of darkness. When Joe first entered the ministry, Ernestine became sick and was diagnosed with stage four bone cancer. They began to confess the word of God, reciting out loud that Jesus had borne their sickness and disease on the cross, and they quoted healing scriptures three times a day, every day. Several months later, Joel had taken Ernestine back to her oncologist, and the doctor had been amazed to see that all the cancer was gone, she had been completely healed. The poor man couldn't do anything but admit that a miracle had taken place, and soon, he became a believer and follower of Jesus!

After consoling Simone, Ernestine led her upstairs and showed her the room she would be staying in. It was right next to the twins. Travis and Trevor were delighted to see Simone again and she gave each of them a hug and kiss. They told her how sorry they were about her sister, and asked if she needed help putting away her things. Touched by their thoughtfulness, she allowed them to help her.

Once all her clothes and toiletries were put away, Simone and the boys went downstairs to the kitchen. Joe's heart warmed, as he watched his boys vying for her attention, while she hung on to their every word. Joel was also watching Joe's new friend interact with his grandsons, and he was pleased by what he saw. He looked over at Ralph, wondering if he had heard a *word* from the Holy Spirit regarding Joe and Simone. Ralph discreetly gave his dad a *thumbs up*. Relieved, Joel relaxed. He was glad that *this* time, his son had chosen wisely.

Joel and Ernestine had been *very* concerned when Joe bought Deidra home with him one weekend, when they were in college. They could see how smitten their son was with the pretty young woman, and even though she said all the right things and behaved appropriately, there was something about her that set off *alarm bells* in both him and his wife. Joel had taken his concerns to the Lord, who confirmed to him that yes, things were not quite as they seemed with Deidra, but Joe would still marry her. The Lord advised Joel to pray for Joe daily, and when Joe announced months later that Deidra was pregnant, the Jenkins were very unhappy about the situation, but they welcomed the young lady into their family with open arms.

Three months later, a very pregnant Deidra walked down the aisle and married the man she wanted. When Joel and Ernestine met her parents, both high powered attorneys from Atlanta Georgia, they finally understood why their new daughter-in-law acted the way that she did. Deidra was an only child and her parents, too busy with their careers, left poor Deidra to be raised with nannies and babysitters. Instead of spending time with their child, her parents showered her with expensive gifts and toys, and never denied her anything she wanted. Deidra was used to getting what she wanted, and when she met Joe at a frat party in college, she immediately set her sights on him. She plotted and seduced him until she became pregnant, confident that the young man would do the right thing and marry her.

Ernestine noticed the exchange between her husband and their eldest child, concerning Joe and Simone, and she was pleased to see Ralph give his father the thumbs up sign. But she already knew that Simone was perfect for her son, the *Holy Spirit* had confirmed that to her at Joe's house the day the *demon* attacked. Glancing at her eldest daughter Magdalene, whom they called Maggie, Ernestine raised her eyebrow. Maggie laughed silently; she knew her mom was telling her to get ready to make another wedding gown. Maggie was a wedding dress designer, having studied in Paris, while in college. Her bridal boutique collection was in *every* bridal magazine. With the help of her husband and family, she had boutiques on the east and west coast, and was currently opening a new store in Chicago, and overseas.

Maggie was a very wealthy woman, and like the rest of her family, she enjoyed giving back to the community. When Daniel told her about his surprise wedding for Hannah, and showed her a picture of a dress that Hannah had circled, Maggie realized that it was one of hers, and had it shipped to him immediately. Maggie quickly sized Simone up, guessing that she was a size ten and in her mind, she began creating the perfect wedding dress for her soon to be sister in law!

Down in Hell, Azazel stalked angrily back and forth in front of the squad of demons that he had sent to stop the pastor and prophetess from marrying. He had just found out about the double wedding and he was furious. "I can't believe that all of you were busy having a good time with that stupid human Sandy befriended, and you missed out on stopping the wedding. Now I have to explain to *him*, that not only did the pastor and prophetess wed, but also the one who got away from us, Daniel James!"

He stopped pacing and looked menacingly at his troops. "I warned you that heads were going to roll for this!" He said, as he nodded at his lieutenant standing behind the squad. The demon leaned forward and produced a huge machete, and with a sweep of his arm, he beheaded the five demons standing in front of him. The twelve remaining creatures, trembled with fear, as they watched five severed heads roll in front of them. Azazel laughed with delight. He still had some explaining to do, but at least he had the satisfaction of knowing the ones who failed him, would *never* be able to fail him again.

Sandy stood among the remaining creatures.

She was terrified that Azazel would find out that *she* was the one who enticed the others to have sex with, and then kill Val. She nervously looked around at the others, but they were too busy trying to keep an eye on the lieutenant behind them. Azazel returned to his chair to think. He needed to find a way to get rid of the pastor and his annoying group of saints, once and for all!

His lieutenant cleared his throat and with a bit of hesitation stepped forward. "Sir, unfortunately there's nothing we can do, since they have already wed, however, we can stop them from having the child that was prophesied. I say we stage an accident and kill her like we did the pastor's first wife." He said cautiously. Azazel gestured for him to continue. "And the human Daniel, I say we **kidnap** him like we did before, and throw him back into the dungeon. We'll make it *appear* that he left his new wife for another woman. That should make them bitter and angry, and they'll stop worshiping *Him*!"

Azazel sat back and thought about this. "Hmm, I like that, I like it a lot. But we must do this quickly before our master finds out that we once again failed in our mission." He told them. Embolden by the acceptance of his peer's suggestion, another demon stepped forward. "Master, should we get rid of the sister of the human we killed? She was *ours* and now has joined forces with our enemies, the bishop and his wife from Raleigh Durham." Azazel was livid. "What! The lawyer, she's a believer? She was so useful, winning cases that *we* shouldn't have won! Where's the human Cynthia, the mother of the *hybrid* Danielle? She knows as much about us as the pastor and his saints." He asked heatedly. Sandy timidly stepped forward. "After we killed her sister, she and the others left New Orleans and returned to Washington, D.C. with the Jenkins family."

The demons shuddered with fear when she mentioned the Jenkins. This new development was Azazel's worst nightmare. The powerful Jenkins family, working with the saints from Grace Faith church! He had tangled with this powerful family before and lost. They had withstood many attacks against them, and none of the demons, especially Azazel was looking forward to battling them again! Azazel looked at his soldiers. "Destroy them all!" He ordered.

On the other side of town, Hannah was busy rearranging her closets and drawers to make space for her new husband's clothes. Daniel was downstairs in the home office calling Joe. During the reception, he had been standing next to Joe when he received a phone call, and Daniel had watched as Joe frantically gathered his dad and brothers together and whispered something to them. Then Joe, Ralph and Marcus quickly left the reception. Daniel had a feeling that what he had witnessed involved Cynthia and her friends, and he was not going to upset his bride on her wedding day. Reverend Rawlins also noticed the commotion going on with the Jenkins family, but like Daniel, the pastor refused to allow anything to spoil his wedding day, and both men knew that Joel and Ernestine were more than capable of dealing with whatever situation was going on.

But with the wedding behind him, Daniel was curious about what happened, so with Hannah distracted upstairs, he decided to call Joe to see what was going on. When his phone rang, Joe looked at the caller ID, and was surprised to see it was Daniel. "Hey man, what are you doing calling me when you have a beautiful wife to occupy your time?" Joe answered teasingly.

Daniel laughed. "*Mrs.* James is upstairs trying to figure out where to put my underwear, so I wanted to ask what was going on with you yesterday at the reception. I noticed you, Ralph and Marcus left after you received that phone call, what's going on?" He asked. Joe told him what happened to Simone's sister in New Orleans, and that she and the other ladies were back in D.C. with him. Daniel was shocked; *they* had attacked again, and each time they were getting bolder and bolder! Joe confided to Daniel his concern that the *evil spirits* were coming after Simone and Cynthia!

Daniel was just hanging up, when Hannah walked into the room to ask him a question, but the look on his face made her stop in her tracks. "What's happened?" She asked anxiously. Daniel rose from his chair and gathered her into his arms. "Simone's sister, Valerie was attacked and killed after they returned home to New Orleans. They were all staying at Simone's house, and the next morning, Simone found her sister dead. Joe received the call yesterday during the reception, and he flew down and brought them all back to D.C." He told her. Hannah was as shocked as Daniel. She looked at her husband. "We need to call Reverend Rawlins." She said. He agreed and picked up the phone to call him.

Chapter Eighteen

Cecilia was making a batch of her husband's favorite snack while he sat at the kitchen table reading the newspaper. When his cell phone rang, he glanced at the caller ID and was surprised to see it was Daniel. Concerned, his wife put a batch of rolls in the oven, wiped her hands and sat down next to her husband as he answered the phone. Daniel told him what happened in New Orleans. William gasped and turned towards his wife. He put his hand over the phone and shared with her what Daniel told him. Cecilia waited patiently while her husband finished his conversation. After William hung up, he looked at his wife. "Sweetheart, would you join me in prayer?" He asked. Cecilia stood and William took her by the hand and they walked back to their bedroom, fell to their knees and began to pray in the *spirit*. Soon the Holy Spirit spoke to Reverend Rawlins, while Cecilia continued to intercede for her husband. Minutes later, William thanked the Lord for revelation. The couple rose and sat next to each other on the bed. He drew his wife into his arms, and held her tightly. "Baby, I've been instructed by the Holy Spirit to contact Joel and Ernestine Jenkins. The Lord wants us to unite with them, and fight this latest threat together. Joel and Ernestine are mighty prayer warriors." He said solemnly.

Cecilia's spirit leaped with joy. She and Ernestine were old friends, and she welcomed the opportunity to spend more time with this mighty woman of God. The two had met decades ago at a women's conference, and had stayed in contact with each other. Suddenly Abby and Greg Taylor popped up in her thoughts. "You should call Greg and Abby honey, so they'll know what's going on." Reverend Rawlins agreed. "How would you feel about having a meeting here this evening? We'll invite the Jenkins, and the rest of the ministerial team. The gates of hell are about to be unleashed against us." He told his wife solemnly. Cecilia squeezed her husband's hand, "It's not a coincidence that the Jenkins are here in D.C. Go ahead and make your calls, honey, invite everyone to dinner. I have a great recipe that I've been wanting to make, and tonight will be perfect." William reached over and drew his wife into a deep loving kiss. "I love you, Mrs. Rawlins." He said tenderly. Cecilia passionately returned his kiss. "I love you too, Mr. Rawlins."

Six o'clock that evening, the Rawlins household was filled with people. Joe, Ralph, and Marcus accompanied their parents to the dinner meeting. Cecilia and Reverend Rawlins served dinner first, and during the meal, William shared with them what the Lord had told him. After dinner, Hannah and Abby helped serve the chocolate Peanut Butter Mousse cake and ice cream, Cecilia made for dessert. Once everyone was served, Reverend Rawlins called the meeting to order and turned the floor over to Joe. The mood was somber after Joe shared with the group what had taken place in New Orleans. When he finished, Reverend Rawlins asked everyone to pray. When they finished, he introduced the rest of the Jenkins family. The members of Grace Faith got excited, anxious to see what they had to say. The couple was well known to the saints, due to their television ministry and the works they have done in Raleigh Durham North Carolina. The Jenkins had been honored twice by President Obama during his two terms in office, and he had personally asked them to assist him in duplicating a federal program similar to what they had created in Raleigh, to stimulate jobs in the United States. The saints were honored to be included in this meeting with them.

Joel stood next to Reverend Rawlins and shared with the group that during his morning prayer, the Lord had spoke to him about joining forces with Grace Faith Church, so he hadn't been at all surprised when Reverend Rawlins called to invite them to dinner. "God wants us to go on the offensive, saints." He said, in his deep soulful voice. "Ernestine and I have decided to stay with our son Joe, until He tells us to return to Raleigh. The Lord also wanted me to share with you that this battle is *His*, our job is to do some serious *warfare* praying several times a day!" As he sat down, the room cheered. For the next two hours they devised a plan to systematically pray and praise the Lord every two hours.

Nudged by the Holy Spirit, Cecilia reached over and picked up her bible. She turned to the book of Job, Chapter 38:12-13, *"Have you ever given orders to the morning, or shown the dawn its place, that it might take the earth by the edges and shake the wicked out of it?"* and verse 51:16 in the book of Isaiah, *"I have put my words in your mouth and covered you with the shadow of my hand I who set the heavens in place, who laid the foundations of the earth, and who say to Zion, You are my people."*

After Cecilia finished quoting these scriptures, the saints held hands and agreed to rise early each morning between the hours of 3-6 am and *command the morning* and *plant the heavens,* so the will of God would be done on earth. It was time for the saints to go on the offensive! Before closing the meeting, Greg stood up and held his hand out for Abby to join him. "We would like to share some good news, God has answered our prayers; we found out this morning that we're having a baby!" He said proudly. All the women squealed in delight, and Abby found herself surrounded by the women, while the men encamped themselves around Greg, slapping him on the back, and congratulating him. Hannah hugged her sister tightly. "I'm so happy for you, sis. Do the twins know?" Abby laughed and nodded. "Actually it was Renee who suggested we pick up a pregnancy kit, so she's thrilled, but RJ is horrified, he thinks we're 'too old' to have a baby!" Everyone laughed.

A few hours after everyone had left, and Cecilia and William were in the kitchen cleaning up, when the hairs on the back of Cecilia's neck rose. She sensed the presence of evil close by. She reached out and grabbed her husband's hand to quiet him. They both stood there quietly, and then William sensed the presence too.

"I bind you *evil spirit* in the name of Jesus, and I command you to leave my house right now. You have no legal right to be here, this house belongs to the Lord" He said loudly and with authority. Within seconds, they felt the presence leave. The evil imp instantly disappeared, then reappeared outside, glaring at the couple through the kitchen window. Then it turned and flew away, determined to tell Azazel everything that it had heard!

Chapter Nineteen

While Joe and his parents were at the Rawlins, Simone, Gayle and Cynthia were spending time getting to know Joe's sisters. When Maggie confessed that she was the owner of *Maggie's House of Brides,* and that Hannah's wedding dress had come from her private collection, they stared at her in shock. Each and every one of them owned a copy of Maggie's catalog, and dreamed of wearing one of her originals down the aisle. They discovered that Joe's twin sisters, Evelyn and Carolyn were also famous. Evelyn was a well known pediatric surgeon and Carolyn was a high profile federal judge.

"When we met Joe, he told us there were two sets of twins in the family, so who's missing? Simone asked, as she helped Evelyn put away the dinner dishes. "John and Luke, they're the youngest and in Dubai, on business. They're architects like Ralph. When they were teenagers, they drove him crazy when he opened his own company. They would draw up plans for houses and buildings, and asked him to build them! He finally challenged them to get their degrees and after they graduated, he would hire them, and that's exactly what they did. They graduated top in their class at Cornell University for their undergraduate degree and first in their class at Columbia for their graduate degree. Poor Ralph had no choice but to hire them, and once he did, they demanded top pay!" Evelyn said laughing.

Gayle smiled, "Yeah Ralph told me about that. When he talks about them you can tell how much he loves those two, he told me he's never seen anyone so gung-ho about drawing up blue prints." She said as she wiped a dish and handed it to Evelyn. When Gayle noticed Ralph's sisters staring at her, she began to feel self conscious. "What?" She asked in concerned. Maggie, Evelyn, and Carolyn looked at each other, then turned back and stared at Gayle, but this time they were all wearing huge grins. Maggie dried her hands with a dish towel and motioned for Gayle to have a seat at the kitchen table. Her sisters also sat and joined Simone and Cynthia, who were already seated. "So, Ralph has shared stories with you about his job?" Maggie began. Still confused,

Gayle nodded. "Actually we've discussed a *lot* of things. Why is something wrong?" She asked. Carolyn laughed, "On the contrary, I think you're the first woman that Ralph has been comfortable with to share *anything* about his life. We never knew how much he enjoys working with the twins; our brother is very quiet and keeps to himself. Seems like you've been able to crack his shell, and honey, we're thrilled." She told her happily. Gayle breathed a sigh of relief. The last thing she wanted was for Ralph's sisters to not like her, because she liked all of them. Gayle had grown up as an only child, raised by a free spirited single mom. She had always wanted siblings, but her mother never married, or had any more kids.

"So what else have you and Ralph discussed, if it's not too personal and you don't mind us asking?" Evelyn asked. Gayle smiled. "He was a bit put out that I didn't tell him I could paint. He really liked my artwork that I had in my condo, and he's interested in purchasing a few pieces for his home and office." She said happily. His sister's once again stared at Gayle. "You're an artist? Do you have something you can show us?" Carolyn asked her. Gayle pulled out her Samsung Galaxy 5 phone, and searched for a couple of pictures, then handed the phone over to Evelyn. Evelyn's mouth dropped open as she stared at the same picture that had captured Ralph's attention, the painting of the family reunion.

Her sisters got up from their chair and crowded around Evelyn as they looked at the pictures on the phone. They were surprised at how talented Gayle was. "These are wonderful. Do you have a gallery in New Orleans?" Maggie asked her. Embarrassed by all the attention, Gayle shook her head. "No, painting is just a hobby of mine, but I do sell them in the boutique I co-own with a friend in the French Quarters." She told them. Evelyn shook her head. Gayle was very talented, and like her brother, she admired a couple of pieces and thought they would love wonderful in her office. Simone looked at her friend, who was glowing from the attention of Joe's sisters. It appeared that Gayle had captured the attention of one of the Jenkins brothers.

Twenty minutes later, the Jenkins arrived back home, and found the women still sitting around the kitchen table, talking. Ernestine joined them at the table, and Gayle's phone was once again passed around so the rest of the family could see her artwork. Ralph's face lit up when his father, after looking at the pictures said, "Wow, you're really talented. I see a couple of pieces I would like to buy for the reception area at work." He showed the pieces he liked to his wife, and Ernestine was amazed at the beauty of Gayle's paintings. She turned to say something to Ralph, and was stunned to see *love* shining on his face, as he stared at Gayle. Ernestine nudged her husband and motioned with her head towards Ralph.

Joel had to stifle a laugh when he looked at his son. He had been concerned about his eldest son, wondering if he would ever find the right woman, and the Lord, being faithful, had brought a beautiful, talented woman into his son's life. Joel looked at his wife and they both grinned. What the devil meant for evil, God had turned the situation around and once again, got the glory! The Holy Spirit spoke deep within Joel's spirit and said, "I see that you're pleased with the women I have selected to marry your sons." Joel excused himself and his wife, and they stepped outside onto the back porch. "Did you hear from the Lord, honey?" He asked his wife. Ernestine looked up at him and nodded. "Yes, I've already told Maggie to start preparing a dress for Simone." She told him. wife, Joel smiled at his lovely wife. "Tell her to get started on one for Gayle too." He chuckled. Ernestine gasped. *"Ralph and Gayle?* Oh praise God! I didn't think that child would *ever* find a wife."

The back door opened and the object of their conversation came out and joined them on the porch. Ralph leaned his large frame against the wooden railing next to his dad. He looked at his parents. "I'm glad to see that you like Gayle. When I was in New Orleans admiring her artwork, the Lord showed me a vision of the two of us together, holding a newborn son." He told his parents quietly. Ernestine reached over and hugged her son. "Praise God! The Lord just confirmed that vision to your father." She told him. Ralph looked over at his dad, and his father nodded. Ralph exhaled deeply. "Thank God. With all the craziness going on, I didn't know if it was God, or a trick of the enemy. I mean, why Gayle? I've dated several born again sisters at the church, and the Lord has never shown me a vision about them, but here comes Gayle, along with all this drama going on. She wasn't raised a Christian, and she's not a virgin, but this is who the Lord has selected for me?" He asked, clearly confused. Joel looked at him. "Son, how do you feel about her?" He asked.

Ralph looked down at his feet, and shook his head, then he looked up at his parents. "I'm **crazy** about her. I've never felt this way about a woman before in my life." He said quietly. His parents looked at each other. "It was the same way between your mother and me." Joel said, as he bent down and kissed his wife. Ernestine hugged her husband. "Honey, *I* was like Gayle! My parents didn't raise me in the church, and I was a **wild child** when your father met me. His parents weren't thrilled at all when we began dating, but the Lord spoke to your grandfather, and finally he and your grandmother gave us their blessings. I had no idea who I was, or what I was capable of doing, until I gave myself to the Lord and told Him to use me for His Kingdom. My life has never been the same since. Your father and I see something special in Gayle, and you do too." His mother said quietly. Ralph nodded. "You're right. When Joe got the call from Simone about her sister, all I could think about was getting to Gayle and making sure she was alright." He told them. Joel nodded, as he held his petite wife in his arms. "Make sure you tell her that son. Let her know how you feel about her. We love you and you have our blessings." Tears formed in Ralph's eyes, as he embraced his parents.

Chapter Twenty

Azazel was furious as he listened to the report of the imp that had witnessed the meeting at Reverend Rawlins home. Abby Taylor was pregnant! This news rattled him so much, that he forgot about the Jenkins. Azazel knew his master was going to be really upset when he found out. Realizing that there was no way he could put off the bad news, Azazel instantly vanished and reappeared in front of his master. After bowing before him, Azazel shared this new development, and just as he feared, Satan was livid.

He threw back his head and howled, *No!* The walls and ceilings shook like a minor earthquake had hit, and he angrily paced back and forth in front of his makeshift throne. Suddenly an idea struck him. The plan was so devious, an evil grin appeared on his face, frightening his loyal soldiers. He turned to Azazel. "Bring me Semjaza!" He ordered. Azazel bowed and quickly vanished. Seconds later, he materialized in Los Angeles, California, in the spacious home of Randy and Candace Nelson, Abby and Hannah's older sister and Abby's ex-husband. Azazel found his old friend in the kitchen, pouring martinis in two glasses, on the spacious granite countertop. After the death of Candace's ex-lover, Leah Lewis, Satan had assigned Semjaza to keep an eye on the Nelson's, whom he was using to run *his* Hollywood talent agency.

Semjaza, in his *human* form, was once again playing the role of Ahmad, the loyal family houseman. But to Randy and Candace, the evil spirit was Randy's *spirit guide*, who once served Randy's father, Richard. Randy was a practicing *warlock* and his wife Candace, was a *Wiccan*. After Randy and Candace were run out of Washington D.C. in disgrace, Satan placed them as high Priest and Priestess in his satanic cult that was the real power behind **Hollywood**. Semjaza allowed them to think that they had successfully summoned him to help them in their new careers as Hollywood talent agents. The powerful couple used him to spy on friends, co-workers and competitors. He controlled **them**, but they believed that they controlled him!

Semjaza loved Hollywood. He had sex with the

actors and actresses his *human pets* represented, he terrorized and even murdered the talent that tried to leave the couple's agency. He also killed anyone who posed a threat to Randy and Candace. Semjaza and his demonic pal, *Zandor LeCray*, the famous Hollywood director, who produced and directed the deceased author, Leah Lewis' novel, **My Demon Lover**, into a blockbuster movie, staged sex and drug orgies with wannabe Hollywood stars and starlets, as they *audition* them for movie roles.

Semjaza had unlimited access to money, drugs and human flesh, so when Azazel suddenly popped up at the Nelson's house, Semjaza was less than thrilled. "The master wants you right away." Azazel said as he glanced around, envying the lovely home his friend was living in. Semjaza rolled his eyes. A popular teen actress was waiting for him upstairs in his bed, and leaving was the last thing he wanted to do, but he nodded to Azazel and they both vanished and reappeared seconds later in front of Satan.

Satan stared hard at Semjaza. "I have an assignment for you and I've devised a plan that I need your help with." Semjaza bowed down before his master and listened intently to Satan's plan.

A couple of weeks later, Abby and Greg were

at her obstetrician's office getting an ultrasound. Her doctor had ordered it to see if she was carrying twins again. Sure enough, they could clearly see two fetuses moving about in the womb. Greg shouted with joy, but Abby was strangely quiet. She was concerned about her age and the trauma her body had sustained when she was physically abused by her ex-husband. She had never told Greg or anyone about what Randy had done to her, the night he drugged and kidnapped her. Her ex had hidden her away in a mental institution for nearly a year, and she had been injected with powerful drugs that nearly destroyed her mind! She was very concerned about the drugs the hospital had given her, and the effects it might have on her pregnancy.

When Greg noticed how quiet she was after getting the news, he held her hand and leaned over her, as she lay on the table looking at the monitor, and the two tiny lives inside of her. "Honey what's wrong? Aren't you excited about having twins?" He asked, anxiously. Abby squeezed his hands. "Yes, but I'm concerned about my age and the drugs that were forced on me. What if they affect the babies? She asked worriedly. Her doctor looked at Abby's chart. She was a colleague of Abby and Greg's friend, Dr. Kenneth John, and he had given her the file from the mental hospital where Abby had been found, and it listed the drugs that she had been given.

"Abby, the drugs that you were given have been out of your system for quite some time. I don't believe they will be a factor in your pregnancy, but I'll monitor you closely during this pregnancy. Don't be concerned about your age, you're only thirty-four years old, and you didn't have any complications with your first pregnancy at eighteen with the twins. We'll do an amniocentesis since you are over thirty, to check for birth defects, but you're healthy and in great shape. I really believe you'll be fine." Dr. Kate Bryant said, as she gently patted Abby's hand. Abby forced a smile and nodded. Dr. Bryant's nurse began unhooking Abby from the fetal monitor, while Dr. Bryant took a cloth and wiped the gel from Abby's abdomen. After she was cleaned up, Greg helped her off the table and kissed her on the forehead. " I'm going to step into Dr. Bryant's office and wait there for you while you get dressed." He informed her. Abby nodded and Greg and the nurse left.

Dr. Bryant had been Abby's ob/gyn for years, and she was also a member of Grace Faith Church, and was aware of the circumstances surrounding Abby's kidnapping. "Okay Abby, I know something's bothering you and you didn't want to say anything in front of Greg, so what else did Randy do to you?" She asked her quietly. Tears glistened in Abby's eyes and she held her friends hand for support. "I've never told anyone this, but the night Randy drugged me, one of those creatures, things that we saw at the church, raped me. Kate, that thing's penis was so huge; he nearly tore me in two!" Abby cried.

Dr. Bryant finally understood why Abby's ultrasound had shown so much scar tissue in her vaginal walls and uterus. The doctor brushed Abby's hair away from her face while she cried. After a few minutes, Abby pulled herself together. Dr. Bryant looked her in the eye and said, "I was wondering where all the scarring I saw came from. Thank God it didn't do any major damage, but I think we should do a C-section when it's time for you to deliver, okay?" Abby nodded. Dr. Bryant cleared her throat and Abby looked up at her. "Are you ever going to tell Greg?" She asked quietly. Abby shook her head. "No, I just want to put my whole life with Randy and his sick, twisted parents behind me. I'm just glad he and Candace live in Los Angeles and the twins don't want anything to do with them. They've forgiven their father and aunt, but they will never forget what they did to me." Abby said heatedly.

When Greg and Abby returned home, they found Renee and her best friend Jada on the front porch playing with a puppy. Greg reached down and scratched it behind the ears. "Who is this?" He asked as the puppy sniffed his hand and licked it. "We found it on the way home from school. We heard something in a bush whimpering, and when we looked, we found this little guy with his foot was stuck in a branch. After we freed him, he followed us." Renee said, as she petted the pup. Greg looked at it closely. "He looks like a German Shepard, maybe about eight months old. Honey, I'm sure he belongs to someone, so don't get too attached, we should try and find his owner." He told her. Renee nodded, but she really wanted to keep the dog.

The dog walked over to Abby and sniffed her shoe. She reached down and patted it gently on the head. "He is a cutie pie, isn't he? Greg, why don't you and the girls take him to the vet and see if he has an *ID* chip?" She suggested. Renee picked the pup up and walked over to Greg's SUV, with her friend Jada right behind her.

An hour later they returned, but they had a doggie bed, puppy food and a book on house breaking and training a puppy. Abby looked at her husband with a raised eyebrow. He grinned at her sheepishly. "Well he didn't have a chip, and the vet said he's very healthy, so I promised Renee that we would take care of him, while we try and find his owner. I'm sorry I didn't clear it with you first, but Renee begged me to let her keep him." He said apologetically. Abby just shook her head and laughed. She was well aware that Renee had her step father securely wrapped around her little finger. Later, RJ came home, and he was just excited as Renee and Greg over the dog, and Abby knew that the cute pup had just become the newest member of their family.

The next morning Abby woke up with the puppy cuddled up next to her, snoring. Abby nudged Greg awake and he was startled to see the dog in their bed, sleeping next to his wife. He frowned, thinking Abby was upset, but when she laughed and began petting the sleeping pup, Greg relaxed. "I thought he was in Renee's room. Wonder how he got in here?" Greg asked as he settled back into his pillow and watched his wife petting the pup. Greg grew up with dogs and had no problem sharing a bed with it, but he knew Abby had never had a pet.

There was a knock on the door, and Renee stuck her head in and saw the puppy on her parent's bed. Feeling guilty, she tiptoed in and picked the pup up, who opened his eyes and yawned. It was adorable and Abby instantly fell in love with him. "I'm sorry," Renee said, as she cuddled the pup next to her chest and kissed the top of his head. "He was in my bed and the door was shut, I don't know how he got out." She apologized. Before her parents could reply, RJ knocked and came into the room. "Oh there he is. I heard him scratching at Renee's door and took him outside around two o'clock this morning so he could use the bathroom, and then I just let him stay in my room. I must have left my door cracked." He said as he reached over and petted the dog.

As Abby watched her kids play with the dog, Abby thanked God for her happy and healthy family. When she was married to Randy, her family never bonded like this. She couldn't put all the blame on Randy. When they were married, he had just won a seat in Congress, and with his dad, Richard's help, Randy was diligently pursuing his way to the White House. Abby was a rising R&B superstar, who became addicted to the glamour and fame and drugs and alcohol. The twins were so neglected by their parent; they were being raised by their nannies. Abby knew that the hell she went through in her first marriage brought her to this place of peace and serenity. This is truly what God's word meant in Romans 8:28 when it says *"And we know all things work together for the good to them that love God, to them who are called according to his purpose."* Abby finally found her purpose after her horrific ordeal, not only was she an award winning gospel singer, but also an associate pastor at Grace Faith Church. She loved working alongside her sister Hannah, who was also an associate minister and Cecilia Ford and of course her spiritual father Reverend William Rawlins.

The biggest thrill however, was discovering that her daughter inherited her singing talent. Renee had no interest in singing secular music, so Abby was able to guide her career as an upcoming gospel singer. In the last CD that the choir had released commercially, Renee had sung lead on three songs, and two of the songs were receiving lots of air time on gospel radio stations. There was even talk going around that her daughter might be nominated for her own Stella music award!

Abby felt her husband's hand slide over her protruding stomach and gently caress their growing twins inside. Greg snuggled closer and kissed the back of her neck, then raised his head and looked at the twins. "Why don't you guys take the dog outside so he can handle his business, then feed him." He said. Before they left, Abby said. "Can you also decide on a name for him? We can't keep calling him the dog!" The twins laughed and left the room. As soon as the door closed, Greg gently rolled his wife over into his arms and kissed her deeply. "I love those two," he said in a husky voice, "but I want some alone time with my beautiful wife." Abby threw back her head as her husband left a trail of kisses down her throat and with his free hands, he began to undress her. Abby shivered in participation, as her husband began to make love to her.

Chapter Twenty One

Kingdom Creations Bakery was the meeting place of choice for the Grace Faith Women's Ministry Association. The members, Cecilia, Katherine, Abby and Hannah, met there twice a month. Cecilia always had her friend's favorite desserts on hand for them to enjoy during the meeting. Today they were munching on her homemade *chocolate gooey butter cake*, a recipe she had brought to DC, from her home town in St. Louis Missouri.

The ladies were busy discussing plans for the annual women's conference and who they wanted to invite as speakers. Abby shifted uncomfortably in her seat, and rubbed the side of her growing stomach. She was now in her fifth month and the twins were very active, kicking and moving inside her. Hannah, noticing her sister's discomfort, began to rub her back, and a grateful Abby smiled at her. "Did I tell you that Renee found a German shepherd puppy last month? We flooded the neighborhood with flyers, but so far no one has claimed him. He's the cutest little thing you've ever seen, but when Greg and the kids leave, he follows me around like I'm his mama." She told the girls with a laugh.

"No, you didn't tell us you had a new family member. Do you think you'll be able to handle dealing with him and twin newborns?" Cecilia asked, as she stood in the bakery's kitchen mixing cupcake batter for a party she was catering later that evening. "We'll even if I can't; it's too late now, because we've all fallen in love with him. Renee and RJ named him Rex. Greg wanted to name him Dexter, but the kids out voted him. He has his own bed in Renee's room, but every morning there he is sleeping between me and Greg, using my belly as his pillow!"

Katherine shook her head. "When Daniel was younger, we bought him a puppy and that animal ended up running the house. He was a water Spaniel named Spanky. I really miss that old mutt. He finally died of old age when Daniel was away at college, he was nearly seventeen years old when he died."

Hannah looked at her husband's aunt in surprise. "Daniel never told me he had a dog.

Hmm, I wonder how he would feel about getting a puppy." She turned to Abby. "Is it okay if we stop by after dinner to meet Rex? Mom and dad never allowed us to have pets, and I've always wanted a dog." She said wistfully. Abby nodded. "Sure, as a matter of fact why don't all of you come for dinner tomorrow?" She looked at Cecilia. "I know you're catering a party tonight, but would it be too much trouble for you to whip us up something tomorrow? It can be something quick and easy, Greg and the kids love everything you cook, and as long as I don't have to cook, it's all good. I'll leave the menu to you." She told her friend.

Cecilia nodded. "Sure. I was planning on cooking fried chicken, mashed potatoes and gravy and buttermilk biscuits for William, so I'll just make extra and bring one of my red velvet cheesecakes for dessert. Will that work?" She asked. The women began drooling. "Oh, Lord, yes. Kenneth and I will certainly be there, it's been way too long since I had your fried chicken and biscuits." Katherine said, as her stomach growled just thinking about Cecilia's food. Abby grabbed her purse, pulled out her credit card and handed it to Cecilia to pay for tomorrow's dinner. "Uh, please make two cheesecakes. One for ya'll and one for me!" She said smugly as they laughed at the pregnant Abby.

The following evening, everyone arrived at the Taylor's house for dinner. Renee answered the door and hugged everyone when they arrived. It had been months since she had spent time with her beloved aunt. RJ went to get the puppy for everyone to meet. When RJ sat him down on the living room floor, Rex looked up at the group of strangers. Seeing that he was on display, the pup lifted his right paw, as if to say hello and RJ beamed. "I taught him that. He's waving hi." He proudly told the group.

Daniel, William and Kenneth watched in amazement as RJ showed them several more tricks he had taught the pup, and soon, the men joined RJ on the floor, and they all played with Rex. Greg grinned at RJ and Abby. It was great seeing his friends enjoying the dog. Abby just shook her head, and went in the kitchen to help Cecilia unpack their dinner.

After the great meal, Renee and RJ took the dog for a walk. Daniel looked at his aunt and uncle. "Remember Spanky? He was a great dog wasn't he? He asked wistfully, remembering the good times he had with his faithful dog. His uncle nodded as he reached for another piece of Cecilia's scrumptious cheesecake. "Yeah, he was a great dog. Well trained, friendly. When you left to go to college, he really missed you. He moped around the house for months, until that cute little terrier moved in next door." He laughed.

Katherine nodded, "We thought he was too old to father a litter, but he ended up having two with that dog! The puppies were the cutest things you ever saw."

Hannah took this opening and looked at her husband. "I would love to get a puppy. I've always wanted one, but because of Mama's allergies, we couldn't have any pets." She told him. Daniel reached over and hugged his wife. "Sure. Tell you what, when we get home, we'll browse the Internet and see what kind of breed we want." He told her, kissing her forehead. Hannah beamed happily.

By the time the adults had finished eating dessert, the twins were back with the puppy. RJ removed his leash and the puppy followed him into the dining room. Abby got up to take her guest's plates back into the kitchen. Rex immediately followed her and minutes later everyone heard a loud crash, followed by Abby groaning. Greg jumped up and ran into the kitchen and found his wife sprawled on the kitchen floor. Greg's heart leaped into his throat. "What happened?"

He asked, as he bent down to pick up a moaning Abby. "I tripped over the dog, he was right behind me and I didn't see him." She groaned anxiously, rubbing her stomach. Rex, with his tail tucked between his legs, fled out of the room.

Abby was visibly shaken and she clutched her stomach, concerned about the babies. Her husband picked her up and carried her into the living room, laying her on the sofa. Dr. Kenneth John ran outside to his car to get his medical bag. Greg moved off the couch, when Kenneth returned. The doctor gently pressed Abby's swollen belly and asked her if she felt any pain. Grimacing with pain, Abby nodded. A very concerned, Kenneth turned to Greg. "Call an ambulance, now" He said tersely. Greg grabbed his cellphone from his pants pocket and called 911. Kenneth asked everyone to leave the room, so he could check to see if Abby was bleeding. When he noticed blood in her underwear, he immediately began to pray and he called out to his wife Katherine.

Abby noticed the look on his face and was scared. Was she losing the babies? Knowing that *life and death are in the power of the tongue*, she refused to speak her concerns out loud. When Katherine arrived, she grabbed Abby's hand and they both began to pray. Kenneth took that opportunity to call the hospital to have them locate Abby's obstetrician. Dr. Kate Bryant returned his call within minutes and with the sounds of the siren in the background, Kenneth grimly advised her of the situation and asked her to meet them at the hospital.

Greg led the paramedics into the living room and once they conferred with Kenneth, they carefully moved Abby onto the stretcher, and whisked her out to the ambulance. Greg climbed into the ambulance with her, and asked Hannah to stay with the twins. A distraught Hannah agreed, but after Greg left, the twins told her they wanted to be with their mom. Hannah finally caved in and the twins jumped in the car with her, Daniel and Reverend Rawlins. Cecilia agreed to stay behind to clean the kitchen and lock up the Taylor's house. While loading the dishwasher, she prayed for her dear friend and the babies she was carrying. After cleaning the kitchen, Cecilia went out the back door to empty the trash, before heading over to the hospital in her husband's car.

With the house quiet, the puppy crept back into the living room and jumped on the couch. He watched from the window as the ambulance and cars quickly drove away. The puppy, Rex laughed. "Stupid humans," he said out loud, as he shape shifted into his true demonic form: Semjaza! At that exact moment, Cecilia, was backing out of the driveway, and happened to glanced at the house out of the corner of her eye. She slammed on the brakes and watched in horror as the cute little puppy dog, that they were all gushing over earlier, transformed into a hideous *demon*! A shocked Cecilia and the demon stared at each other.

Semjaza panicked, he thought everyone had left. Cecilia panicked; she realized that this *thing* had been living with the Taylors for months! Suddenly the Holy Spirit spoke to her, "***Leave, now***!" Cecilia slammed her foot on the gas pedal and peeled out of the driveway and down the street.

Agitated that his cover had been blown, Semjaza called out to Azazel. Within seconds, Azazel and a battalion of imps appeared at the Taylor home. After Semjaza told them what happened, the demonic spirits immediately took to the sky, in the form of huge black ravens to search for Cecilia. Driving as fast as she could to the hospital, Cecilia looked up and saw that the sky was suddenly filled with large black ravens! She began praying in tongues, asking God to help her, because she knew those were not ravens!

"Pull into that car wash at the next corner and stay there until you see them fly over you." She heard the Spirit say. Cecilia quickly turned the corner and cried out in relief when she saw the semi-empty car wash on her left. She pulled into one of the empty bays, and immediately turned off her car. Leaning her head back against the head rest, she watched as the swarm of ravens flew right over her. Cecilia grabbed her cellphone out of her purse and quickly dialed her husband. She nervously tapped her nails against the steering wheel, waiting for him to answer, and kept a watchful eye on the skies above, to see if the birds would circle back to look for her.

When William finally answered, Cecilia told him what happened at the house and the subsequent chase. Shocked by what his wife was telling him, William quickly waved Daniel and Hannah over, and they stepped out into the hallway. In a hushed tone, with his wife still on the phone, William told them what Cecilia told him. Stunned, Daniel and Hannah looked at each other. *Oh no!* The enemy had infiltrated the Taylor household in the form of a harmless puppy. Hannah looked over at her niece and nephew, and her heart went out to them. She knew how devastated they were going to be when they found out that the enemy had used Renee to plant one of their own in the Taylor house! Suddenly Hannah remembered Abby telling her about waking up every morning to find the dog lying with its head on her stomach, the enemy could have killed the twins at any time! Hannah felt sick to her stomach and with her hand over her mouth; she rushed into a bathroom, and violently threw up the wonderful meal Cecilia had prepared earlier!

Back at the car wash, Cecilia spoke quietly to her husband on the phone. She still hadn't seen any sign of the ravens, but she feared they were nearby, waiting for her. She didn't know what to do. There was no way she was going to lead them to the hospital, fearing they would attack Abby again, so she prayed in the Spirit, while her husband listened quietly on the other end. Then the Holy Spirit spoke to her. *"Cecilia, your prayers have been heard, and God's army of angels are engaging the demonic horde in battle at this very moment. You're surrounded by your angels and they will safely escort you to the hospital. I have sent hundreds of thousands of them to surround the hospital, all of you are safe, my love."* The Spirit said deep within her.

Cecilia visibly relaxed and relayed the information to William, who assured her he and

Daniel would be waiting at the front entrance when she arrived. Cecilia started her car and slowly pulled out of the car wash and headed over to the hospital, unable to see her *guardian angel Raphael*, sitting on the hood of her car, with his swords held at the ready!

Two hours later, Dr. Kenneth John and Dr. Kate Bryant walked into the waiting room to speak to the family. Greg was with his wife, refusing to leave her side. Kenneth went over to Katherine and gently took her in his arms. She anxiously searched his face for any sign of Abby's condition and he smiled down at her and nodded. "Abby's going to be fine," Dr. Bryant told them. "The bleeding has stopped, but we're going to admit her overnight just to be on the safe side." Dr. Bryant looked over at the twins. "I know how much you two love that new puppy, but until your mom has the babies, I think it will be best if the dog stayed outside." She said solemnly. Both RJ and Renee nodded, as the adults looked at each other uneasily. How could they tell the twins that the puppy they had fallen in love with, wasn't really a puppy at all?

A few hours later, the twins, their aunt and uncle and William and Cecilia returned to the Taylor house. RJ went to look for the puppy, but he wasn't anywhere in the house. Renee joined in the search and together they called for him. Cecilia, praying for forgiveness, quietly walked over to the kitchen door and opened it slightly, and then called the twins. When they arrived in the kitchen, Cecilia looked them in the eye and lied. "I'm sorry; I just noticed that I accidently left the kitchen door open when I took out the trash. I have a feeling the puppy got out." She said solemnly. RJ and Renee were so upset, they told the adults they were going out to search the neighborhood.

After they left, Cecilia looked at the adults, and grimly shook her head. "I just didn't have the heart to tell them about the dog. I know Renee will blame herself for bringing the dog home and causing this accident to happen, and I just couldn't do that to her." She explained softly. Everyone nodded, they felt the same way, but they knew that ell Greg and Abby what really happened to the dog, once Abby was home and feeling better.

Chapter Twenty Two

Simone stood in the kitchen of her newly decorated apartment in D.C. After burying her sister, she sold her house and her share of the law firm and asked Joe to help her find a two bedroom apartment close to him and the boys. Gayle also decided to relocate, as her feelings for Ralph grew. She returned to New Orleans with Simone for the funeral, and sold her condo, packed up her paintings and headed back to D.C.

After the Jenkins purchased a majority of her paintings, Gayle stepped out on faith and purchased a cute little warehouse that Ralph and the twins designed and converted into a condo/ art gallery for her. Gayle and Simone joined Grace Faith Church, and Simone decided against joining another law firm. The idea of giving up her personal life again for work, no longer appealed to her. Now she wanted to be free to spend as much time as she could with Joe and his sons, so after discussing her options one Sunday over dinner with Joe, at Daniel and Hannah's house, she agreed to work with Daniel and Hannah at the church's center.

Joel and Earnestine decided to buy a nice 3 bedroom garden style condo close to Reverend Rawlins and Cecilia. Joel and William hit it off so well, William asked him to preach at the church for two weeks, while he took his new bride away for a well deserved honeymoon. Before leaving, Revered Rawlins and Cecilia told Greg and Abby what *really* happened to the dog. When Cecilia told the Taylors about seeing the dog turn into a demon, Abby, knowing how close that dog-thing had been to her and her babies, nearly fainted.

Once she got over her initial shock, Abby realized that the enemy wanted to destroy her babies, and the *warrior* in her came out! She increased her prayer time and asked the Holy Spirit for wisdom and discernment so that she could protect her family.

Greg and Abby sat down with the twins and told them the truth about the dog. At first, RJ refused to believe it, until his sister reminded him about the demonic shape shifting they witnessed when they lived with their father and Aunt Candace. RJ had blocked out most of the stuff he had seen at the Brotherhood lodge meetings with his father, but once he was reminded about what he had witnessed, he started having nightmares, which made his sister feel guilty for reminding him about the past.

When Hannah and Daniel found out about the dog, they decided that maybe now was *not* a good time to purchase one! Unbeknownst to Abby, Hannah and Cecilia made a pact to stay close to her until the babies came. They were determined to thwart the enemies plan to hurt or kill Abby's babies. Greg conducted his business from his home office, and put his top man, Roger Bacon, in charge of the office and the field operations.

Six weeks later, Dr. Bryant released Abby from bed rest, and the ladies resumed their monthly meetings back at the bakery. Cecilia invited Ernestine Jenkins to join their group, and to mark the occasion of her friend's first meeting, Cecilia made Ernestine's favorite dessert; peach cobbler and homemade chocolate fudge ice cream. When Cecilia served the homemade cobbler and ice cream, she and Hannah quickly devoured theirs, then helped themselves to seconds. The other women watched in amazement as the two women demolished their cobbler and ice cream. "Uh, are you two okay?" Katherine asked in concern. "I've never seen you eat this much."

Hannah was trying to restraint herself from licking her bowl, so she settled on licking the remaining cobbler off her spoon. "I can't help myself," She said happily. "This is one of the best cobbler's CeeCee has made, and the ice cream..." Hannah just shook her head and turned to Cecilia. 'Please tell me you have another cobbler and ice cream, I would love to serve it tonight after dinner." Cecilia laughed. "For some reason, I'm craving peaches and ice cream; I made five cobblers and five quarts of ice cream yesterday. Last night I served this to William and I ate three helpings! I don't know why I'm craving sweets." She said as she spooned a third helping onto her plate, and reached for the homemade ice cream. Seeing her host go for thirds, Hannah joined her and they both sat back and ate with relish.

Abby, Katherine and Ernestine looked at each other. Suddenly a thought popped into Abby's head. She looked over at Hannah and Cecilia. "You two are eating like you're pregnant." She said with a smile. Hannah and Cecilia's spoons stopped midway to their mouths. "What?" They said in unison. They lowered their spoons and looked at each other, as they tried to remember their last menstrual cycle. "Oh my," they said in unison again.

Cecilia bowed her head and consulted the Holy Spirit, who didn't say anything, but joy flowed through her body. The same thing happened to Hannah, and with tears glistening in her eyes, she quickly finished her ice cream and grabbed her purse. "I'm going to the drugstore and pick up a pregnancy kit." She said excitedly. "Wait for me!" Cecilia yelled, as she gobbled up the last of her cobbler and ice cream, grabbed her purse and ran after Hannah.

Before she reached the door, Cecilia turned towards the three women sitting at the table and asked, "Can you stay here until we get back?" They nodded and she quickly followed Hannah out of the bakery. Ernestine looked at the other two ladies and helped herself to more cobbler. "Why I wouldn't miss this for the world!" She laughed.

Hannah and Cecilia returned thirty minutes later. Cecilia headed for the staff bathroom and Hannah went into the public one. Within minutes the ladies came out with huge grins on their face and positive sticks in their hands! After showing and conferring the results with the others, Cecilia and Hannah hugged each other and cried with joy. Their fondest wish had just come true, they were having a baby!

Later that night, all four wives shared the wonderful news with their husbands. Hannah told Daniel he was going to be a father over a romantic dinner she prepared. As soon as William walked in the door, Cecilia met him at the door and told him that they were having a baby. After Abby left the bakery, she raced home to share the news with Greg. Since the twins were still at school, they celebrated the good news by **christening** every room in their house! Katherine's husband was working an evening shift, so she stopped by the hospital, and invited him to lunch. While eating his favorite meal, she told him that he was about to become a great uncle, and his longtime friend and pastor was going to be a daddy again. While everyone on earth and in the heavenlies was busy celebrating, the imps assigned to keep an eye on the saints, flew off to share the grim news with their leader.

Chapter Twenty Three

Back in Los Angeles, Ahmad was in the Nelson's pool drifting lazily on a floating rubber lounger and sipping a martini. Nicely tanned and wearing a tight Speedo that left absolutely nothing to the imagination, he looked like a movie star. He stood well over six feet six inches tall, and his body was lean and fit. His six pack abdomen and his fashionably long, thick black hair, were two of his best features. His green eyes were hidden behind an expensive pair of Louis Vuitton Evasion sunglasses. Suddenly a shadow appeared over him. As Ahmad snarled, furious that someone was intruding on his private time, a large hand reached out and flipped the floating device over, and Ahmad tumbled into the water. Gasping for air, he resurfaced, and whipped off his shades, ready to kill the person responsible, but when he saw who stood before him, he quickly wiped the snarl off his face and hauled himself out of the pool and stood trembling before Satan.

The evil fallen angel glared at the trembling creature before him, and with a wave of his hand, he transformed Ahmad back into his natural form. The other demons laughed, as Ahmad's Speedo bikini snapped in two. Exposed and humiliated, he tried unsuccessfully to cover himself while Satan walked around him with a snarl on his lips.

"So is this how you waste your time, Semjaza, as we wage war with the saints of God?" He barked at him. Semjaza cringed. "No master, the humans are out of town and I was contemplating how to save your television series. Yesterday, the star of your hit teen comedy overdosed." He said quickly.

That information stopped Satan in his tracks. "What happened to the actress?" He asked sharply. Semjaza snapped his finger, and his tattered wings fluttered open and covered his body. "She was found dead from a heroin overdose. Candace blames Randy because he was the one who forced her to use heroin so she could lose weight, and Randy blames Candace because Candace's lover was hired to be the girl's manager, and she and Candace were busy having sex when the girl overdosed in her apartment!" He told him.

Satan laughed. He hated humans, but he had

a soft spot for Randy and Candace. They were both so depraved and self serving, it was easy to influence them to do his bidding. Satan shook his head and returned to the reason why he appeared. "It has come to my attention that not only is Abby still pregnant, but so is her sister Hannah. But my main concern is that *His* prophecy of a child for that annoying pastor and that stupid prophetess, Cecilia Ford-Rawlins, has come to pass, she is also with child!" Satan fumed, as he once again began to pace. "I refuse to allow this child to be born." He turned back to Semjaza. "You remain here and keep an eye on my investment, that show is too important to me. I can't afford to let it fall apart. Find another actress to replace the dead one as soon as possible. Did you tape enough episodes so we can find a way to write her out and find a replacement?" He asked. Semjaza nodded, relieved that he had convince Zandor to do just that. "Yes, Zandor is returning home tonight, and we'll start searching for a replacement immediately, Master."

Satan nodded and with a sweep of his long cape, disappeared, along with his entourage. Semjaza shape shifted back into Ahmad and with a longing look at the pool, he turned and went inside the house to search for a suitable actress for his masters top rated television show, **The Shadow Hunters**.

Satan returned to his lair, and sat sullenly upon his makeshift throne. He was determined to get rid of the dreaded child that Cecilia was pregnant with! He finally decided to take matters into his own hands, and he quickly vanished, then reappeared at the Rawlins home in the form of his alter ego, **Beelzebub, the fly!** He buzzed around and found Cecilia alone in the kitchen, cooking.

Beelzebub telepathically sent out a call to every fly in the area and soon thousands of flies gathered around him at the Rawlins residents. He silently commanded them to swarm every room in the house and they obeyed him. Cecilia was checking on her pot roast when she heard a buzzing sound. She closed the oven door and looked around the neat clean kitchen. Her mouth dropped open when she saw at least a hundred flies buzzing around her kitchen. Cecilia reached into the utility closet and grabbed a can of bug spray. She stood in the middle of the room, and released a steady stream of spray. Several flies drop dead instantly, but many of them flew towards her, attacking. She swatted at them with her hands, and continued to blast them with the spray. She chased them into the dining room, and her heart nearly stopped when she saw thousands of them in there and the adjacent living room! Beelzebub ordered them to attack and the swarm turned on her!

Cecilia fled. She ran into her bedroom and locked the door. A couple of flies flew into the room from underneath the door, and she swatted at them as she grabbed her cell phone to call her husband. "William," she cried out frantically, as she continued to swat at the flies with her free hand, "there are thousands of flies in the house, attacking me. " She shrieked into the phone when he answered.

William immediately sat up in his office chair. "What? How in the world did flies get in the house?" He asked, puzzled. Cecilia swatted two flies with a newspaper she found in the room. "I have no idea; I was in the kitchen cooking and heard a buzzing sound and when I looked up there were in the kitchen. When I sprayed them, some died, but the others flew at me and I chased them into the dining room and there were *thousands* of them in there. I ran and locked myself into the bedroom, but some of them followed me in here, from underneath the door." She explained. Suddenly she heard buzzing at her window and when she turned she stared in disbelief. The bedroom window was covered with flies! She relayed this information to her husband, who was walking out of his office, to head home. He mouthed to Alice, his secretary, that he was headed home as he listened to his wife. "Baby, I'm on my way," he said, as he jumped in his car and sped out of the church's parking lot.

Cecilia hung up the phone and sat at the foot of their bed. She calmed herself down and sought the Holy Spirit to find out what was going on. Within seconds the phrase *demonic attack* came to mind. Realizing that the enemy was messing with her mind, Cecilia fought back. "I bind you Satan from attacking me and my home, and I cast you out of my house right now, in Jesus name!" Then she reached over and turned on her CD player and blasted Grace Faith's latest CD throughout the house! She grabbed a bottle of anointing oil that she kept on the nightstand, and defiantly opened her bedroom door. She began flinging oil on the flies, as she commanded them to leave. The flies slammed against the windows, doors and each other, trying to escape the oil Cecilia was throwing on them.

Cecilia walked over to the windows and opened them as the flies made a beeline out of her house!

Beelzebub glared at the mighty woman of God, and flew out of the house along with his swarm. Within minutes the house was completely bug free and when William arrived a few minutes later, Cecilia was back in the kitchen, transferring her perfect pot roast onto a platter and humming along with the CD.

"What happened?" William asked, as he set his briefcase down on the kitchen island and walked over to embrace his wife." Cecilia laid her head on his chest and said. "After I hung up with you, I asked the Holy Spirit to reveal to me what was going on, and I heard demonic attack. Then I went on the offensive and commanded Satan to leave this house, I got the oil and began anointing the house and I put on the church's new CD and blasted it! Baby, those flies couldn't get out of here fast enough!" She said cheerfully. William laughed as he hugged his warrior wife and kissed the top of her head. He glanced into the dining room and just like his wife said, there were hundreds of dead flies lying in oil. "I'll sweep up the rest of these flies, while you finish dinner. Baby, I truly love you, I'm going to have to include this episode in my spiritual warfare class next week." He chuckled, as he pulled the broom out of the utility closet.

Meanwhile on the other side of town, Satan, still feeling the sting of defeat from the Prophetess, transformed into a crow and searched for Hannah. It was time to show her some of his wrath. He spotted her car coming down a busy intersection and with an evil smile; he swooped down and landed on top of a car heading towards her in the opposite lane. As the car passed Hannah's car, Satan, the bird, let out a loud squawk, startling the driver who lost control, and his car swerved into Hannah's lane.

Hannah saw the car coming towards her and her heart skipped a beat as she grabbed the steering wheel and swerved onto the shoulder, to avoid the car. But unfortunately, she was headed right for the guard rail! Hannah quickly called out, "Please help me, Jesus!" A large **invisible hand** reached down and extended the shoulder so Hannah wouldn't hit the guard rail. Once Hannah straighten her car and was out of danger, the hand returned the shoulder back to its original size. Hannah stopped, and turned her car off, trying to collect herself. "Thank you precious Lord," she whispered gratefully. After a minute, she started her car and made it home safely. Satan was beside himself with anger. He **hated** these humans, and he was even more determined to destroy them all! He glared at Hannah as she pulled into her driveway and fell into her husband's arms. Satan realized that he was going to have to really step up his game if he was hell bent on destroying these saints, because they knew exactly **who** they were and who they **belonged** to! Defeated, he turned and flew away.

Chapter Twenty-Four

The next day, Simone was in the office she shared with Daniel, checking her emails. She really enjoyed working with Daniel, he had a brilliant mind when it came to the law, and unlike her and her former partners in New Orleans, he refused to compromise his integrity to win a case. She quickly realized that her boyfriend and his friends didn't just talk the talk about being a Christian, they **lived** it, everyday.

Satan, again in the form of **Beelzebub,** was sitting on top of a bookshelf in the office, undetected, watching her carefully and **invading** her thoughts. Being a new follower, she couldn't sense the presence of evil in her office, but she did feel uneasy. Suddenly she heard Joe's voice in the hallway, and a sense of relief overcame her. She looked up and saw him chatting with Hannah. The two were standing very close to each other, sharing a laugh, and as Simone watched them, a twinge of jealousy stabbed her heart. Hannah had everything Simone wanted, a handsome devoted husband, a career that she loved, and carrying her first child.

Aware of what she was feeling, the evil fly smiled. He flew off the bookshelf and landed on the window behind her and began filling her mind with inappropriate images of Hannah and Joe, filling her mind with suspicion and insecurity. *Why is Joe always hovering around Hannah, whispering and laughing? Where they talking about her? Laughing at her?* A startled Simone caught herself, surprised at what she was thinking. She knew how much Joe adored her, and Hannah and Daniel were happily married. But still, she thought, as she watched the two of them, uneasily from her office. *Was something going on between them behind her and Daniel's back?*

When Joe finally entered Simone's office, she had an attitude! She wanted to tear into him, for spending so much time in the hallway chatting with Hannah. "Hey beautiful lady, are you free for lunch?" He asked, as he came around her desk and planted a sweet kiss on her lips. Simone's anger melted, and she chided herself for thinking bad thoughts about him and Hannah. "I'm all yours, sweetie," she answered, as she reached into her desk, and pulled out her purse. As they left her office, they passed Hannah in the hallway. "Enjoy your lunch, you two." Hannah said. Joe grinned, "Would you care to join us?" He asked politely, as Simone stiffened beside him. Hannah waved a handful of folders at them, "Maybe next time, I've got too much paperwork to do." Joe nodded, but Simone glared at Hannah, and reached out and took Joe's hand. "C'mon honey, I'm starving" She said impatiently. As she watched them walked out the door, Hannah stared at Simone's back with her eyebrow raised, "What's eating her?" She mumbled to herself. Beelzebub watched the exchange between the two women and grinned. Now this was more like it! He flew off, eager to put the next phase of his plan to work.

His next stop was Grace Faith church. He flew in as the choir was rehearsing. He landed on a pew and searched the congregation intently. His eyes narrowed with hatred as he watched a pregnant Abby chatting with Cecilia. He looked around and bingo! He spotted one of the women in the choir, glaring at Cecilia. The *fly* listened to the woman's thoughts: ***It should have been me that Reverend Rawlins married. I asked God over and over to bless me with him as a*** *husband, but instead he once again blessed Cecilia! Why didn't God bless me?* The poor woman thought to herself.

God doesn't love you as much as he loves Cecilia. Never believe the like that he's not a respecter of person. Cecilia has everything, and you can barely keep your lights on at home! God allows the pastor to use you and the rest of the congregation to pay for their extravagant lifestyles. Did you see the new car Reverend Rawlins just bought Cecilia? Look at the old beat up car you're driving! But you faithfully give ten percent of your paycheck to the church, and he uses it to buy his wife whatever she wants! The fly whispered in the woman's ear. The woman fumed as she listened to the voice inside her head. *Maybe you should have the board look into the church's finances to make sure Reverend Rawlins isn't using your money to spoil his wife!*

The woman grabbed her purse and hurried out of the sanctuary. She was going home to make some phone calls. There was no way she was going to let Reverend Rawlins and Cecilia rob the church blind, not on **her** watch! The evil fly threw back his head and laughed as the woman stomped out of the church. Oh this was going to be so much fun!

Later that evening, while William and Cecilia were enjoying dinner, the phone rang. William excused himself and answered it. He was taken aback when the President of the church board asked to meet with him tomorrow evening to discuss the church's finance. "William, we're concerned about some large withdrawals from the church's bank account. These withdrawals were never discussed or approved by us, and you know that's against church policy." The man said sternly.

William was shocked. "I haven't written any checks that the board has not approved," He said sharply. "I would never do that!" The man on the other end of the line rolled his eyes, as he waved away an annoying *fly* that was in his study. "Well we just had an emergency meeting today, after this was brought to our attention, and we have removed your name from the account. Meet us tomorrow night at 7pm sharp at the church." The man said abruptly, and slammed down the phone. When William returned to the dining room, Cecilia was concerned by the look on his face. "Honey, what's the matter?" She asked, as she put down her fork and looked at her husband. William sat down. "That was Lee Johnson from the church

261

board. He accused me of taking large sums of money from the church without their approval. Sweetheart, apparently they voted today to take my name off the account, and ordered me to meet with them tomorrow night at the church." He said, still stunned.

Cecilia looked at her husband in shock. "They think you stole money from the church?" She asked in disbelief. William nodded as he picked up his fork, "Yep, it appears that's exactly what they think!" He said, unsettled. The fly watched the flustered pastor and his upset wife, through their dining room window. Satisfied, that he had thrown them for a loop, he went after his last target.

Abby was getting ready for bed when her phone rang. Thinking it was her sister Hannah, she picked up the phone without checking the caller id, and was startled to hear her ex-husband, Randy Nelson on the line.

"Hello Abby" Randy said, when Abby answered. The hairs on Abby's neck stood straight up! "What do you want?" She asked harshly. Randy laughed. "Now, that's not very **Christian** of you. I can't call the love of my life and ask about my children?" He asked, nastily. Abby rolled her eyes. "You haven't called to ask about **my** children in over two years, why are you calling now?"

The large black *fly* watched Randy as he sat in his office, twirling a pen around in his hand. Abby's voice bought back memories of their time together, and he was shocked to realize just how much he missed her. The fly projected images in Randy's mind about the good times they shared together. *Abby will always be the love of my life. I made a big mistake letting her go, and marrying Candace.* Randy thought, as grief overcame him. He sighed heavily into the phone. "I miss my kids and I want to see them." He said softly. Abby gripped the phone so hard, she was afraid she would break the receiver in half.

"Trust me Randy; they don't want to see you." She said evenly. She looked around for Greg, then remembered that he was at his office, meeting with his agents. "Abby, I spoke with my attorney, and he said I have a right to visit my kids. I'm going to be in Washington tomorrow, and you can either bring them to my hotel or I can come to your house. Either way, I'm going to see them, or I'm going to haul you into court for violating our custody agreement." He said quietly.

Abby panicked. She knew he was right, their custody agreement stipulated that he had visitation rights. Abby silently prayed to the Holy

Spirit for guidance. Randy waited for her to say something, but when she didn't, he said, "Are you still there?"

Abby sucked in her breath and said, "Yes, hold on. I'll let you talk to the twins and they can decide if they want to see you or not." She replied, following the advice the *Spirit* gave her. She called the twins into her room. When they arrived, she put the receiver against her chest. "It's your father; he wants to talk to you two." Renee backed away from the phone. "I don't want to talk to him! What in the world is he doing calling us?" She asked hotly. RJ looked at his twin. "I'll talk to him and find out what he wants." He held out his hand and Abby gave him the phone. "Hey dad," he said evenly, "how you doing?" Tears came to Randy's eyes as he heard his son's voice. Randy missed his kids, especially his son, who was named after him. "My God, you sound like a grown man, your voice has changed so much." Randy said. RJ chuckled. "Well it has been a couple of years since we've spoken, and I've grown a couple of inches as well. How are you and Aunt Candace doing in Los Angeles?" He asked. Abby and Renee were amazed at how calm RJ was, as he chatted with his father. Fear rose in Abby. Did RJ want to see his dad? Lord, please don't let him want to live with his father and my sister. She prayed. RJ had been exposed to the evil side of his dad and aunt's lives, and he **embraced** it, while his twin, Renee, **rejected** their lifestyle and them.

"Son, I'm going to be in Washington tomorrow, and I want to see you and your sister. Unfortunately, your aunt and I have separated, so it will just be me, but I really want to see you. If you two don't want to see me, I understand, and I won't bother you again, but you're my only children and I miss you. I want to apologize to what I did to you, your sister and your mother. Are you ready to forgive me?" Randy asked hesitantly.

RJ looked over at his mom and his sister. He knew how hard this was for them. "Dad, Renee and I are born again Christians, we love the Lord with all our hearts and souls. Forgiveness is paramount in our relationship with the Lord, so yes, I would love to see you. I can't speak for Renee, but I do want to give you a chance to apologize." RJ turned and looked at his sister.

Renee lowered her head and studied her shoes. She knew that forgiveness was indeed something Jesus taught, and being a follower, she had to do what was right. Finally, she lifted her head and took the phone from RJ. Taking a deep breath, she said, "Hi dad," into the phone. Randy closed his eyes as he heard his daughter's voice. She sounded so much like Abby that he thought his heart would break. "Hi sweetheart," Randy said emotionally, "Baby, I'm so sorry for everything Candace and I put you through. Please give me a chance to make things right." He pleaded.

Tears came to Renee's eyes and she nodded. "Okay, but you'll have to come to the house, and mom and Greg have to be here." She said softly. Randy exhaled a sigh of relief. "I can do that, and I promise you won't regret it." He replied. Renee looked over at her mom. "Mom, is it okay if dad came for dinner?" Defeated, Abby just nodded. "Okay dad, here's the address and we'll see you about seven okay?" As Renee gave her dad the address, RJ sat down on the bed next to his mom and put his arm around her.

"Mom, I know this is going to be hard for you, because you suffered the worse at the hands of our father, however, you and Reverend Rawlins have taught us about forgiveness. Do you think one day, you'll be able to forgive dad too?" Her son asked her. Abby hugged her precious son and said, "I'm certainly trying, darling."

After Randy hung up, he picked up his glass of whiskey, and downed the contents in one gulp. He turned to Ahmad, who had been standing in the doorway watching and listening. "Okay, it's done. I'm having dinner with Abby and the kids at her house tomorrow evening." Ahmad smiled at his boss. "Good." He turned and left the room.

Randy fixed himself another drink and took a key out of his pants pocket and unlocked a desk drawer. He pulled out a picture of him, Abby and the twins. The babies were about six months old, and he and Abby were very happy. Tears rolled down his face as he stared at the picture. **Beelzebub** panicked, as he stared in disbelief at Randy. He quickly flooded Randy's mind with images of Greg making love to Abby, and the twins calling Greg dad. The images made Randy grip the half full glass in his hand in anger and he threw it against the fireplace mantel. He was going to make Greg Taylor pay for stealing his family!

Chapter Twenty-five

The next evening, Reverend Rawlins and Cecilia meet with the Grace Faith church board. The tension in the air was palpable as the members glared at the reverend and his wife. Lee Johnson, the board president, shoved the cashed checks in William and Cecilia's face that had his signature on them. They totaled over twenty-five thousand dollars. The board members grilled the couple about the purchase of Cecilia's new car, and she pulled out her profit and loss statement from her bakery, that showed her income surpassed what the board was paying Reverend Rawlins. She vehemently denied that her husband used church funds to pay for her car. Finally fed up with the boards grilling and insinuations, William stood up and told the board about the investments he had made over the years. He and Cecilia were very well off and didn't need to steal money from the church. He called his investment broker and put him on the speaker phone, and the man verified what the pastor told them.

The proverbial fly on the wall, also attended the meeting, and he delighted in sending angry darts of **envy** and **jealousy** amongst the board members, when they realized how wealthy the Rawlins were. Lee Johnson glared at the pastor, and told William he needed to explain how his signature appeared on the church's checks. When William honestly told them he didn't know, Lee scoffed at him, and motioned for a vote among the members, to remove William as pastor of the church. Cecilia was **floored** and William was beside himself with anger!

When the motion passed, the vindictive board president also called for a vote to have William arrested and charged with embezzlement of church funds. The Rawlins watched in horror as the vote passed unanimously! One of the members of the board was a police officer and he called the station and asked that a police officer be dispatched to the church and Cecilia nearly passed out as her beloved husband was handcuffed, read his rights and hauled off to jail!

Cecilia left the church in tears, and immediately called Daniel and Hannah told them what had transpired in the meeting. Daniel was stunned and he told Cecilia he would meet her at the police station. With the good reverend behind bars, **Beelzebub**, took off and headed to the Jenkins house. Simone was there having dinner with Joe and his sons, when Hannah called. She told Joe what was going on at the church and asked him to call his parents. Joe told her they were back in Raleigh Durham, visiting. Hannah asked Joe if he could come by her house until Daniel returned from the police station, so they could try and figure out what to do. Joe immediately grabbed his coat and asked Simone if she could stay with the boys, while he went to Hannah's. The fly grinned as Simone gritted her teeth in anger, but not wanting to alarm the boys by starting an argument with Joe; she agreed, and asked Joe to call her as soon as he had more information.

Hannah then called Abby and Greg and was shocked to hear that her sister's ex-husband was in town and was coming over for dinner. Greg wanted to support Reverend Rawlins, but there was no way he was leaving Abby and the twins alone with Randy Nelson. He did tell Hannah to call him after the meeting and keep him in the loop. When he hung up, he called his brother Al, who was a detective on the police force, and one of his best investigators, to look into the charges against Reverend Rawlins.

Abby was upstairs in her bedroom, consoling a distraught Cecilia on the phone when Randy arrived for dinner. Greg greeted him warmly, but warily. The twins did the same. They were all sitting in the living room chatting with Randy when Abby came down to join them. Randy's mouth dropped open in astonishment when he saw her huge swollen belly. "You're pregnant?" He asked in surprise. Abby nodded and walked over to her husband who placed his arm around her. "Greg and I are expecting twins. I'm due in a couple of months." She answered quietly. Anger quickly welled up inside Randy, but he fought to keep himself in control. "Congratulations." He said evenly. He turned to Renee and RJ. "So I guess you guys are excited about the babies?" He asked. Renee's eyes lit up. "We can hardly wait; they're going to let us name them." She said excitedly. RJ grinned. "Yeah, we're thinking Moses and Solomon if they're boys and Esther and Ruth if their girls. If they're fraternal twins like me and Renee, then it'll be Moses and Esther or Solomon and Ruth" He said proudly. Randy pretended to be happy for them, but inside he was seething! He couldn't stomach the thought of Abby having anyone's baby but *his*! He was amazed at how lovely she looked, she hadn't aged at all and she glowed with happiness. Randy knew it was going to take everything in him to stay in control, and be cordial towards the man who stole his family, he was more determined than ever to destroy Greg Taylor!

A couple of hours later, after a wonderful dinner, Randy prepared to leave. He turned to his kids and hugged them. "I love you guys and I hope we can get together again. If your mom is okay with it, I would love to have you guys come out and visit me in Los Angeles. With Candace gone, the house is very empty and lonely." He said as he tried to play on their sympathy. RJ and Renee hugged their dad again. "We'll think about it, but if we do, it will be after the twins are born. There's no way we're going to miss their birth." RJ told his dad. Randy nodded, waved good bye to Abby and Greg and left.

While the kids were in the kitchen cleaning up, Abby whispered in her husband's ear. "Did you buy any of that?" She asked. Greg kissed his wife on the top of her head and whispered back, "Not for a minute. He's up to something!" Abby sighed, and leaned against her handsome, strong husband. "Don't worry honey," Greg said, as he rubbed her back, "I have my men following him twenty-four seven while he's in town. If he tries anything, we'll know!" He assured her.

When Randy returned to his hotel suite, Ahmad was there waiting for him. "How did it go?" Ahmad asked, as he helped Randy out of his coat and handed him a drink. Randy gulped down the whiskey in one swallow before answering. "She's pregnant with twins! Can you believe that, she's having his babies and my kids are thrilled?" Randy asked furiously. He was so angry, he needed to destroy **something**, anything, but he controlled himself. He paced back and forth in the spacious room, finally he turned to Ahmad. "Help me Ahmad. Please help me get Abby and my kids back." He pleaded, and then he broke down in tears. Ahmad looked at the pathetic human and sneered.

Humans were so weak, they made him sick! He couldn't understand God's fascination with the creatures. When God made the angels, submissive to humans, he and thousands of other angels, joined Lucifer's rebellion that led to the unsuccessful *coup d'état* in Heaven!

Ahmad withdrew from the room, leaving Randy weeping, on the plush carpeted floor. He went to his room and pulled out his cell phone and called Candace. When she answered, Ahmad got straight to the point. "Ms. Candace, your husband really needs you." He said quietly. He heard Candace sigh in exasperation on the other end. "What's wrong, is he drunk again?" she asked nastily. Ahmad wanted to chuckle. Randy's drinking was the main reason she finally left him. "We're here in DC and he just came back from visiting his ex-wife and their kids. He's upset because Abby is pregnant and expecting twins with her new husband." Ahmad told her.

The gasp from Candace was priceless. Ahmad was truly enjoying himself. Candace's inability to *have* children was one of the reasons why Randy began drinking heavily! Ahmad knew that Abby's pregnancy was going to rock Candace's world and she didn't disappoint him. "What! She's pregnant with twins, again?" She wailed pitifully into the phone. Ahmad smiled, as he heard her voice catch in her throat, then he dug the knife in deeper. "Randy has decided that he still loves **his** wife, and he wants her back." He told her smugly. Candace grabbed a glass snow globe off her desk and hurled it across the room, smashing it to smithereens. Ahmad pushed the mute button on his cell phone and erupted in laughter. He composed himself, and put the phone back up to his ear, and heard Candace ranting and raving like a lunatic. "*She* is not his wife, *I'm* his wife and if he thinks I'm going to divorce him so he can go running back to her, he's got another thing coming. I'll kill them both before I allow that to happen!" She screamed into the phone. Candace was beside herself! She didn't want to be with Randy anymore, but she would **not** give him his freedom so he could go running back to her sister. Candace hated Abby with every fiber in her being, and knowing that her sister was happy and having babies with her new husband, put her right over the edge. Ahmad cleared his throat, and continued tormenting her. "I'm afraid she's not the only one pregnant, your sister Hannah and her husband Daniel are also expecting." He quipped.

Candace moaned in sheer agony, which totally made Ahmad's day! Not her mousy little sister too! She had heard from her old high school friend, Winnie that Hannah had married Daniel James. Daniel had attended high school with them, and she remembered the very attractive, albeit moody freshman that stayed in and out of trouble after the death of his parents. Candace also remembered Abby's husband Greg Taylor. They sung in the choir together when they were teens, and she wasn't at all surprised when he was the one, who found Abby at the mental facility, then later married her. Greg used to *moon* over Abby when they were kids and their dad kept a close eye on him because, Greg was twenty-one and Abby was only seventeen. But Candace remembered how fine he and his brother Al were. Al was smitten with Lynn, one of Abby's friends, and after they graduated high school, Lynn and Al got married and were now the parents of a couple of teenagers.

Tears of frustration and defeat ran down her face. Why did *they* all have such great lives and she couldn't even have a baby? She couldn't take hearing anymore news. "Ahmad, I gotta go, I'll call you back later, just don't let him get anywhere near my sister or those kids of theirs. Do you hear me Ahmad?" She fumed into the phone. Ahmad grinned, "Yes, I'll do what I can." He said, trying to sound sincere.

After she hung up the phone, Candace dropped her head on her desk and burst into tears. It just wasn't fair that Abby and Hannah were both pregnant. She and Randy had tried every fertility treatment available, spending thousands and thousands of dollars, but she never conceived. Randy had finally asked her if she wanted to use a surrogate, but the thought of another woman carrying his child turned her stomach. Her refusal to use a surrogate to give Randy the child he so desperately wanted, drove him to the bottle and back into the arms of other women. When Candace found out he was cheating on her, she retaliated by cheating on him with other women! That had been the state of their marriage for the last couple of years. Things finally came to an abrupt end when the star of their top rated television show was found dead of a heroin overdose a few days ago.

When Randy found out that the girl overdosed because Candace and the woman they hired to keep an eye on her, were off having sex at a hotel, he hit the roof, and immediately contacted his lawyer and filed for divorce. The divorce papers were served to Candace the next day at their office; and she was furious at Randy for embarrassing her in front of their staff and clients! They had a huge fight and Candace moved out of their house the next day and into a hotel before finding a condo to rent, until the divorce was settled. She hired a well-known celebrity divorce attorney, Gloria Allison and Randy hired his own celebrity attorney Raul Punzino.

Both attorneys were known for fighting dirty, and soon news began leaking to the media from each camp: Candace's lesbianism and infidelity, and her attorney leaked: Randy's drinking and drug usage. It was ugly and it was dirty!

Candace wanted to move her new lover, in with her, but her attorney advised against it, since Randy was divorcing her on grounds of infidelity. So Candace hired a private investigators to follow Randy around 24/7 to dig up dirt on him! The two had been apart for nearly three months, when Randy was arrested in a drug bust. The Brotherhood moved quickly to have all charges against him dropped, and Candace began buying up stock in the company, to force her husband out. When Randy found out about that, he vowed to hire someone to get rid of his wife for good!

Candace was furious to hear how happy her two sisters were, while her life was filled with chaos and drama! She called her brother Michael, who lived in New York City, to complain about her situation. When Michael answered the phone, Candace immediately began to cry. Alarmed, Michael panicked, thinking something horrible had happened between her and Randy. Frankly, he was worried the two would wind up killing each other, but when Candace finally stopped crying, she told him about Abby and Hannah.

Michael and Hannah were twins, and he

couldn't believe that she hadn't called to tell him she was pregnant. He was still upset that he hadn't been invited to her wedding, but he couldn't fathom her not sharing her pregnancy with him. Michael and his wife, Georgia had been married for years, and like Candace and Randy, they too were childless, unable to conceive.

At the beginning of their marriage, Michael's wife wanted children, however, after many years of trying, Michael finally confessed to her that he really didn't want to have children, so Georgia let go of the idea of being a mother. She was disappointed, but she truly loved Michael and they enjoyed a very extravagant lifestyle. Michael spoiled her outrageously, buying her anything she wanted.

Michael ran the east coast division of the **N.A.A.** talent agency, while Georgia was the owner/ broker of a real estate company Michael bought for her after she became a licensed broker. She also oversaw the huge *Wicca* community in their area. She was a *High Priestess* and Michael was a *High Priest* in the Brotherhood organization. After Michael's parent's murder-suicide, Randy's father, Richard Nelson had taken the young man under his wing and taught him everything about the Brotherhood. When Richard and Melina died, a heartbroken Michael relocated to Los Angeles, to help Randy and Candace start the **N.A.A.** talent agency. Because of Michael and Randy's contacts in the Brotherhood, the agency quickly grew into a multimillion dollar business, and was touted as one of the best talent agency in Hollywood. Actors and actresses from New York, overseas, and well-known figures in the music and sports industry, fought to be represented by them.

Once the agency was profitable, they took the company public and made even more money! Michael took his share and relocated to New York, and opened up the east coast office. Within two years, he had expanded his operation and was representing, singers and wannabe reality stars. He and Georgia hung out with big name celebrities, and they enticed them to join their secret society, *The Brotherhood.*

With the help of his *spirit guide,* he not only controlled his client's money, but also their personal lives by handpicking wives, husbands and groupies for his clients without their knowledge. Some of the most powerful couples in Hollywood, and in the music industry was *arranged.* Michael and Georgia were the most powerful couple in town, they often participated in matching some of their favorite supermodels up with world class athletes, or up and coming actresses with music moguls. Michael and Georgia shared *everything* together, so infidelity and boredom was never an issue for them. They vacationed on their own private island, or one of their many estates around the world, so they didn't have to worry about the prying eyes of the media.

As Michael listened to his older sister whine about her miserable life, he rolled his eyes and stared out the window of his Upper West side office. There was a time when he looked up to his sister and brother in law, but now they appeared weak and ineffective to him. He had toyed with the idea of stealing their share of the company way from them, but his lawyer had found out that his sister was buying up stock, so she could force Randy out of the company. Michael's spirit guide appeared, along with a huge black fly that Michael couldn't see. He abruptly put his sister on hold. "Tell your sister she should go to DC and fight for her husband." His guide advised him. A stunned Michael looked at the dark shadowy figure in awe. How did it know what Candace was ranting about? He started to ask, but stopped himself. His guide always knew what was going on, so Michael told Candace that she should fly to DC and try to save her marriage. Candace was surprised. "What?" She gasped.

"Well you certainly don't want him going back to Abby, do you?" Michael asked smoothly. Dumbfounded, Candace remained silent and listened. The guide nodded at Michael and Michael surrendered his body to his guide.

"If I were you," the guide continued, using Michael's voice, "I would fight for my husband and get rid of Abby for good, that way she will no longer be a threat to you." Candace picked up her glass of wine, and sipped it, while listening to her brother. What he said made sense to her drunken mind. This *was* all Abby's fault. Her sister was once again trying to come between her and Randy. Candace listened as the thing **possessing** Michael's body continued to speak. "You and Randy need to join forces and make sure Abby and her husband or no longer a threat to your marriage. I'm just saying." The shadowy figure said softly.

Candace nodded to herself as she continued to sip her wine. After thanking Michael, Candace hung up and called Ahmad back. "Is he still there?" She asked in a slurred voice. Ahmad assured her that he was still there, asleep in his suite. "Well I'm taking the company jet, and coming out

283

there. I'll be staying in my husband's suite. Don't tell him I'm coming, I want to surprise him." She ordered.

"Okay, Ms. Candace, I will prepare for your arrival. I'll call the pilot for you and tell him to pick you up at five o'clock and I'll order a car to drive you to the airport. That should give you enough time to eat some lunch, take a quick nap, and then you'll be all fresh and ready for your reunion with your husband; he really misses you, Ms. Candace." Ahmad lied smoothly. Tears came to Candace's eyes as she listened to her butler. "Thank you Ahmad, I don't know what Randy and I would do without you." She sniffed. She hung up the phone and promptly passed out on the couch.

Ahmad smiled as he peeped in at his sleeping master. "No worries Ms. Candace, I'm not going anywhere!" he laughed to himself as he dialed the pilots number and told him to get the plane ready to fly Candace out to DC at five p.m. and then he called the limousine service and requested a car for her. "Please make sure the bar is fully stocked for Mrs. Nelson." He told the customer service agent.

Later that evening, Greg received the phone call he had been dreading since Randy Nelson arrived in town. One of his investigators called to warn him that Abby's sister Candace had just pulled up in a limousine at the Ritz Carleton-Georgetown Hotel! Greg ordered him to follow her and report back to him immediately. After he hung up, Greg leaned against the wall of his home office and sighed. He knew he had to tell Abby that her sister was back in town, but he was worried about how the news would affect her and their unborn twins. He bowed his head and prayed for guidance. Soon he heard a still small voice say, **"Do not be afraid, I'm with you and nothing by any means can hurt you or your family."** Relief flooded through his body and Greg whispered, "Thank you, Lord," then he went to find Abby.

His wife was lying upstairs in their bedroom, reading. He sat at the edge of their bed and took her small hand in his. "I just received a call from Roger; he spotted Candace arriving at the Ritz Carleton hotel in Georgetown where Randy is staying." He told her softly. Abby lowered the magazine and stared at her husband. A *spirit of fear* tried to overcome her, but Abby rose up from her bed and said boldly, "I am *not* afraid of those two. There is nothing they can do to us." Greg drew her into his arms and held her tightly. He truly loved this mighty woman of God. "That's what the Lord said to me, do not be afraid, I'm with you and nothing can hurt our family." Greg told her. They held each other and finally Abby received a word from the Lord. "Honey, find out what room they're in, we're heading over there to confront them, now!" She said emphatically. Greg nodded and pulled out his cell phone and called Roger back. Roger picked up on the first ring. Greg asked him if he had a room number for him and Roger told him the two of them were staying in room 1209. While Greg was talking to Roger, Abby got up and headed over to her closet. She picked out her favorite maternity suit and quickly got dressed. When she was ready she looked at her husband. "Let's head over there before the kids get home from school." She said grimly.

Twenty minutes later, Candace and Randy where in the middle of a bitter argument when they heard a knock at the door. Thinking it was room service; Candace opened the door without bothering to ask who it was or look out the peep hole. She was shock to find herself staring at her sister and brother in law. Abby glared at her and pushed her way into the room. Randy was staring out the window with a drink in his hand. He turned to see who was at the door, and was surprised to see Abby and Greg enter the suite.

Abby didn't waste time with pleasantries. "Why are you two here in D.C.?" She demanded.

Candace and Randy stared at her in surprise. A defiant and confident Abby was not at all what they had expected. Candace actually stammered as she responded to her sister. "I came here to work things out with my husband." She said, as her eyes roamed over Abby and her swollen belly. Jealousy ripped through Candace like a knife. Abby was even more beautiful than she remembered, and her skin glowed with her pregnancy. Randy gulped down his drink and looked at his ex-wife and her husband. 'I didn't know she was coming here." He said harshly. "I was in my bedroom asleep when I heard her in the living room." Candace turned on him. "You weren't sleep; you were passed out drunk." She said nastily. Randy glared at her. "I'm a drunk because you're a slut, and I can't stand the sight of you." He roared back at her.

The hatred in his voice, caught Candace off guard; she couldn't believe he just disrespected her like that, in front of her sister. Devastated by his words, tears rolled down her cheeks. "That's not true; you drink because I can't get pregnant. You *hate* me because I can't give you a baby!" She yelled at him, and ran out of the room. The truth in her statement hit Randy hard, and he sat down on the couch, and stared down at the drink in his hand. For the first time in a long time, his heart ached for Candace and he realized that he *had* been punishing here because they were childless. He held his head in his hands, and began to cry.

Abby and Greg stared at each other in surprise. This was not at all what they had expected. Even more surprising, Abby heard the Holy Spirit say to her, *Go to your sister.* Abby squeezed her husband's hand, and went to search for Candace. As Greg looked at a sobbing Randy, he heard the Holy Spirit say, *Minister to him.* Amazed, Greg walked over and sat down next to Randy on the sofa. Greg prayed and asked for the words to say to the man, who had tried to destroy the woman he loved. Finally Greg heard, *forgiveness*, and with a heavy heart, Greg obeyed the Holy Spirit. He cleared his throat and said, "Randy, I forgive you for what you did to Abby and God wants you to know that He loves you." He said to the lost and broken man.

In the rear of the spacious suite, Ahmad and the fly, peeped through the adjourning door between the two bedrooms, eavesdropping. He watched in disbelief as Abby approached her sister, who had thrown herself across the king size bed, sobbing her heart out. The Holy Spirit whispered to Abby, *forgiveness*, and she reached out and gently began to stroke her older sisters back.

Tears tumbled down Abby's face as she thought back to their childhood. She and Candace had never gotten alone, and Abby remembered praying over and over again for her sister to love her. Suddenly, as if she heard what Abby was thinking, Candace turned and flung herself in her sister's arms. Abby was shocked, but happy. "Help me Holy Spirit; please give me the words to say that will heal my sister's heart." She whispered. Candace heard her, and cried even more. She couldn't believe that her sister was praying for her, and comforting her, after everything Candace had done to her.

"Candace, God loves you and He loves Randy too. I really believe He wants your marriage to work, but you have to let go and let God be front and center in your life and then He will bless you with the desires of your heart." Abby said softly. Candace stopped crying and listened to her sister. "I just want a baby. I want what you and Hannah have." She admitted softly. "You can have what we have; you just have to trust God. He only wants what's best for you, sweetheart." Candace was quiet for a minute. Then she pulled herself out of her sister's arms and wiped the tears from her face. "Help me Abby; help me get closer to God. I gave up on God a long time ago, and my life has been hell every since! I can't take it anymore, please help me." She asked sincerely. Abby gently turned her sister's face towards her and led her to Christ with the salvation prayer.

Ahmad's mouth dropped open in astonishment as he heard Candace give her life over to their **sworn enemy**. He and Beelzebub immediately vanished from the bedroom, and reappeared unseen, in the living room and watched Greg and Randy, as they sat on the sofa, quietly talking. They couldn't believe their ears, as Randy poured out his heart to Greg, admitting that he truly loved Candace and wanted to make his marriage work. "I see how happy Abby and my kids are with you, Greg and to be honest, my intentions were to come out here and try and win them back and destroy your life. But seeing the pain in Candace eyes just now, I know how much I've hurt her, and how much I really do love her. She's the one I want to be with, not Abby."

Greg nodded. "What can I do to help you?" He asked. Randy stood up and walked over to the bar to fix himself another drink, but he stopped himself. Candace was right, he was an alcoholic and it was time for him to get some help and hopefully save his marriage. He turned towards Greg and lowered his head in shame. "I need help. I need to get sober and learn how to be a husband to my wife and a father to my children. I want me and Candace to have a marriage like you and Abby. Can you help me do that?" Randy asked quietly. Greg stood up and walked over to him. "All things are possible with God. Abby and I have a good strong marriage because we put God first in our lives, so do the twins. If this is what you really want, Randy, you have to give your life to God and make Him front and center." Greg told him honestly.

Randy returned back to the sofa and sat down. "I was taught that God wasn't real, and that it was *my* responsibility to make things happen in my life. I've tried that and look where it's gotten me. I'm ready to try this God of yours, to ask Him to help me, get my life together. What do I need to do? He asked sincerely. "Just repeat this prayer after me: *I believe that Jesus Christ is the son of God, that He died on the cross for my sins, and that He was raised from the dead, and now sits in Heaven at the right hand of the Father. Lord, come into my life.*"

Ahmad and Beelzebub stood in shock as Randy

Nelson gave his life over to their sworn enemy. Ahmad tried desperately to possess Randy's body, but he couldn't. Suddenly a cool breeze entered the room and they turned around and saw Michael, Gabriel and Raphael, the archangels. They grinned at a furious Beelzebub, as he and Ahmad looked up, and saw a book appear in the air, and float down into Gabriel's hand. With great joy, Gabriel wrote Randy and Candace's name in the *book of Life*. Beelzebub and Ahmad could hear the saints in heaven cheering, and with a scowl on their face, they glared at the three angels and immediately vanished!

Suddenly, Randy felt a tremendous weight depart from him, and he hugged and thanked Greg. Then he went off in search of his wife, and found her and Abby, laughing and hugging each other. When the sister's looked up at him, he marveled at the glow on his wife's face. He walked over to the bed and fell on his knees in front of his wife and laid his head in her lap. "Candace, please forgive me for hurting you, I love you so much. I'm sorry that I abandoned you when you couldn't get pregnant. If we can't have kids, as long as you're my wife, that's all I need."

Candace stared down at her husband in shock. She couldn't believe her ears. Abby stood up to go, so that the two could have some privacy, but Randy stopped her and called out to Greg to join them. When Greg arrived, Randy was still on his knees and he turned towards Abby. "Abby, I pray that you too, will forgive me for everything I did to you and our kids. I want you to know that I did love you when we were together, but Candace is the real love of my life and I never told her that." He turned back towards his wife and said, "When we were dating in high school, I had never been happier in my life, but when you went away to college and refused to come home, you really hurt me. When I spotted Abby one afternoon, I decided to date her to make you jealous, but you still didn't come home, until after she and I were married. I should have told you this a long time ago Candace, you were my first true love." He admitted passionately.

Candace hung her head in shame and then confessed. "I never told you the real reason why I refused to come home. I fell head over heels in love with you when we were dating in high school, and when I went away to college, I was terrified that you would meet someone else and dump me. I couldn't bear the thought of you telling me you didn't want me, so I decided to end the relationship myself. It was the stupidest thing

I've ever done, and I truly regret it. " She told him honestly.

Abby smiled at her sister. "I'm a witness at just how heartbroken Randy was when you refused to come home for the holidays. We only got together because he wanted to get back at you, and I was angry with our parents because they had forbidden me to go to Grace Faith Church . I became rebellious and started drinking and doing drugs to mask the pain, then Randy came along, and well, the rest is history, but sis, it was really you that he loved not me. Randy and I made each other miserable." Randy looked up at her and grinned. "We did, didn't we?"

They both laughed and Randy stood up and hugged Abby. "Greg was the best thing that ever happened to you and the twins. I'm really happy that you found what you were looking for." Abby hugged her ex-husband back, and reached down and pulled her sister into the embrace. After all these years, they had finally put all the anger, and bitterness behind them.

Greg stood back with a smile on his face. What the enemy meant for evil, God was getting the glory as everyone forgave each other. Randy reached out for Greg and clasped his hand in friendship. "Abby, your husband has helped me find my way to Jesus Christ and I gave my life to him in the living room." Candace looked at her sister and then her husband. "Abby did the same for me. Oh praise God." She said happily.

Abby invited her sister and her ex-husband to their home for dinner. When she arrived home, she also called and invited Hannah. When Hannah and Daniel arrived, Hannah was shocked to see Candace and Randy laughing and chatting with Abby and the kids in the living room. When Candace looked up and saw her baby sister, she rose from the couch and walked over and gave her a warm hug. Hannah was stunned. "Congratulations on your marriage and your baby, Hannah, I'm really happy for you." Candace said sincerely. "Uh, thanks," Hannah stammered in confusion. She looked at Abby and Greg. Abby nodded at her reassuringly. Candace introduced herself to Daniel as she waved her husband over. Randy reacquainted himself with Hannah, remembering her as a young girl and then shook hands with Daniel.

"Dad and Aunt Candace have given their lives to the Lord!" Renee said as she ran to Hannah and hugged her. Hannah stared at Candace in disbelief. "Is this true?" She asked. Candace nodded. "Thanks to Abby and Greg, God used them to lead us to Him and to give our marriage another try." She said excitedly. They all sat down in the living room and Randy turned to his kids. "I'm an alcoholic and I'm going to check myself into a treatment center in Maryland and stay there until I'm well. After I'm released, I would like to start over with you two and be a part of your lives. Candace and I have renounced the evil lives we led, we want to be happy and whole so that we can be a family." He told them humbly. Renee and RJ hugged their father and stepmother. "We'll be praying for both of you, and we'll be here for you." They said tearfully. Candace looked at her two sisters. "Hannah, Abby has forgiven me for everything I've done to her and her kids, and I hope you can forgive me too." She said quietly. Hannah hugged her sister and said, "We love you Candace, and we've all been praying for you. God has a plan for you and Randy." Candace broke down and wept, while her two younger sisters comforted her. Raphael and Phanuel hovered above the family, from the ceiling. They rejoiced along with Abby and Hannah, that their sister, who was once lost, had found her way back home. They two angels tilted their heads to the side, and listened to the saints in heaven joyously shouting!

Chapter Twenty-Six

William was spending his second week in jail. The prosecutor considered him a flight risk, and asked the judge to deny him bail, and the judge, who was a secret member of the **Brotherhood**, agreed. When Cecilia heard the judge deny her husband bail, she nearly fainted. She returned to an empty house and cried herself to sleep.

Assuming that the woman was vulnerable, Satan attacked Cecilia's mind like he had in the hospital, gloating and taunting her with visions and images about her husband and child. He tried his best to convince her that she would be forced to raise their child by herself, and William would spend the rest of his life in prison. He tortured her with dreams of their son, William Jr, turning bitter and resentful towards them. Satan placed images in her mind about her son turning to drugs and alcohol, and eventually to a life of crime, because she and William were failures as parents.

But this time, a strong and defiant Cecilia was ready for him. Each time he sent these thoughts and images to her mind she loudly quoted Genesis 17:6-8 out loud. *I am God almighty, walk before me faithfully and blameless. Then I will make a covenant between me and you and will greatly increase your numbers. I will establish my covenant as an everlasting covenant between me and you and your descendants and their children after you for the generations to come, to be your God and the God of your descendants after you!* She also took great pleasure in *reminding* Satan about his defeat at Calvary, and he would angrily disappear.

Satan was determined to make Cecilia lose her baby by stressing her out, so he changed tactics and went after William. He arranged to have a dangerous and deranged man placed in William's cell. When Daniel found out about his pastor's new cellmate, he petitioned the court to either have William or the man removed, but his petition was denied. Concerned, Daniel called an emergency meeting of all of Reverend Rawlins supporters, who were dwindling in numbers each day, due to the extensive negative news coverage, as the lead prosecutor leaked information daily to the press.

When Daniel finally secured a court date for his pastor, he and Cecilia headed over to the prison to share the good news with William, and he surprised *them* by introducing his *violent and dangerous* cell mate to his wife and friend. The man told Cecilia and Daniel how Reverend Rawlins had cast out the demonic forces that had taken over his mind, and led him to the Lord. He told them that once he was released, he was looking forward to becoming a member of Grace Faith Church. Everything Satan tried to do, was thwarted by the saints of God!

Joel and Ernestine Jenkins arrived back in D.C. and met with the pastors supporters. Afterwards, Joel went before the board, and was asked to take over, until a new pastor could be found.

Joel agreed, but only because he wanted to make sure that Pastor Rawlins would get his church, back once this mess was over. Simone and Daniel worked diligently on Reverend Rawlins defense, interviewing and questioning witnesses, while Greg and his agents investigated the missing money. They were determined to find out who was actually embezzling money from the church.

A few days later, Ernestine had an appointment to meet with Hannah at the center, and she noticed tension between Hannah and Simone. She asked the Holy Spirit to reveal what was going on, and it wasn't long before the *Spirit* revealed to her that Satan was up to his old tricks, playing mind games with an insecure Simone, about her relationship with Joe. Ernestine shared this information with her husband and together, the two prayed for guidance. Finally, the Holy Spirit prompted Ernestine to have a heart to heart with Simone, so Ernestine invited her out to lunch.

Once they were seated and had placed their orders, Ernestine got right to the point. "I noticed some tension with you and Hannah at the center. What's going on?" She asked her. Feeling uncomfortable, Simone shrugged, and tried to play it off. "It's nothing, I think we're all on edge because of Reverend Rawlins situation." She said evenly. Ernestine nodded and took a sip of her ice tea. The waiter arrived with their food and after serving them, he left. They dug in and both expressed appreciation for the wonderfully prepared food. After a couple of bites, Ernestine put down her fork, and gazed at the young lady seated across from her. "Simone, as the wife of a pastor, I've had to deal with my share of women trying to get too close to my husband. In the early days of our ministry, I allowed the enemy to fill my mind with all kinds of thoughts and images of Joel and other women. It almost drove me crazy, and it created problems in our marriage. One day, I was in a book store and the Holy Spirit led me to a book by Joyce Myers, the book was entitled, *The Battlefield of the Mind.* She's an evangelist from St. Louis Missouri. When I got home and began reading it, I realized that the enemy was **attacking** my mind, filling my head with all kinds of lies! That's when I really began to study **Ephesians 6 verses 10-12** *"Finally, my brethren, be strong in the Lord and in the power of His might. Put on the whole armor of God that you may be able to stand against the wiles of the devil. For we do not wrestle against flesh and blood, but against principalities, against powers, against the rulers of the darkness of this age, against spiritual hosts of wickedness in the heavenly places"*

I shared the book with Joel, and we read it together. *Spiritual Warfare* was something we had never been taught before, so we purchased hundreds of copies of the book, and made them available for our congregation." She said quietly. She paused as she took a bite of her delicious baked chicken. Simone sat quietly, thinking about what Ernestine said. "Did it sound like *someone or something* was whispering things in your ear, and you just found yourself agreeing with it?" Simone asked. Ernestine nodded, as she took her napkin, and wiped her mouth before continuing. "Yes and sometimes a thought would just **pop up** in my mind out of no where, and within minutes. I would get angry at my poor husband, who hadn't done anything wrong!" She laughed shaking her head at the memory.

Simone put down her fork and lowered her head. These crazy thoughts about Joe and Hannah, started just recently, and she realized that Ernestine was right, someone or somebody was messing with her mind! "So you don't think anything is going on between Hannah and Joe?" She whispered.

Ernestine shook her head. "No honey. My son loves you, besides, he and Daniel have been best friends for years. He would never flirt or sleep with another man's wife, especially his friends." She said kindly. Filled with guilt and relief, Simone leaned back against her chair. "Wow, I feel so silly." She confessed. Ernestine reached into her purse and pulled out a book, and handed it to her. "Don't be. Remember, you're a new *Christian in Christ* and the enemy's job is to confuse and frustrate you. He's going to try and make you think, that what God has for you, is not yours. I want you to have my copy of **Battlefield of the Mind**. Read what I put on the inside." Simone took the book and opened it and read, "To my beautiful Simone, welcome to our family." Tears glistened in Simone's eyes and she held the book against her chest. "Thank you so much, I will treasure this forever." Ernestine reached over and gave Simone's hand a gentle squeeze. "You're more than welcome!"

The huge black *fly* on the wall above them, fumed. Once again his plan to cause trouble had been prevented. **Beelzebub** glared at Ernestine Jenkins and flew out of the crowded restaurant.

Chapter Twenty Seven

Detective Al Taylor, stared at the church embezzlement file on his desk. Al and his partner had successfully got a warrant to seize the church's financial records from the board, and what they discovered, just didn't make sense. Just as the board president said in his statement, the checks in question all bore Reverend Rawlins signature, however, what puzzled the detective was the fact that the checks were out of numerical sequence. He had questioned Agnes, the church secretary, and she provided him with a copy of her signature and even offered to take a polygraph test, but he told her it wasn't necessary, his handwriting analyst was convinced the checks were signed by a male.

Al had questioned every member of the deacon board and the board of directors, and each of them provided copies of their signatures, but the only signature that came close to the forged checks, was Reverend Rawlins. Al had known the reverend since he was a young boy, and he believed his pastor and friend, but unfortunately it wasn't looking good for the pastor. Deciding to call it a day, Al locked up the file in his desk and was about to leave, but at the last minute, decided to take the file home with him. He didn't know why, but he felt compelled to keep the file in his possession.

After enjoying a wonderful dinner, prepared by his wife Lynn, Al went into his study to go over the file once more, he was convinced that he was overlooking something. Hours later, Lynn tapped on his door and bought in a tray of decaffeinated coffee. She poured them both a cup and sat across from her handsome husband.

"Baby, I know I'm missing something." Al said, as he leaned back and took a sip of his coffee. "This is driving me bananas. I know Reverend Rawlins didn't steal this money, but all the evidence points right at him." He said frustrated.

Lynn sipped her coffee and silently prayed, *Holy Spirit, let there be light on this situation. Bless us with your wisdom.* After a few minutes of silence, Lynn cleared her throat and said, "Honey, only those that had access to the check book are your primary suspects right?" Al nodded. "Remember the movie we watched years ago, the one with Kevin Spacey, I think it was called The **Usual Suspects**, what if you're looking in the right direction, but the wrong people? Maybe the culprit is someone you would never suspect." She said quietly. Al got up and began to pace around the room. Pacing is how he did some of his best thinking, and he considered what his wife said. Lynn watched her husband walk back and forth, deep in thought. She loved how he shared his work with her and took to heart the insight she provided.

Suddenly, he stopped pacing and looked at her. "Sweetheart, you might be on to something." He walked over to his desk, and picked up his list of people that had access to the church on a regular basis. He began to check off the names of people he had already cleared, and was left with a list of people that didn't have access to the check book, but did have access to the office, and *bingo*! One name stood out and it made perfect sense, Otis, the janitor. Otis had access to the office, but didn't have a key to the safe where the books were kept. Otis only had access to the office a couple of days a week, since he was part time, and that could account for the checks being out of order. Al noted in one of his officers report that Otis had been interviewed, but since he didn't have access to the safe, the questioning officer never asked Otis to provide his signature.

Al grinned over at his wife. "Lynn, I think you may have solved this for us." She stood up and walked over to her husband, and gave him a hug and a long, lingering kiss on the lips. "I just asked the Holy Spirit for a little light on the situation and some wisdom." She admitted softly. Al took her into his arms and kissed her deeply. Thank God for praying wives.

Al was so wrapped up in the sensuous kiss that he didn't hear his cell phone ring, but Lynn did, and she reluctantly broke free from her husband's passionate embrace and handed it to him. Al rubbed his hands through his short curly hair, and took the phone from his wife. He sat on the corner of his desk, with his lovely wife between his legs, with her head leaning against his chest, as he answered his phone.

It was his brother Greg, checking to see how the case was going. The brothers frequently worked together on cases, and Al enjoyed moonlighting on his days off from the force, and working for his brother. Al shared his hunch with his brother that the real culprit might be the janitor. Ten minutes later, Greg and Daniel were knocking on Al's door. Lynn greeted her brother-in-law, and led them to her husband's study. She left so the men could concentrate on the case. They sifted through the evidence that the police and prosecutor had complied, and decided to shift the investigation towards the janitor.

Meanwhile on the other side of town, a miserable and depressed Cecilia arrived home,to an empty house. Before preparing dinner, she felt led by the **Spirit** to read the book of Acts, chapter 12. Making herself comfortable on the sofa, she picked up her bible and began to read.

Suddenly her heart filled with joy, she immediately called Ernestine, and Hannah and Abby, and invited them over for dinner and to join her in praying for William. After she hung up the phone, Cecilia hummed to herself as she prepared dinner for her guest.

After everyone arrived, she told them that the Holy Spirit had led her to Acts 12 and she was sure God was instructing them to pray for William's release. They came into agreement with her and they began to pray in earnest. An excited Abby and Hannah looked at each other. They knew that their husbands were checking out a lead on the case, but they decided to keep that information to themselves until they heard from Greg and Daniel.

While the saints were busy praying, Greg, Daniel and Al drove over to the home of Otis, the janitor. Otis' wife opened the door and invited them in. "Is Brother Otis here?" Al asked her. His wife nodded, and called out to her husband, who was in the kitchen. Otis walked into his living room, and was surprised to find the Taylor brothers and Daniel waiting for him. He greeted them warmly, and waved his hands towards the couch, offering them a seat.

Once seated, Al got right to the point. They all knew Otis from church and hated suspecting him of stealing, but they had to know. "Otis, we have to ask you some questions, and I have to advise you, that we're here on official business. This is about the embezzlement case against Reverend Rawlins. If at any time you want to speak to an attorney, just let us know, okay?" Al asked him. Otis was taken aback. An attorney, what in the world would he need an attorney for? He nodded and motioned for Al to continue. Al stood up and began pacing the small, but tidy living room. "Otis, we know that you work part time cleaning the church a couple of evenings a week, right?" Al asked him. Otis nodded. "Do you have access to the pastor's office?" Al asked. Again Otis nodded and said. "Yes, it's my job to clean his and Sister Agnes' office." He told him. Al nodded and continued to pace back and forth in front of the man. "Do you have access to the safe in the pastor's office?" He asked him, bluntly. Confused, Otis looked at him, and then shook his head. "Why would I have access to the safe? I don't need to clean that." He said honestly. Al stared at the man. "Otis, have you ever seen Reverend Rawlins or Sister Agnes open the safe, or leave the safe open while you were there?" He asked him. Otis shook his head. "No, Brother Al. Cleaning the church is my part time job." He looked over at Daniel. "Brother Daniel, you and Sister Hannah helped me start my part time janitorial business, and I have contracts to clean the church and the training center, you two helped me bid on both jobs. My wife and I have been cleaning them for nearly two years." He said, getting upset, as he realized the detective's investigation was now focused on him!

Al nodded and sat down. He looked over at Greg and Daniel, wondering if they believed Otis like he did. A frustrated Greg took over the questioning. "Brother Otis, do you have a set of keys for the church and the training center?" He asked. Otis nodded. "Yep, Sister Hannah gave me a set of keys for both, when I won the contract. I clean the offices when I finish my day job, my wife and I usually arrive at the church around six in the evening, and the agency around seven thirty or eight. We only clean on the days the church doesn't have anything going on." He stated. "Does anyone else have access to the keys?" Greg asked him.

Otis was about to shake his head no, but hesitated, as he remembered something. "Well last month, when I was cleaning the pastor's office, Brother Johnson stopped by and said he needed to get some paperwork out of Reverend Rawlins office for a board meeting. I didn't think anything of it, so I let him in, and told him to lock the door when he was finished. Then I went back down the hallway, to clean the restrooms. He was in there for about ten or fifteen minutes. Did I do something wrong? I mean Brother Johnson is the president of the board, and this wasn't the first time he asked me to let him into the pastor's office." He told them.

Al, Greg and Daniel looked at each! Lee Johnson **never** mentioned having access to the Reverend's office, when he was questioned by the police. Al stood up. "Thank you Brother Otis. We really appreciate you taking time to speak with us about this. Please don't share this conversation with anyone, not even your wife." He asked him. Otis also stood up. "I promise I won't say a word. My wife likes to talk a bit too much to the other ladies at church, so I'll have to figure out what to tell her about why you came by, because I know she's going to ask." He said grimly. Greg looked at him and smiled. "Tell her I'm interested in having you come by next week to give me an estimate about cleaning my offices. The contract I have with my present janitorial service is about to expire and I haven't been exactly pleased with their work." He told him.

Otis' face immediately lit up. "Really? Wow that's great! Business is going so good; I'm seriously thinking about retiring from my fulltime job, and devoting all of my time to my own business. It's just like Reverend Rawlins said, *God wants to have ownership here on earth. You can't live the abundant life Jesus died on the cross for us to have by working for someone else!*" He said enthusiastically. Greg nodded in agreement.

"I hear ya my brother. It was Reverend Rawlins teaching about ownership that made me look at my own situation and start my own investigation business. I'm glad I did and have never looked back since." He said proudly.

After Otis thanked them, and let them out, his

wife immediately rushed into the living room. "What did they want?" Was it something about the pastor and the stolen money?" She asked, eager for information that she could share with her girlfriends. Otis looked at her and grinned. "Actually, Brother Greg wants me to stop by next week so I can give him an estimate for cleaning his offices. Look like we're getting another contract!" He told her happily. His wife squealed with delight and hugged her husband tightly. "Oh baby, that's awesome. If you get this one, you can retire from the post office." She told him. Otis hugged his wife and kissed her. "Yep, that's the plan!"

Al, Greg and Daniel climbed into Greg's SUV and Al checked his watch. It was nearly nine-thirty, but there was no way they were going to let another night go by with their spiritual leader and friend in jail! Al called his captain and told him what Otis shared with him. He also asked that a search warrant be issued, to search the home and business of Lee Johnson, the church board president. Within thirty minutes, Al received a call back from his captain, who had called in a favor that a judge owed him. He told Al that a warrant had been issued and he was sending it with an officer who would meet them at Lee Johnson's home.

It was eleven-thirty in the evening when Al and the police officer with the warrant knocked on the Johnson's front door. A disgruntled Lee answered the door, and was surprised to see the police. The officer showed Lee the warrant and politely asked him to step aside while they searched his home. Lee Johnson was about to protest until he looked over the officer's shoulder, and saw three more police cars pull up in front of his house. Six officers made their way up the driveway and one was carrying a battering ram!

A nervous Lee, quickly moved away from the door, and the officers came in and began a thorough search of the house. The sound of sirens aroused the neighbors and within minutes, lights blinked on in each house on Lee's street. His neighbors stood outside in their robes, as they watched the events going on at the Johnson house. One of the neighbors grabbed his video camera and began taping the scene.

An hour later, a police officer yelled out, "Al, I think I've found something." Al quickly made his way over to the officer, and bent down next to him. The officer had found a small safe, hidden in the back of Lee Johnson's closet. The safe was filled with stacks of money, and checks that had been torn out of the church's check book! Elated,

Al waved over the officer that had brought the warrant, and the policeman immediately cuffed Lee, and read him his Miranda rights.

As the disgraced man was led out of his house in handcuffs, loudly protesting his innocence, his wife, children and neighbors looked on in disbelief. The neighbor that had been videotaping the raid, ran up to one of the policemen, camera in hand, and asked the officer if this had anything to do with the pastor who was in jail for embezzling money from his church. The officer winked at him, as he assisted Lee into the police car. "No comment," the officer told him cheerfully. The neighbor realized this was indeed connected to the case against the pastor, so he raced home and uploaded the video to a local news station and his *YouTube* account!

The police car, with a dejected Lee Johnson in it, pulled off, and Al called his captain. "We got him and all the evidence we need to indict Lee Johnson on embezzlement charges. Is there any way we can get Reverend Rawlins released immediately?" He asked. "I'm calling the prosecuting attorney right now; we should have him released within the hour. Good job, Taylor." His captain said happily.

Cecilia and her dinner guest had eaten the

delicious dinner she had prepared, and were taking a break from praying. They were sitting in the living room drinking coffee when they heard someone insert a key into the front door. Their mouths dropped open in astonishment as Reverend Rawlins, the Taylor brothers, and Daniel walked into the house. Cecilia stood up and stared at her husband. With tears streaming down her face, she ran over and threw herself in his arms. Reverend Rawlins hugged her tightly and wiped the tears from her face. "It's over honey; all the charges against me have been dropped." He said happily.

The group shouted with joy, and began praising God! The scene was like a modern day version of Acts 12, after Peter was supernaturally released from prison. While the rest of the saints celebrated in the living room, Cecilia pulled her husband into the kitchen and kissed him deeply. During the kiss, the baby kicked and moved. William lowered his head and kissed his wife's swollen belly, as tears formed in his eyes. "Hello little William, I've missed you two so much, son." He cried softy. Cecilia hugged him tightly. "Honey, God told me to read the book of Acts, chapter twelve and to call our friends over to pray, just like when He released Peter from prison, and now you're here, free! Praise God, praise God! He's so faithful!" She said joyfully.

In the living room, Al was telling everyone what had transpired that evening when his cell phone rang. It was Otis, calling to tell him to turn on the local news. Al turned on the television, and they watched as Lee Johnson was escorted out of his house in handcuffs, and placed into the back seat of a squad car. The neighbor who shot the video was heard asking if this arrest had anything to do with the pastor who was accused of stealing money from his church, and they all laughed as the police officer winked and said, 'no comment." After the broadcast went off, Cecilia told Al, Greg and Daniel how the Holy Spirit lead her to the book of Acts, and instructed her to call the others to come and pray for William. They all joined hands and bowed their hands and gave thanks and praises to the Lord. Reverend Williams had indeed been delivered!

Chapter Twenty-eight

Back in Virginia, Candace was on the phone with her brother Michael. "I did what you suggested Mike, I followed Randy to D.C. and confronted him about wanting to end our marriage. In the middle of our argument, Abby and her husband Greg Taylor showed up. She's pregnant with twins again and she looks beautiful and happy." Candace told her brother.

Michael was half listening to his sister. His spirit guide had already informed him about her and her husband's defection to the other side, and it was taking everything in him not to threaten her life and hang up. "I also saw Hannah, and she's pregnant too. She and her husband Daniel, are thrilled about becoming parents. Michael, you should see how happy our sisters are. I think you and I made a huge mistake joining the Brotherhood, and denying Christ." She said quickly, before losing her nerve. "Randy and I are both in rehab for our addictions. He's doing a 30 day inpatient treatment for his alcoholism and drugs, and I'm doing an inpatient treatment for my sex addiction. I can't tell you where we are, but I'm calling to see if you want to purchase our half of the agency. We no longer want to be a part of that culture. I know you're disappointed, but please believe me when I tell you, this is the best thing to ever happen to me and Randy." She finished quickly.

Candace waited with bated breath for his reaction. Michael was a High Priest of the Brotherhood, and she knew that their defection could be punishable by death! For several minutes there was silence on the other end of the phone, finally her brother asked her, "How much do you and Randy want for the company?" He asked quietly. Candace grabbed the paper they had drawn up, that showed the value of the company. They didn't want to be greedy, but they did want their fair share of the company they started. "We think twenty five million is fair. We show that the company is worth nearly eighty million dollars." She stated. Michael wrote the figure down. "That's fair, but we'll need to meet to sign the papers." He said calmly.

Fear gripped Candace heart as she heard the

coldness in her brother's voice. "Our attorney is capable of handling it, I'll have him call you and set up a meeting." She said. Michael chuckled. "Sis, sounds like you and hubby are afraid to meet with me. Why?" He asked slyly. His tone sent shivers up Candace spine, and she felt the urge to get off the phone with him, *now*! "Well like I said, we're in treatment, so meeting you in New York or LA would be impossible." She said, trying to sound calm. Michael chucked again. "Very well, we'll do the deal with your attorney, but Candace, you know we don't take members leaving *lightly*. You and Randy have been at our *sessions* when we've punished members and their families who wanted out. Even as High Priest, and your brother, I can't guarantee that the Brotherhood will not retaliate against you two, so I advise you to watch your back." He said grimly, and hung up the phone.

Candace stared at the dead phone in her hand, as fear gripped her. Was her brother warning her that she and Randy were in danger? Candace quickly called her husband at the rehab. When he picked up the phone, she told him about her conversation with Michael. Fear gripped him, because he knew what the Brotherhood was capable of. "Baby, we just have to trust that God will protect us. Call Morey, and tell him to draw up the papers for the sale. The sooner we get this over with, the better! Candace, honey be careful, don't forget that Morey is one of them too." He reminded her. Candace assured her husband that she would indeed be careful, she hung up with Randy and called her sister Hannah. Hannah was surprised to hear from Candace, but after Candace told her why she was calling, Hannah became concerned. She didn't want Candace meeting with her attorney alone, so she told her sister to have the attorney meet her at the agency, that way she and Daniel would be there with her. A grateful Candace thanked her sister, and later, called Morey to see if he was available to meet her the following week.

After Morey hung up with Candace, he looked over at her brother Michael. He had been sitting in his office listening to the conversation on the intercom. "Insist that both parties are present to sign the paperwork. Once they have signed the papers, kill them." Her brother ordered the man dispassionately. Morey nodded and bowed down to his High Priest and left.

Chapter Twenty-nine

The next week, Randy received a day pass from the rehabilitation center and he and Candace met with their attorney at the church's training center. Greg and his brother Al also showed up.

When Morey arrived, Daniel escorted him to the agency's large conference room. Unbeknownst to the attorney, the room was being monitored by Greg and Al via video surveillance. Morey cheerfully greeted his clients, then expressed remorse about their decision to sell the company and leave the organization. He reached into his briefcase and pulled out the paperwork for them to sign.

While Candace and Randy were looking over the paperwork, Morey casually reached for the coffee pot and poured himself a cup. He then asked the couple if they wanted a cup and both said yes, so he grabbed two more cups and poured coffee in each and handed it to them. He leaned back and sipped his coffee, while the two continued to look over the paper work, and after seeing that everything was in order, Candace and Randy both signed the documents and handed them back to Morey.

Morey looked over the paperwork and nodded his consent. He reached into his briefcase again and pulled out an envelope and handed it to Randy. Candace reached for her coffee and took a few sips, while Randy opened the envelope and saw the cashier's check from his brother-in-law. He handed the envelope to Candace, and then reached for his coffee. Candace was elated to see the cashier's check from Michael Harris for twenty-five million dollars. She reached over and hugged her husband. They were finally free from the Brotherhood and were ready to start a whole new life.

Morey stood up, and gathered his briefcase. He shook hands with his clients, and left the conference room. Minutes later, after the sleek black town car drove off, everyone at the center exhaled in relief. They gathered into the conference room with the couple, and congratulated them, glad that there wasn't any trouble.

Randy turned to his wife. "Baby, I love you, I ..." Suddenly, he went pale, grabbed his chest and keeled over. Candace stared down at him in horror. "Randy! No, baby what's ...."

Hannah watched in horror as her older sister grabbed her chest, and with a stricken look, she collapsed on the floor. Greg and Al leaped into action, kneeling down beside the incapacitated couple, searching for a pulse. Daniel quickly pulled out his cell phone and dialed 911, while Hannah stood frozen in shock, staring down at her sister in disbelief. Reverend Rawlins went to console her, and held her in his arms, while Al and Greg began administering CPR to the couple.

Within minutes the ambulance arrived, and the paramedics took over from the brothers. As they tried to resuscitate the couple, two more paramedics prepared IV's and inserted them into the couple's arms, while a third pulled Daniel to the side and quietly asked him what happened. As the medic quickly jotted everything down, he asked if the couple had ate or drank anything. Alarmed, Hannah and Daniel looked at each other! Had Morey somehow managed to poison the couple while they were in the conference room? Greg told the medic that the couple and their attorney each had a cup of coffee. The medic took the coffee pot and the three cups as evidence and then they rushed the couple to the nearest hospital.

The saints followed in their cars, and Greg called Abby to tell her what was going on. Abby nearly fainted when she heard the news and she insisted on driving to the hospital to be with her sisters. By the time Abby arrived at the hospital, the look on her husband and sister's face stopped her in her tracks. "No, no, please no." She cried softly, shaking her head in denial. Greg pulled her into his arms and rocked her back and forth. "They did everything they could for them, but it just wasn't enough. They're gone, sweetheart." He said quietly. Abby cried and reached out for her sister Hannah. They stood in the middle of the hospital floor, crying over the loss of their older sister. Abby immediately thought about the twins, Renee and RJ, how in the world was she going to tell them that their father and aunt was dead?

When the twins arrived home from school that day, they were surprised to see several cars in their driveway. Thinking their mom had gone into labor while they were at school, they rushed into the house, but the first person they ran into was their mom, still pregnant, but with red swollen eyes. They could tell she had been crying and when they looked around the living room, they noticed that Reverend Rawlins, and his wife, and their Uncle Al and his wife were also there. Renee immediately looked for her aunt Hannah, and when she didn't see her or Daniel, an uneasy feeling began to settle in her spirit. She prayed that nothing bad had happened to Hannah and the baby.

Abby hugged her twins and asked them to sit with her on the couch. The others got up and went into the kitchen, leaving Abby and Greg alone with the twins. With a heavy heart, Abby told the twins about their dad and her sister. The twins were so shocked, they were speechless.

Later that evening, the television and the Internet was filled with reports about Randy and Candace Nelson's sudden death. Reporters gathered outside the hospital to talk to Dr. Kenneth John, the attending physician who was on duty when the couple was brought in. After leaving the hospital, they showed up at Greg and Abby's house, and Greg agreed to speak with them alone, telling them that his wife was overcome with grief and was unable to make a statement. A couple of days later, one of the major news organization, on orders of the Brotherhood, began releasing articles about the ugly history of Randy and Candace's marriage. They interviewed the deceased couple's co-workers, and the actors and actresses they represented, who couldn't wait to share the juicy gossip about the couples infidelity, drug usage and impending divorce.

Three days later, Abby and Hannah buried their sister and brother in law. RJ was one of the pallbearers and Reverend Rawlins conducted the eulogy. During the service, Renee sang a solo, *I Dreamed of a City Called Glory* that brought the church and members of the press, who attended the funeral, to their feet! They all marveled at the young girl's voice.

The next day, the media and the Internet buzzed with excitement about the young singer, as local, and cable news pundits compared Renee to her famous mother. A YouTube video of the young teen singing at the funeral, received millions of hits, and Abby and Greg suddenly found themselves having to fend off music producers interested in signing Renee to their label.

Michael did not attend his sister and brother in law's funeral, but he sent one of his representative to make sure the couple were indeed dead. He also called his sisters to express his condolences, however, when he spoke to Hannah, who was still hurt and confused about her sister's death, she angrily accused her twin brother of killing their sister. Michael laughed at her and hung up!

The hospital did conduct an autopsy on Candace and Randy, and the results showed that the two had died of heart attacks. Since there was no foul play indicated, there was no investigation into the Nelson's death. A week later, Morey, the couple's attorney, was found dead in his bed by his housekeeper. According to the coroner's report, he too, died of a heart attack.

Michael took over both the West Coast and East Coast offices of N.A.A. Talent agency. He and his wife moved back to Los Angeles, fired all of Randy and Candace staff, and installed their own people, who transferred from the New York offices.

Four weeks later, on April 24th, Abby went into labor and gave birth to two healthy babies. Each infant weighed five and a half pounds. As promised, Abby and Greg allowed the twins to name the babies, so they named their baby brother, Solomon and their little sister, Ruth. The birth of the twins bought so much joy to Renee and RJ, that it eased the pain over the death of their father and aunt. Greg vowed to God and Abby that he would protect and raise all of his kids to serve the Lord!

Four months later, in August, Cecilia and

Hannah went into labor and Cecilia gave birth to a healthy baby boy, just as God prophesied to William, and they named him William Eugene Rawlins, Jr, and five days later, Hannah gave birth to a beautiful baby girl, that they named, Antoinette Suzanne James, after Daniel's mother.

In September, Joe Jenkins proposed to Simone and she happily accepted, and Ralph proposed to Gail, who also accepted. They decided on a double wedding to take place on Christmas day! Joel and Ernestine decided to move to D.C. permanently and they turned the church over to their son Marcus, who asked Cynthia to move to Raleigh Durham with him as his wife. They were married within a week!

Chapter Thirty

Satan was furious! All of his plans had been thwarted by the saints of Grace Faith Church, and when Azazel flew in and reported that Cecilia, Abby and Hannah had all given birth to healthy babies, he was beside himself with rage. Demons scrambled to get out of his ways as the dark lord stomped back in forth in his dark, fiery lair in Hell. He seized the ones that didn't get out of his way fast enough, and violently threw them through the walls.

Azazel and Semjaza watched their crestfallen leader carefully. They all trembled with fear as the dark lord finally sat down on his makeshift throne, thoroughly defeated. No one had a plan or idea that they dare mention to him.

Suddenly a bright light came shining into Hell. Terror gripped the group of creatures as they looked up and saw an object floating down towards Satan's throne. As it came closer to their master's hideous face, they realized it was a huge hourglass, and it was half full as sand slowly filled the bottom half. The hourglass hovered right in front of Satan's face, and they all heard a familiar voice from Heaven say:

You were loosed for only a short time and your time is nearly up! The image of the hourglass vanished, and an image of the lake of fire appeared. ***Your destiny awaits you Satan, you and your angels!*** The booming voice informed them.

Satan trembled and paled as he stared at the shimmering image of the lake of fire. Every demon in Hell trembled with fear. Ages ago, they had followed the archangel Lucifer in his rebellion against God, and waged war with Jesus and the angels, and were kicked out of Heaven, they knew what fate held in store for them!

A fearful, yet defiant Satan stood up and yelled towards Heaven, "I will not fail! Do you hear me Father? I will destroy your precious mankind before my time is up and those I can't destroy, they will share my fate in the lake of fire! I will deny you, Father, these animals you call humans, which are so precious to you. They will never live in Paradise with you, never!" He shouted angrily. The image of the lake of fire disappeared along with the bright light, and once again darkness descended over Hell.

Incensed, Satan motioned for Azazel and Semjaza to come forth. With trepidation the two demons walked towards the dark lord and kneeled in front of him.

"Round up the Brotherhood and meet me in Switzerland. It's time to put my final plans in motion. I will show Father just how easy it is for me to destroy his precious mankind and make them curse Him to His face." Satan snarled. "What I did to his precious *Job* will pale in comparison to what I have in store for these vile creatures that He dared to love more than us!" He roared in anger. All the demons in hell, encouraged by their master's boldness, clapped and cheered!

Two days later, all the High Priest and Priestess of the Brotherhood gathered in the Embassy Ballroom at the Badrutts Palace in St. Moritz, Switzerland. Many of them were Presidents, and ex-Presidents, Vice Presidents, Senators and Congressmen from the United States and Kings, Queens, heads of states, and clergy men and women. Also in attendance were CEO's of Fortune 500 companies, and Wall Street executives, technology billionaires, doctors, and lawyers. There were also music moguls, movie stars and superstar athletes. Over twelve million men and women were in attendance and they were all puppets for the puppet master, always eager to do his bidding!

Satan was attired in **his** black Brotherhood robes, his face was concealed by the large black cowl hanging loosely from his head. Seated at the head of the tables, he tapped his crystal wine goblet, and rose as silence fell over the room. "My brothers and sisters, the time has come for us to activate my master plan. Our enemy will be sent a very powerful message about who is *really* in control of this planet!" He said boldly. The members stood up and cheered. Satan allowed them a few minutes, and again tapped his goblet. The cheers quickly died down and the members took their seats and waited.

"Each of you has a sealed envelope on your table. I want you to open them now." He sat down and picked up his wine goblet and took a sip, enjoying the fine, expensive Chablis. As each member tore open their envelopes, and read the contents, he heard them gasp and cry out in disbelief, at the directives they held in their hands. The members looked at those seated around them, their eyes filled with terror.

The President of France stood up; he was

shaking with anger, as he held his directive in his hand and looked towards the head table. "Your Eminence," he began, as he bowed down towards Satan. "I can't in good conscience fulfill your mandate, this will destroy my country." He stammered, as he waved the paper in front of him. Murmurs of agreement filled the room.

Satan looked at the man and smiled. "Yes, it will, Henri." He said quietly. The Frenchman continued. "I just can't do this to my people, your Eminence." He said boldly. Satan looked over towards one of the guards stationed in the room. He nodded at him and the guard walked over to the French president, removed his pistol from his holster, and shot the man in the head, killing him instantly.

A stunned silence fell over the room, then a woman screamed, "You're a madman!" Several of the men stood up, ready to attack the guards, and the madman at the head table, when Satan suddenly stood up and whipped off his robes, revealing his true nature. His guards morphed into huge twenty foot tall demons, and so did the creatures now seated at the head table with Satan. "Sit down and shut up!" Satan roared to the crowd as the demons took flight and flew around the room, intimidating the terrified members.

Satan was delighted to see fear in each and every one of their faces. "I'd like to remind each and every one of you, that in exchange for the wealth and power you enjoy, you pledged total allegiance to me." Horrified, the German chancellor looked at the creature in front of her. "Who are you?" She whispered fearfully. Satan grinned down at her. "Well I have lots of different titles, but my given name is Lucifer, however, since I've been exiled to this filthy planet, I'm now called Satan, or most commonly, the Devil. But you will still address me as Your Excellency, since I own you body and soul." He said triumphantly.

Each and every member shuddered in terror and disbelief. They never believed in God or the Devil, and they truly believed that their *secret society* was just a global network of wealthy citizens destined to rule the world. They had enjoyed the power of being held in such high esteem by this organization, feeling superior to those around them who weren't involved in the Brotherhood. Now the truth had finally been revealed, they had sold their souls for power and wealth and this thing, this *creature* was determined to extract payment from each and every one of them!

Michael and Georgia Harris sat glued to their chairs, terrified with fear. Michael immediately remembered his upbringing at Grace Faith church back in D.C. and he realized that everything Reverend Rawlins had taught was actually true. Even as a young boy, church was just a complete waste of his time, and now here he was sitting here being threatened by Satan, the *Devil*. He gripped his wife's hand and did something he hadn't done in almost thirty years, he began to pray.

Confident that he had the attention of each and every human in the room, Satan and his demons reverted back to their human form. "For many years, you and your families have enjoyed the best this world has to offer. Now it is time for you to fulfill your end of our bargain. Before I leave is there anyone of you who feels like our late friend Henri that you can't do what I've assigned you to do?" He asked the crowd. No one said a word. "Good. Each of you have one week to put my plan in action. Now enjoy the rest of your evening." Satan gulped the rest of his wine, and left the ballroom.

The members stared at each other, too shocked and afraid to say anything. The totality of what they traded for wealth and power hit them hard. They were so upset they ignored the gourmet meal the waiters carried in and placed in front of them. One by one they rose from their tables, and left the ballroom to return to their rooms. They quickly packed their bags and made arrangements to return to their own countries. The weekend of fun they had envisioned with their fellow Brotherhood members, had instead turned into the weekend from Hell, literary.

An hour after the Brotherhood meeting was over; Reverend William Rawlins received a phone call. Sitting in his office were Cecilia, Greg, Abby, Al, Lynn, Daniel, Hannah and Joel and Ernestine. As he listened intently to the voice on the other end, his face turned ashen. He quickly grabbed a piece of paper and began jotting information down. Five minutes later, he stopped writing and dropped his head onto his chest as he silently prayed for strength. "Thank you so much for alerting us. Take care of yourselves and stay safe." He said, before hanging up the phone. Everyone in the office waited for the pastor to tell them what was going on. With a huge sigh, he turned towards them and relayed the information that was just given to him. They all gasped in disbelief. The enemy had made his move, now it was up to the saints to trust in God, and His Word that He would protect them and supply all of their needs.

After the man hung up the phone with Reverend Rawlins, he walked over to his wife and held her in his arms and said grimly, "It has begun." Candace shuddered in Randy's arms. They were hidden away in a safe house Greg had provided for them, grateful to be alive. The day before their meeting with Morey, one of Randy's friends in the Brotherhood had contacted him and warned him that he and Candace had been targeted for murder! When Randy relayed this tidbit to Greg and Al, they devised an elaborate scheme to fake the couple's death to protect them from Michael and the Brotherhood. Randy and Candace were well aware of the methods the group used to kill members who tried to leave, so when Greg alerted him, through a wire he was wearing at the meeting, that the attorney had poisoned the coffee! He and Candace had pretended to drink the coffee, but the two swallowed a pill instead, that made them ill.

Once they arrived at the hospital, Greg and Al immediately spotted two men that were trying to blend into the background that the Brotherhood had sent to confirm the two were truly dead. Doctor John, who was also involved in the plot, had his team ready in the OR, and the doctor temporarily stopped the duo's heart, making it appear like the pair had died of heart attacks.

Later, while Doctor John was in the visitor's waiting room telling the family that the couple didn't make it, Randy and Candace were being whisked away in a laundry van and sent to one of Greg's safe houses. When they arrived, Randy and Candace fell to their knees and thanked God, grateful that He had used the saints of Grace Faith church to save them.

The same friend that alerted Randy about the assassination attempt, told him about the meeting he had just attended, where Satan revealed himself and his diabolical plan. The man finally revealed to Randy that he was an undercover agent assigned to take down the Brotherhood, but even *he* didn't have a clue that the **Devil** himself was running the organization! The agent asked Randy to share the information with someone he trusted, because he was also fleeing to an undisclosed location. The agent discovered some of his superiors were involved in the Brotherhood, and he could identify several of them. After receiving the information, Randy called Reverend Rawlins on the secured cell phone Greg had given him to use.

A week later, a press conference was held and a tired, and haunted looking President of the

United States of America, announced that China was calling in all the money the US owed them, and every bank and credit union were calling in **all** consumer and business loans. Every citizen that had a mortgage, car loan, credit cards or business loans had to pay them off in full, or risk losing their homes, businesses and cars! Two hours after that announcement, several top CEO's from around the world, announced major layoffs. Chaos ensued as people began losing everything they owned, and they took to the streets to protest. The military was called in to keep order and marshal law was put in effect all over the world.

Millions of citizens around the world lost their jobs, homes, and healthcare benefits, as companies continued to lay off workers. Thousands committed suicide and murder suicides, killing their families and then themselves. Soup lines, food pantries and homeless shelters were filled to capacity, as supplies dwindled daily. The churches were bombarded by people looking for help, and soon they were overwhelmed, as they tried to help as many people as they could. People that had denied God or hadn't prayed in years began to cry out to Him.

Reverend Rawlins and the members of Grace

Faith church and hundreds of other churches, that had heeded God's word and had preached faith and trusting God, were more prepared than others. Church members opened their homes to loved ones, who had lost theirs, and the training center was able to keep people working as Joe and his brothers taught others how to build their own homes, and businesses. They slowly rebuilt the communities. Membership at Grace Faith grew, and soon Joe and the others were building a bigger church to accommodate all of their members. God was faithful to those that had been faithful to Him, and even in the midst of this chaos, Grace Faith members continued to prosper.

Epilogue

As the years passed, the saints at Grace Faith church, Reverend Rawlins, Cecilia, Abby, Greg, Hannah, Daniel, Al and Lynn died, and went home to be with the Lord. Their children took over the ministry, which continued to grow and prosper. Reverend William Rawlins Jr. married Hannah and Daniel's eldest daughter, Antoinette. Renee married and became the minister of music, and led the choir, just like her mother did, and her twin brother RJ, was also married, to one of the choir members and associate minister of the church.

One night, a loud sound erupted on planet earth! And with a blink of an eye, the church was gone, raptured. Billions of saints worldwide disappeared and reappeared in the sky with Jesus! When the saints of Christ arrived in Heaven with Jesus, they rejoiced as they reunited with their loved ones! Heaven was just as the Bible said it was. The streets were paved in gold, and each one of the adults had their own mansion, built to their specifications, because Jesus knew what they liked!

Oh it was joyous in Heaven, but down on earth things had become much worse! Earthquakes devastated the planet, killing millions, and those that didn't die began to wish they had, because they were under the control of a madman!

The world's economy never returned to its previous prosperity, and many countries including the United States, looked like a third world countries. With state and local governments losing tax revenues in the millions, illegal drugs were legalized and taxed. Desperate citizens around the world, unable to find work, a decent place to live, drowned their sorrows in drugs and alcohol. Many people died, the cemeteries were filled to capacity, so they began burying the dead in empty fields and lots. Homeless children were being kidnapped, killed, and their body parts sold for food!

In Hell, Satan sat on his throne, and watched in delight as chaos engulfed the rest of his Father's precious pets. Everyday, as people lost everything, they would cry out to God and when they didn't receive help, or an answer right away, they began to curse Him. Satan threw back his head and laughed each time. But he wasn't finished yet, not by a long shot. He had one more trick up his sleeve, to strike a final blow to destroy mankind. He turned to Azazel and said, 'Fetch your boy, now." Azazel bowed and vanished. He reappeared seconds later, with his teenage son. CJ was delighted to see his dad, and his old friend, Satan. He bowed down to his master and Satan motioned for the boy to approach the throne. "Son, it's time. Release the **Nephilim**!" The Tribulation had begun!

The End

I hope you enjoy the Invisible Enemies Series. It's my pleasure to write it and entertain you with it. Please tell your family, friends and co-workers about the series.

Lynda D. Brown

Lynda D. Brown

I hope you enjoyed the Invisible Enemies Series. It was quite a ride writing and publishing it, but my prayer is that our churches will begin operating like Grace Faith Church, using all the dominion and authority that God gave each and every one of us!

If you have any questions or would like to comment on the series, please follow us on Facebook: https://www.facebook.com/invisibleenemiesseries

Please remember the series is available in paperback, eBooks and audio! You can purchase a copy from all major online book stores!

Lynda D. Brown
Spoken Word Press Publishing

www.ingramcontent.com/pod-product-compliance
Lightning Source LLC
Chambersburg PA
CBHW062008170626
46813CB00001B/75